SELF-MADE BOYS

BOYS

A GREAT GATSBY REMIX

ALSO BY ANNA-MARIE McLEMORE

ANNA-MARIE McLEMORE

SELF-MADE BOYS

A GREAT GATSBY REMIX

FEIWEL AND FRIENDS

New York

Content warning: This book contains references to
racism, colorism, transphobia, queerphobia, and sexism
in the context of the 1920s, and references to soldiers'
experiences during and after World War I.

A Feiwel and Friends Book
An imprint of Macmillan Publishing Group, LLC
120 Broadway, New York, NY 10271 • fiercereads.com

Our books may be purchased in bulk for promotional, educational, or business use. Please contact your local bookseller or the Macmillan Corporate
and Premium Sales Department at (800) 221-7945 ext. 5442 or by email
at MacmillanSpecialMarkets@macmillan.com.

Library of Congress Cataloging-in-Publication Data
Names: McLemore, Anna-Marie, author. | Fitzgerald, F. Scott
(Francis Scott), 1896–1940. Great Gatsby.
Title: Self-made boys : a Great Gatsby remix / Anna-Marie McLemore.
Description: First edition. | New York : Feiwel & Friends, 2022. |
Series: Remixed classics ; vol 5 | Audience: Ages 13 and up |
Audience: Grades 10–12 | Summary: "Three teens chase their own
version of the American Dream during the Roaring 20s in this YA remix
of The Great Gatsby"—Provided by publisher.
Identifiers: LCCN 2021062266 | ISBN 9781250774934
(hardcover)
Subjects: LCSH: Rich people—Fiction. | First loves—Fiction. | LCGFT:
Psychological fiction. | Romance fiction. | Novels.
Classification: LCC PZ7.1.M463 Se 2022 | DDC [Fic]—dc23
LC record available at https://lccn.loc.gov/2021062266

First edition, 2022
Book design by Veronica Mang
Feiwel and Friends logo designed by Filomena Tuosto
Printed in the United States.

ISBN 978-1-250-77493-4 (hardcover)
1 3 5 7 9 10 8 6 4 2

To CGM,
who was still looking at the stars

So he invented just the sort of Jay Gatsby
that a seventeen-year-old boy would
be likely to invent.

—F. SCOTT FITZGERALD, *The Great Gatsby*

————————— ❖ ❖ ❖ —————————

I am a self-made man, born with
my two hands.

—JOE STEVENS, "Ghost Boy"

Ms. Daisy Fabrega-Caraveo
East Egg, New York

Dear Daisy,

They said no. More exactly, Papá said he didn't think it was a good idea, and Mamá said I'd go to that godforsaken city over her dead body, and even in that eventuality, her alma would haunt me into staying in Wisconsin.

Dais, this might be the best chance I ever get. How many New York finance men do you think loiter around Beet Patch? If he hadn't blown a tire, he never would have stopped.

Ever since my parents helped me become Nicolás Caraveo, I've been wondering how I was ever going to pay them back. If I take this job, I could. Papá could stop fixing things around here with string and axle grease and have them properly repaired. Mamá could buy the medicine she needs. She still gets that cough but won't see to it because she says the roof's hanging on by its last shingle and that we need to save for the day it lets go.

And before you say anything, I know you've tried to help, and I know they won't take it. You're always good to them. That dress on Mamá's birthday, the hat and boots for Papá *at Christmas. And they love you for caring so much, but I know they draw the line at you giving them money and that they're going to draw it forever. So it's got to be me.*

And it's got to be me anyway. What they did for me, Daisy . . . I have to find a way to repay them. I have to do this for them. I could make real money in New York. Maybe not real money to you, not like Tom has, but enough to make a real difference here.

Daisy, if you tell me to forget this, I will. You're the one who told me to tell them I was a boy, and when you did I thought you'd dropped your good sense to the bottom of the pond, but I did it, and you were right.

So what should I do now? What would you do?

Nick

Mr. Nicolás Caraveo
Beet Patch, Wisconsin

Dear wonderful Nick,
You just leave everything to me.

Your favorite cousin,
Daisy

Mr. and Mrs. Agustín Caraveo
Beet Patch, Wisconsin

Dearest Tío y Tía,

By my lights, this letter finds you in a quagmire of a decision. One which I, your favorite niece—don't pretend I'm wrong, and don't worry, I'll never tell my sisters or primas—am writing to help you solve.

As you know, your Nicolás and I have kept in touch by letter while I was in Chicago and then when I came to New York. I know all about what a genius he is (he hates when I use the word, but we all know it's true). He's so painfully modest, I had to pry from him that the school had run out of math classes for him by the time he was fourteen. So you can imagine what quicksteps and waltzes I had to perform to get him to tell me what happened with the stockbroker. (Is it really true that he offered Nicky the job because of some trick with a chessboard? I couldn't make sense of that part of Nick's letter.)

Tío y Tía, I know you worry about sending your dear boy east. But the thing he'll never tell you is just how badly he wants to go. He wants to put that head for numbers to good use, and he'll never leave the farm unless you tell him to.

Just consider it. I'd look after him myself. I may have only a year on Nicky, but it's enough for me to play the big sister. And I hope you won't fault your favorite sobrina the slightest presumption, because I already found the sweetest little cottage for him. Close enough to the train into the city but with plenty of space around, no neighbors crowding him. And he'd be near me, just across the sound! You could skip a stone between us.

Please let him come to New York? I promise, he'll have the gayest of times.

Yours, with deepest affection,

Daisy

CHAPTER 1

"West Egg."

At the conductor's call, I shuddered awake, becoming aware of three sensations at once. First, the soreness from folding myself against my seat. Second, the leaf-green light of the world outside. Third, the indentations left on my palm from the chess piece I'd been holding, off and on, since Wisconsin.

Before Papá saw me off at the station, he'd given me some advice, knowing I'd think about it as the scar line of railroad tracks wound east.

"Recuerda esto, Nicolás," he said. "The world may look at you and see a pawn"—he pressed a carved piece of wood into my palm—"but that just means they'll never see your next move coming."

I didn't uncurl my fingers until we were almost to Chicago. But I could recognize the shape by touch, the contours of the felt coin at the bottom, the pillar base, the notches of the horse's head. It was a knight, in deep-finished wood.

My father had just left his own chess set incomplete in service of making his point. He'd have to add in a saltshaker now.

Papá had always been one to give advice, even back when he thought I was a girl. But last winter I had told him and Mamá that I was boy. I said it in halting words, as though admitting an awkward, inconvenient fact, like a sweater a relative had knitted me didn't fit. And ever since he and Mamá had given me my new name and the shirts and trousers to go with it, he'd been working twice as hard at this dispensation of wisdom, like a priest administering Communion at double speed.

I put the wooden knight in my pocket, the shape of the whittled features still pressed into my fingers.

The West Egg station had a plain, unadorned look not so different from where I'd started. But around the edges was the glint of wealth—there, in a freshly painted bench, or over there, in a square of well-tended violets.

It was the possibility of such wealth that had lured my cousin away from Wisconsin in the first place. Her efforts had gotten her an emerald ring, the promise of an eventual New York engagement, and money to quietly send back home to her family in Fleurs-des-Bois, a town little different from Beet Patch except in name.

I rubbed sleep from my eyes as I got off the train, squinting into the lemon-meringue light. So I didn't recognize the woman on the platform until she flung her arms wide and yelled, "Nicky!"

At the sound of my cousin's voice, I braced for her shock. She knew I'd been living as the boy I was for a while now. But if the few relatives I'd seen were any indication, no amount of explaining in letters could prepare them for the cropped hair, the suspenders, the hands in trouser pockets.

Daisy threw her arms around me, the smell of lilies drifting off the brim of her hat. "You're here, and you're so impossibly handsome; I refuse to believe it."

I tried to arrange my face into something other than being stunned, but it resisted.

Daisy's skin was a few shades lighter than the last time I'd seen her, as though she'd spent months in a windowless parlor, or tried those awful tricks of lightening it with lemon. Her once-dark hair was now pale as honeycomb. When the light hit it, it looked the same shade as masa, frizzing at the edges from how she must have bleached it.

"I know," she said. "Don't I look wonderful?" She twirled, her skirt a whirl of yellow. "I'm a brownette now!"

I didn't mean to check for who might be staring, but I did. Anyone who was—men rushing for their cars, old ladies conferring about the afternoon—looked charmed for having witnessed Daisy's turn.

"A what?" I asked.

Daisy stopped spinning. "They call us brownettes." She

led me away from the station's bustle. "Us girls of light-brown hair and intermediate coloring."

She stopped in front of an open-topped roadster in a color I'd never seen on a car, like the sheen of a blue-gray pearl.

"Don't you adore it?" She posed alongside, flipping up a buckled shoe. "The first man tried to sell me a color called florid red, can you imagine? He said it was perfect for women with the Latin kind of coloring."

I opened my mouth to remind her that *she* had once been a woman with a *Latin kind of coloring*.

Except she wasn't anymore.

My cousin Daisy looked white.

CHAPTER II

As Daisy drove, the leaf-filtered light spilled over her bleached hair. The wind twirled a chiffon scarf away from her neck.

"You'll just adore the cottage, Nicky." She reached across the seat and tapped my upper arm. "It's divine."

The sun slipped through branches in fragile ribbons, and in the distance, a great mansion loomed beyond the summer trees. If an Irish castle had an affair with a cathedral, that might be the house that came of it.

Daisy slowed the car, suggesting that the house down the lane was the cottage, and that the castle-cathedral held my nearest neighbor.

"U-um," I stammered. "Daisy?"

"Oh, I know," she said. "Garish, isn't it? I don't know who he is, but they say his money is fresh as lettuce and just as soft."

"What if the man who lives there doesn't like having a neighbor like"—I gestured to myself—"me?"

"He'll never know, Nick." Daisy cast me a glance from under her hat brim. "You've invented yourself splendidly, right down to the walk."

"I—I didn't"—again, I stammered—"I meant someone brown," I said. "People like that are used to us serving their food and cleaning their floors, not being their neighbors. What if he doesn't like me right on his property line?"

"Then I'll simply ask Tom to have him killed." Daisy gave that high bell ring of a laugh. "He won't notice you. No one looks at anybody anymore. They're too taken with themselves."

The turn of Daisy's head, and the salt perfume of tidewater, made me look right.

An ocean I had never seen was so close I could have thrown my suitcase into it from the car. The piercing blue of the water, paler than Lake Michigan, stretched out toward another finger of land across the bay.

"I'm just over there." Daisy pointed. "At night you can see a little green light—I had that put in there, don't let Tom take credit for a second. That's how you'll know it's me. I'm practically in the next room from you."

Boughs of juniper brushed the sides of Daisy's car as we came to a stop. The cottage looked sweet enough to be made out of gingerbread, and I felt the unease of having invaded some feminine space, like Daisy's old lace-curtained dollhouse.

We were barely out of the car before her shoes were tapping across the flagstones.

"Don't you adore it?" she asked.

An arch of roses and trailing blossoms framed the front steps. Neat yellow awnings topped the windows. Inside, pale blue light from the water and pale yellow light from the sun brightened the antique wood and dust-dulled carpets. Apples and oranges gleamed to a higher shine than their pewter bowl, like they'd been waxed. A short vase burst with roses that matched the ones along the front walk. I imagined my cousin cutting the roses, speaking endearments to the thorns pricking her fingers.

Daisy Fabrega-Caraveo made things beautiful, starting with herself, her efforts then billowing ever outward. Anything close enough for her to touch came away dusted with perfumed powder and magic.

She darted around the house, showing me the biscuits and coffee she'd tucked into the cabinets, a teapot in the same understated blue as the bay, the crisp linens on the bed. Her shoes clicked out her excitement with the clarity of a telegram.

She clasped my hands, dark eyes wide and serious as she said, "Nicolás Caraveo, I have a question to ask you, and I demand you tell me the truth."

When it came to Daisy, such an introduction could preface anything, from *What do you think of the Temperance Union? No, I mean it, what do you really think of it?* to *Tom says I look like Marion Davies, don't you think I look a little like Marion Davies?*

"Are you still using elastic bandages to bind?" she asked.

"Well, yes," I said, conscious of the sheen of travel sweat under mine right then.

"Nicky," Daisy said with high, sparkling concern as she rifled through her handbag. "You could bruise a rib that way." As though producing a magician's rabbit, she held up a white garment with laces on two sides.

"It's called a Symington side lacer, and it's a wonder," she said. "I wear it right under a fitted chemise. All the girls with chests like mine wear them. And I see no reason a boy like you can't use one for your purposes. It's a world safer than what you're doing. And I found plain ones special for you. You can wear them right beneath your undershirt. They're terribly comfortable, you wouldn't believe."

"You wear them?" I asked.

"Of course." Daisy shimmied one shoulder, then the other. "The fashion of the moment doesn't like us girls with curves, so we have to flatten ourselves out. No more corsets pushing up heaving bosoms. It's considered garish these days to emphasize our chests, so we do what we must. It's not as though the dresses will change for us."

"I'm sorry," I said. I was uncomfortable enough binding down the body I had so I could be the boy I was. I barely understood Daisy doing it to be a particular kind of girl.

"Give it a few years." She flapped a hand, and her polished nails gleamed. "It'll all change again." She folded the side lacer and another like it and tucked them into the top drawer of a high dresser. "Anyway, I bought you two. I ordered more, so if you like them, there are three more on the way to you. They're very boring, the most boring ones they had. Just plain white and tan and beige. Mine are much more interesting. Pink satin and peach lace. I'd fall asleep while dressing if I had to wear ones like yours."

"I think I'll manage to stay awake," I said.

"And first thing tomorrow we're getting you fitted for a proper suit," she said.

"That's really all right," I said.

Her letters spoke of bold East Egg men wearing orange or fairway green. I'd have rather stayed with the secondhand suits I'd come with.

"Oh, don't worry," she said. "Nothing bright. Maybe navy or gray. Though I'd love to see you in something two-toned. They're doing that now, you know. Jacket different from the trousers, or vest different from the jacket. You'd look very sharp, I think."

Our cousins said a lot of things about Daisy. That she was vapid, shallow, *lovely as an angel but stupid as a basket.* But Daisy had never flinched at who I was. And she showed a consideration that was hard to come by, one held as much in the plain cloth of the side lacers as in the roses trimmed and arranged in delft-blue vases.

"I'm glad you're here," I said.

She pulled a millinery flower from her hat and pinned it to my shirt. "I'm glad I'm here too."

CHAPTER III

The sun threw silver coins across the water as Daisy drove us from West Egg to East Egg.

"Tom's just mad to meet you," she said. "He doesn't know any of my friends except the ones I've made here."

"Friends?" I asked.

Daisy kept her eyes on the road. But I noticed the slightest pursing of her lips, the same tell as when she used to lie to her mother about whether she was wearing rouge.

"Daisy," I said, my voice low under the roar of the engine and the snapping current of the wind. "Does Tom know I'm your cousin?"

She flashed me a guilty smile, as though she'd swiped a finger of frosting off a cake. "Tom doesn't know me as anyone other than Daisy Fay. As anyone other than, well"—she glanced down at her dress, her newly pale forearms—"this. So if you don't mind the tiniest lie, could we not tell him?"

"What will you say when he asks how we met?" I asked.

"Don't you worry," she said. "I've got it all figured out."

My neighbor's castle could have vanished in the shadow of the Buchanan estate. Grass so green it looked dyed carpeted the ground from the beach to the marble-pillared mansion. In the distance, against the sculpted hedges, Tom Buchanan sped forward on a horse.

"He never realizes I'm alive when he's playing polo," Daisy said.

"You can play polo with yourself?" I asked.

Daisy cackled. "Playing polo with yourself. Doesn't that sound indecent?"

So many people dashed around the mansion I thought there might be a party going on until I realized they were all workers in uniform. One man rushed to open Daisy's door. A woman with a ballerina's posture walked around the side of the house, bearing a stack of what I took to be tablecloths. Two men carried in fish on snowdrifts of ice.

I tried to catch a few of their eyes by way of greeting. But the older, more polished ones looked at me as though I had just failed some test, and the younger ones looked away as though intent on not failing ones of their own.

Daisy led me from the car around to an ivy-veiled stretch of the mansion. She regarded a white wrought-iron table and its candlesticks with mournful disdain.

"Candles, always the candles," Daisy said. "Tom thinks I like them."

"Don't you?" I asked.

"When it's dark, yes. But it's summer, so it's practically light until midnight." She snuffed one out with her fingers. "It's such a pity Jordan couldn't join us. Tournament in the morning, you see. She's just a paragon of virtue—the face of an actress, the self-discipline of a nun. At least if there's not a party she can't miss. Anyway, you two will get on like an engine and a purr, you just wait. I can feel it. I know these things, Nicky. Go on, sit down. You're not waiting for the queen."

Daisy held up an amber bottle. "Wine?"

"Where did you get that stuff?" It was a tactless way to ask where she'd bought illegal alcohol, but the question had tumbled out.

Daisy smiled. "Corner drugstore."

"No, thank you," I said.

"A young man of such virtue." Daisy's voice blended with the splashing of wine into faceted crystal. "Didn't I say you and Jordan would be a pair?"

Tom came in from the polo match with himself, smelling of sweat and leather and distilled musk, as though the exercise had made his cologne stronger. He was tall and wide-shouldered, as I'd expected, but his manner had an air of boredom.

He noticed me and said, "Oh," with casual consideration, like Daisy had left out some fundamental fact about me.

I was forever gauging strangers' reactions to me, both to my brownness and to the kind of boy I was, though the former was much more obvious than the latter. The vacant registering in Tom Buchanan's face made me sure it was my brownness, but even that was fleeting. He seemed to forget me as fast as he'd seen me. He had the look of a man who thought he always deserved to be somewhere better, as though the world should come up with something more worthy of him than acres of rosebushes and a sunken garden and a marble terrace.

Over dinner, Daisy's shimmering chatter saved me from having to talk much or often.

"Tom, you have to see the cottage," Daisy went on. "It's the perfect little dream."

"Thank you," I said, in as deferential a way as I could to Tom.

"It was nothing," Tom said. "The family that owns it are friends of my parents. No one uses it much anymore. High time someone blew the dust off." In one long swallow, he drained half a glass of wine. "Though if you want to know the truth, I doubt we've done you any favors. You have a dreadful neighbor. Some Gatsby fellow."

"Gatsby?" Daisy's eyes followed a candle flame. "What Gatsby?"

"That's who bought that carnival palace," Tom said. "The eyesore. You've seen it. You can't miss the thing unless you look straight up."

"Who is he?" I asked.

"New money." Tom took a bite of his steak and kept

talking while chewing. "Reeks of it. You can smell it all the way across the sound."

"What does he do?" I asked, and knew instantly that it was a crude question in rich company. It was the sort of fact you waited for someone to offer rather than asking.

"I heard he might've been some kind of child spy during the war. But here's the thing I meant to warn you about, Nick." Tom pointed the tines of his fork at me. "He throws these god-awful parties every weekend. You can hear the damn jazz all the way across the bay."

"No, you cannot," Daisy said. "You're imagining it. I told you you're imagining it."

Tom kept both his fork and his eyes on me. "Ten to one you'll be swimming across to us just to get away from the noise."

Daisy turned her gaze on me. "Don't you love the cottage?" She set a hand over mine, her fingers cool and smooth as cream. "I thought it looked just like the little house your mother kept on the estate."

"The what?" I asked.

"Oh, you remember it, don't you?" Daisy asked. "It had climbing roses just like that."

"Who's his mother?" Tom asked.

"Nicky's mother was one of my family's maids, Tom," Daisy said, as though reminding him.

As though she'd told him this lie before.

CHAPTER IV

My stomach hitched in time with the flicker of the candle-light. It was a flash of shock, like when I lost my hold on the All Cotton Elastic and the bandage snapped against my body.

My cousin hadn't so much been asking permission to disavow me as she was warning me she'd already done it. How else to explain the presence of an unfamiliar brown boy than to cast him as the son of the family maid? Not even *the* family maid, apparently, but one of a few.

The truth was that her own mother had worked as a seamstress for most of her life, straining her eyes over other people's stitching.

"Most caring woman in the world, Nicky's mother," Daisy said. "I wanted her to be my governess, but Father insisted on one who spoke French."

Her father—my uncle—was a balding man as sweet and unthreatening as condensed milk. My aunt went with him whenever he had to buy anything, knowing her husband's honest, unguarded face inspired price hikes. She enjoyed thwarting any predatory merchants so viciously that they offered apologetic discounts when they saw her coming.

Daisy was still talking, but the waves outside spoke over her. The billow of the tide whispered the truth through the sheer curtains.

Daisy hadn't written to my mother and father because she missed me. She hadn't gotten Tom to arrange for the cottage because she was lonely for family.

I was the brown boy who stood as proof of the lies she'd told. And now I was trapped, unable to correct her without ruining her and myself.

Daisy glanced toward me, one hand under her chin. That glance told me that if people like us wanted to make something of ourselves in a world ruled by men as pale as their own dinner plates, we had to lie.

Daisy would help me make my way in New York. Her price would be the two of us erasing ourselves from each other's blood.

"She must be so proud!" Daisy grabbed my hand. "Her son, a newly minted stockbroker!"

"I'm not a stockbroker." This, Daisy couldn't lie about. Tom knew where I'd been hired and could check up if he wanted. "Quantitative analyst. Different kind of work."

"Tell Tom what it is you'll be doing," Daisy said. "I love the way you tell it."

"It's just different kinds of math," I said. "Looking at

quantities in relation to each other. Studying trend lines. Formulating models."

"Sounds awfully dull," Tom said.

"Oh, I think it sounds a world more exciting than yelling numbers across a trading floor," Daisy said.

"You can't make any money in mathematics," Tom said. "When you want a real job, you tell me. We'll find you something."

"Tom could make you the deputy mayor," Daisy said. "Tom and his eating club rule half of Manhattan."

"Eating club?" I asked.

"For God's sake, Daisy." Tom looked toward another room as though a train might pull in. "You didn't teach him a thing about Yale, did you?"

"Nick doesn't know a thing about the stock market either, and they hired him right off," Daisy said. "That's how smart he is."

"How do you plan to work there if you don't know about it?" Tom asked.

"Uh . . ." I stalled by taking a sip of water from a glass as heavy and faceted as a jewel. "The man who hired me said he likes taking on a few men who don't know the markets. He says it means we come at it with a more objective eye. We don't get attached to certain names, certain companies. We just see the numbers."

But Tom was already turning to Daisy. "You can't bring him around once my parents are back."

"Tom," Daisy said.

"Oh, don't look at me like that, you know *I* don't care. But *they* can't see one of them sitting on their furniture."

Daisy's voice sharpened. "Tom."

One of them.

The water from the crystal glass grew bitter on my tongue.

"Listen." Tom turned from Daisy to me. "You seem decent, and if Daisy likes you, that's more than enough in my book. It's just my parents, you see. They think we're approaching the end of the Nordic race, which I can't understand, because we're ruling this country same as we always have been."

With the next snap of the candle's flame, my mind blinked back to my ancestors, in the place now called Texas. I thought of land we'd sown for hundreds of years and then lost, the border of the United States crossing us long before we ever crossed it.

I could have said something just then, and maybe I should have. But all through these rooms, I saw things I wanted for my family. Not so much the overpriced vases or the glasses etched with peacock feathers. It was more the things the Buchanans wouldn't have given a second thought. I wanted my family to have the comforts of sealed iceboxes and reliable heat, level floors and freshly painted walls.

If I wanted to give them these things, I would have to make my way in New York. And if I wanted to make my way in New York, I had to play nice with every Tom Buchanan

I met. And sometimes, like this minute, that would mean shutting up.

Daisy again offered me a glass of wine, and this time, I took it and drank it.

"And my mother's not too keen on Daisy, so I'm trying to smooth things over," Tom said. "You understand."

Daisy licked her fingers and snuffed out a second candle. "I'll win her over. If you'll just let me at that dreary little room over there, I'll work wonders. It'll be a surprise for her when she gets back."

"My mother's not going to take well to you changing anything around here," Tom said.

"Well, then why'd you put me here in the first place?" she asked.

"You two are here by yourselves?" I asked.

"Until Mr. and Mrs. Buchanan return home in August," Daisy said.

"Nick's going to get the wrong idea if you don't explain," Tom said.

"It would be too much of a scandal to have us both here," Daisy said. "So Tom gives me the run of the place while his parents are gone, and he stays in the city. Very gentlemanly, don't you think? Tom doesn't want anyone implying anything about my virtue."

"So you're here all by yourself," I said.

"She'd be less by herself if she didn't tell the staff to go home every time I leave," Tom said.

"I'm not Anne Boleyn," Daisy said. "I don't need a house-hold to get me into my dress and bring me apples. It doesn't seem fair to just make them wait around."

"My family's still paying them, Daisy," Tom said. "Even when you send them away."

"So we all get time to relax, then," Daisy said. "Not a wrinkle in sight."

"A wrinkle?" I asked.

"No wrinkles means no chaperones," Tom said. "By which she means my parents. Never mind her. She talks like a girl."

Daisy snuffed the third candle between her fingers. "I *am* a girl."

"You're eighteen," Tom said. "That's a grown woman."

"Tom doesn't like that I make him feel old," Daisy said. "Apparently being twenty-one makes you ancient. He can't even appreciate having all this. It's like having an Italian villa to ourselves."

"I grew up here, Daisy," Tom said. "It's nothing as excit-ing as all that for me. And the only Italian around here was the man polishing our silver."

"Tom has no sense of excitement at all," Daisy said. "That's why he won't let me have a debut."

"Not this again," Tom said with impatience but not with-out affection.

"What's a debut?" I asked.

Tom gave a huffing laugh. "See? Nick doesn't even know

what it is. If it's so important, how does such a good friend of yours not even know? We men know what's important, don't we, Nick?"

He winked at me in a way that made dinner lurch in my stomach.

Daisy turned to me so quickly that for a moment her curled hair drifted like hanging blossoms. "I'll tell you all about it," she said. "But for now, just so we don't put Tom to sleep at the table, it's a marvelous night where a young woman is presented into society."

So a debut was a debutante ball. I'd heard about those fluffy white affairs put on in the London court and imitated in New York and Chicago. I'd just never heard of it called a debut.

"It's silly, Daisy," Tom said.

"Then why does every girl who knows anyone have one?" Daisy asked. "Your sister included."

"I just threw you that party, didn't I?" Tom turned to me. "Nick, you should have seen it. Oysters and champagne to the rafters. And the pearls! Daisy, tell him about the pearls."

"Did they come out of the oysters?" I asked.

"This necklace I bought her, it cost $350,000," he said. "All French and Italian pearls."

It took effort, but I successfully stopped myself from spitting out water at the number.

"My neck could hardly hold the thing up," Daisy said.

"Of course, it's somewhere on the bottom of the sea now," Tom said.

"Poetic." Daisy smiled at me. "Don't you think?"

"What happened to it?" I asked.

A look passed between Tom and Daisy, and the subject was cast aside.

"It's just silly to debut now," Tom said, more to his dinner than to Daisy.

"Why?" Daisy asked. "I'm the right age, aren't I?"

"You're not a single girl," he said. "Those things are for single girls."

"I'm not engaged though, am I?" Her smile might have been meant to soften her look at him, but it sharpened it.

"I gave you that ring," he said. "I thought it would keep you happy for longer than this."

"It's not an engagement ring," she said. "You made quite the point of that. Just like that party wasn't an engagement party."

"It's as close as we can get right now," he said. "My family's got to warm up to you. Just give them a chance."

I knew he hadn't proposed, but I didn't know it had become this tense thing between them.

"Wouldn't they warm up to me better if I was a proper society girl?" Daisy asked. "And don't you want a debutante wife?"

"I want *you* as a wife," he said with unexpected tenderness. Just as quickly, it vanished, and he went back to cutting the meat on his plate.

Daisy licked her fingers and snuffed out the last candle.

When she refilled her glass and then mine, I didn't stop her. And I didn't stop her when she refilled it again.

But Daisy had more practice at this and drank faster than I did. She got a glass ahead of me, then two, and eventually wilted onto a sofa.

"Tom, dear." She leaned her head back. "I'm under the table. Would you mind terribly taking Nick home?"

The breeze through the sheers took on a chill.

Before I could catch Daisy's eye, Tom was through the open French doors. "We'll take the runabout."

* * *

To my truest heart in the world,

All good men of Yale will be out of the house tonight for an hour. What mischief shall we make?

Did you know that in his sister's bathroom there's a spout especially for salt water? Rushes right into the tub! Can you believe it? She insisted on it for her sixteenth birthday, swearing up and down that she needed a cold salt rinse to look her most beautiful. But according to Tom, she used it about three times before she moved out.

I haven't seen her in months. She doesn't come home much, still trying to catch that Icelandic millionaire. But from what I saw, the salt water didn't do her any great favors. Oh, I know what your face is doing right now, and yes, I'm a mean little thing. But you met her, didn't you? She always looks like she's trying to place a bad smell. You could fill your bath with the whole sea and it wouldn't make a difference so long as you're sneering at everyone like they've ruined your view of the scenery.

Come over tonight if you can get away. We can sneak into her room and try it out. I'll be wearing my Louise Boulanger; you know the one. The taffeta bouffant with the organdy flowers, the one in all those shades of peach with names like honeydew and bud of romance. Now that I think of it, don't you have one just like it? Cornflower blue with the jade lining? I could swear you have one just like it.

Yours eternally,

Daisy

CHAPTER V

"You know, I think I like you, Nick." Tom's voice roared over the motor cruiser's engine. The boat threw off a spray that grabbed the moonlight and left crystal beads on my forearms. "You're an honest one, I can tell. A good one. They're not all like you."

"Brown people?" I asked.

I was drunk enough not to know whether I'd spoken out loud, but not too drunk to realize that Tom was taking something out so he could show it to me. Was this the engagement ring he'd have in hand to propose to my cousin?

But the thing he was showing me was a small pistol.

I stumbled back hard enough that I was lucky not to go overboard, and then I considered that maybe going overboard would have shown some degree of wisdom. I'd always been a good swimmer and better at holding my breath than any of my cousins.

"Do you think she'll like it?" Tom asked, with such earnest

hope that I paused my deliberations about whether I could swim to West Egg when I was this drunk.

"Pardon?" I asked.

"What," Tom said.

"I said *pardon*," I repeated.

Tom laughed to rival the engine. "No, I'm telling you to say *what* instead of *pardon*. You say *pardon*, you sound like an amateur. Like you're putting on airs." He handed me the gun, grabbing my hand to make me accept. "Don't be so jumpy. It's not loaded yet."

The pistol was smaller than a butter dish, the body polished wood, the handle iridescent like the inner curve of an abalone.

"Shell-handled Remington," Tom said with admiration. "An antique. I wanted to get her something for the anniversary of us meeting, and she said she wanted to learn."

"Learn to fire a gun?" All my practice with dropping my voice failed me on the last word, so for a second I sounded like a boy of twelve or thirteen, not seventeen. How had Daisy passed herself off as not knowing how to shoot? She was the one who would drive off the wolves and foxes, but her heart couldn't bear hurting a living creature, so she always fired and missed on purpose. Her father was immensely proud, and no one understood why. They didn't realize it took a better shot to miss by just a little than to hit.

Tom took back the gun. "She's something, isn't she?" he said, and I couldn't tell if he meant the pistol or my cousin.

Then he put it away, and his face was so wistful I knew he meant Daisy. That look was always about Daisy. She'd left it on men who met her once and never forgot her. For Daisy, the act of enchanting was so frequent that it must have seemed ordinary.

Tom pulled alongside the dock, and I got out so fast I clattered against the boards.

"Do you want me to walk you back?" Tom asked. "You don't seem used to the wine."

"No, I'm all right." I stumbled away from Tom and his runabout and his *gift* for my cousin.

"A self-sufficient man. I knew I liked you," he shouted as he pulled away, the wake kicking up foam. "I always tell Daisy, I just have a sense about people."

I stumbled off the dock and onto the grass. The world looked blurred, as if wine had spilled on it and made the ink of everything run down toward the bottom of the page.

The one point that didn't blur was the figure of a man. Or a boy? He didn't look much older than me, but he held himself upright as though ready to meet the world. He stood in the grass, hands in the pockets of his trousers, and stared out over the bay, eyes fixed straight across.

"You waiting for the next boat?" My hands in the grass broke my fall forward. "Because I don't think it's coming."

"Are you all right?" he asked.

I nodded. "It seems I can't walk a straight line, so I think the thing to do is face the trees, and that should mean I'll stagger true toward the house." The words made sense in my head, but they sounded muddied and strange out loud.

He approached, his pressed shirt brightening under the moon, cut by the two dark straps of his suspenders. "I think you're a little tight right now. Can I help you get home?"

"Home is Wisconsin," I said. "I'm trying to get over there."

Before my next fall, he caught me with one arm around my waist. "Okay, let's go." He took one of my arms over his shoulder and helped me walk. "Have you got a name?"

"I am Nicolás Caraveo of Beet Patch, Wisconsin, of the Beet Patch Caraveos." I said it with the grandeur of announcing my own entrance into a ballroom. "Do you like beets?"

"Not especially," he said.

"Me neither," I said. "Not my mother or father, either. I think it's in the blood. My family came to Wisconsin as betabeleros. Once you work so hard at something that it starts breaking your body, I think it just doesn't taste very good anymore."

"No," he said. "Not so much."

He smelled like rose water but with something else there. Something wild-growing and green. Nothing as prim as a mint sprig. Maybe bay leaves, or overgrown rosemary. I still hadn't figured it out by the time he got me through my door and was cueing me to drink water.

"Do you want an apple?" I asked from the sofa. "Or a biscuit? Or a vase of roses?"

But he was already at the door, closing it behind him with a soft laugh. "Good night, Nicolás Caraveo."

— ⦿ —

To Mr. Nicolás Caraveo of the Beet Patch Wisconsin Caraveos,

A pleasure meeting you last night.

I'm having a little party tonight, so if you should find yourself without diversion this evening, please do stop by.

Your neighbor,

Jay Gatsby

CHAPTER VI

The minute I woke up, my head thick with last night's wine, I suspected.

When I found the invitation outside my door—fountain pen ink on heavy linen stock—I knew.

The man looking out over the bay had been my new neighbor, and his first impression of me was as an underage drunk.

There was no use trying to correct the impression outright. Telling him I'd never had more than half a glass of stolen Communion wine was a good way to sound like a liar. The best I could do was show a sober face tonight.

Gatsby's pristine handwriting called it a "little party," but every coming and going I saw from the cottage window said otherwise. Crisply suited musicians carried violas and saxophones. Men piled up crates of oranges and grapefruits and lemons with smoother rinds than I'd ever seen, as though they'd been buffed. The strings of lights were as numerous as the strands of spider silk in a web, and all in colors I had never known light bulbs could come in. Lavender, rose, pale blue and gold against the deep green of the hedges and trees.

I had one shirt that might pass for good enough. I could prop the collar taut with stays, and if I didn't move too much, no one would notice the tiny hole I'd darned up just under the arm. I put it on over one of the side lacers Daisy had given me, and I crossed the shorn green velvet of the grass between the cottage and Gatsby's mansion.

Guests spilled out of shining cars, and with every new set, Gatsby's blue gardens grew louder and brighter. Trumpets joined the saxophones. Women flashed fingernails painted with question marks or renderings of their own faces. They wore eyeliner in the creases of their eyes, blinking as they threw tinseled confetti and lit each other's cigarettes. Daisy had written to me about how many women in New York smoked in public and about the cigarette company advertisements telling girls to favor lighters over desserts. But it hadn't caught on back home quite the way it had here.

This sense of being out of place lessened only with the revelation that there were other guests who weren't white.

Two men with skin a darker brown than mine were talking about some telegraph magnate.

Two Black women laughed in a way that fluttered their eyelashes.

There was a woman another guest said was Chinese American, but it was a white man who said it, so I didn't assume he was right. Back home, such men referred to neighbors whose families had come from Guatemala and Peru as *Mexicans* without ever bothering to check.

The woman stood next to a white woman, the two of them skeptically studying a tube of orange lipstick.

"Tangee color-changing."

"It doesn't go on tangerine, does it?"

"It's not supposed to. It says it shifts to the right color for your lips."

A Black man wearing a tie threaded through with silver explained to a group why scientists thought the universe had been expanding since the start of the cosmos. He said it with the wistful admiration of someone describing a lover's beauty.

A semicircle of brown-skinned women showed off their latest manicures, cuticles and tips left blank, only the middle of the nail painted peacock green or plum. I thought I heard one of them say something in Spanish, but I couldn't be sure, and I didn't dare ask, and how would I ask anyway? Say something in Spanish and risk a blank look? Or worse, ask, *Are you like me?*

But even if I couldn't be sure whether this woman or that man over there was the same kind of brown I was, I knew this: If Gatsby's mansion was a place where more than just white people were welcome, maybe I didn't have to draw myself as tight as a violin string.

A waiter passed by, and I stared at the glasses he carried on a polished tray.

"Delft blue?" he offered. "Jenever, crème de violette, elderflower, and a little bit of pepper. It might sound strange, but I tried it earlier—you'll like it."

"No, thank you," I said. But I kept staring, not because of the blue purple of the drink or even the perfect curl of lemon peel floating on the surface.

The glasses seemed to be tilted, as though melting to one side.

"Oh, they're made that way." The man laughed. "When it looks straight, you know you've had enough!" Then he was on his way, the crowd so thick he vanished in seconds.

A blonde stopped in front of me. She touched the curls arranged around her face and shoved an empty glass into my hand. "Refresh that for me, would you?"

I stopped still, wondering if it was more how I looked or how I was dressed.

Then I realized that the men's shirts were as colorful as the women's dresses, in shades that matched the citrus rinds and cocktails. Crimson dots, patterns of green and yellow, and brilliant blue stripes stood in contrast with the flawless black dinner jackets. (Were those dinner jackets? I was guessing.)

The only men wearing what I was wearing—a white shirt and black pants—were the waiters. I had not only embarrassed myself, I was probably also causing the catering team some confusion.

I'd known West Egg was no place for my denim and twill work shirts, and I thought knowing that was enough. But it turned out I didn't know anything.

"Come on, speed it up," the woman said. "Don't you know how to do what you're told?"

A second woman came between me and the blond one. She had her hair pulled back, as dark and smooth as the bay at night. Her posture was so straight she looked like a painted portrait of a duchess greeting a crowd. Her eyes were a brown as deep as my own, but something about the cool tone of her gaze made it different from mine. The brown of my eyes held wet earth and worn barn wood. Hers held the richness of fountain pen ink and nail lacquer.

"He's not a waiter," this woman said.

The blond woman cast a glance down at my shirt. "Isn't he?"

The dark-haired woman plucked the glass from my hand and placed it back in the blond woman's. "Go put this somewhere, would you, dear?"

The blond woman's mouth rounded open in such offense, she looked like a startled doll.

"Sorry about all that." The dark-haired woman clasped both my shoulders. She walked me through the crowd, the air sugared with a hundred perfumes. "Don't mind her."

Sometimes, when I met someone else who I thought might not be white but I didn't know for sure, a wondering turned on at the back of my mind. If I hadn't known better, something about this woman's features and coloring would have done it. Her skin was light, but not the flour-pale of the blond woman now flouncing away.

"I'm Jordan, by the way," she said.

The wondering faded. That sense at the back of my mind had been because I'd seen her face before, in photographs. I placed her picture in newsprint, smiling from under a hat, a clean-lined skirt skimming her calves.

"Jordan Baker?" I asked. "The golfer?"

"A fan." She smiled. "I like you."

No, of course she was white. If she wasn't, she wouldn't have been allowed in half the tournaments. My father couldn't play on the closest course back home, even if he could have afforded the greens fees.

"Any boy who recognizes me so fast gets a prize," Jordan Baker said. "You're coming to my next tournament as my guest."

"I don't think that'll go over so well," I said.

"Anyone wants to say anything about it, I'll accidentally knock my putting cleek into their heads," she said. "Now tell me your name."

"Nick," I said, wincing at the memory of how I'd introduced myself to Gatsby last night. "Caraveo."

"Oh." A light came on in Jordan's voice. "So you're the boy Daisy lured all the way to New York."

"You know Daisy?" I asked.

"We go months back," Jordan said. "Though we can't stroll along the park without someone taking our picture."

"All the sports pages want to know what you're driving, and all the ladies' magazines want to know what you're wearing?" I asked.

"Oh, they're after Daisy's picture almost as much as mine." With a smile at a passing caterer, Jordan accepted a purple drink with violets floating in the glass. "She's nearly as famous these days."

"Because she's with Tom?" I asked.

"That, yes," Jordan said. "She's engaged to be engaged to Tom. We'll get into that nonsense some other time. And it's because she's so lovely. But so many girls here are lovely. What really did it was the incident on the boat."

"What incident?" I asked.

Jordan paused in the middle of her sip. "Don't you know?"

She told the story in that rush of all party conversations. And it was in this way that I learned my cousin had come by her status partly through beauty, partly through her impending engagement to a Buchanan, and partly by an accident on a yacht.

During a party on Louis Becker's yawl, Daisy had fallen overboard wearing the $350,000 pearl necklace. My cousin was a good swimmer, the only one who could rival me at our breath-holding contests in the pond. But upon hitting the water, the weight of so many French and Italian pearls threatened to drag her into the depths.

"She thought she might drown," Jordan said. "She says she would have, but an angel of God must have unfastened it. Or a mermaid."

Tom had dispatched every lifeboat and man in reach to look for his not-quite-fiancée.

"He didn't go into the water himself, of course," Jordan said. "Couldn't ruin his suit."

But it wasn't one of Tom's patrols that rescued Daisy Fay. She wasn't lifted from the waves by strong, certain arms. Daisy swam to shore herself, rising from the surf. The family whose estate sat on that stretch of beach had been playing croquet when they spotted her. She was wide-eyed and frightened, but something about her inspired awe, as though she had fought the sea for her life. It seemed equally likely that she had either wrestled down the waves or charmed them into giving her up.

That image of Daisy, emerging from the ocean like Venus on her shell, left her name on every tongue. It set her star among the constellations of famous socialites.

"We still don't know what exactly happened on that boat, how Daisy ended up in the water," Jordan said. "That's part of why everyone thought it was so delicious. Was it one of Tom's old flames? A jealous girl who resented this new intrusion into the East Egg set? There were a hundred theories, just as many as there are about Gatsby. And speaking of him, come this way. We're finding our host."

I had so many more questions about Daisy and the yacht

and the sea. But Jordan took my hand as though we were paired up for a dance.

"Who is he?" I asked.

"No one knows," Jordan said. "Isn't it marvelous?"

"But you know him," I said.

"We were fast friends," Jordan said.

"So, who is he?" I asked.

"Oh, I heard he kills people for money, or struck oil, or imports contraband champagne. It's all nonsense. Rumors." She flashed a grin over her shoulder. "I hope the one about the champagne's true though. I'd believe it. Jay!" she shouted over the bustle. "Jay!"

She shouted louder, lifting a hand. How did such delicate fingers and forearms accomplish the golf swing she was famous for?

I only found my neighbor by how he turned, and stilled, in the roiling crowd.

Jordan led me toward him. "Jay, will you get this boy in a different shirt before Carolyn tries to make him fetch her hat and coat?"

My throat turned sour. If I had to change my shirt, I'd have to make a good excuse for why I needed to do it behind a closed door. I had an undershirt on over the side lacer, but anyone looking closely might ask, *What have you got under there?* And I'd have to sell a lie about a recent injury or operation.

"Jay's got about a thousand of them." Jordan touched a

hand to my arm again. "He collects shirts. He wouldn't even notice one gone."

"I'm glad you two met." Gatsby's delight seemed so genuine it was my instinct to look for the calculation in it. "Nicolás is my new neighbor."

"Yes, the cottage boy," Jordan said. "And a math genius, I've heard."

Then Jordan was gone, and Gatsby was leading me toward a marble staircase. Guests crowded halfway up the steps, so Gatsby didn't take his arm off mine until we were through.

"You really don't have to," I said. "I don't want you to go to any trouble."

"It's no trouble at all," Gatsby said.

Under the brass lamps, I could see him more clearly than under the moon and the dock lights. He couldn't have been older than eighteen, maybe nineteen. His hair was an even lighter brown than Daisy had turned hers. It took on a gold cast at the edges where the light hit it. Strands of tinsel had landed in his hair and stayed, like veins of ore in rock.

The central rooms of the house were done in so much royal blue and copper that it took me a minute to adjust to the palette of Gatsby's bedroom. The space was gray satin wallpaper and autumn-leaf wood, gray bedding and gilt edging, a mix of masculine and glittering I had never seen.

He opened a set of double doors, revealing a closet of deep wood shelves. A full column held shirts in pristine squares.

Each folded stack of blue and purple or pink and tan stood a measured distance from the next, and alongside them sat accompanying stacks of pocket squares and handkerchiefs, the edges folded so neatly they looked sharp.

"Do you have a favorite color?" Gatsby asked.

"I guess I like green," I said.

He pulled a forest-green shirt from a stack and tossed it to me. It unfurled in midair. I caught it by the sleeve but didn't put it on.

"In fact, I'm considering a costume change myself." He flicked at a damp spot on the otherwise-immaculate yellow of his shirt, and then unbuttoned it. He took down his suspenders to get the shirt off.

It took effort for me not to gasp in recognition.

I only saw the vague shape of it beneath his undershirt. If I hadn't known what it was ahead of time, I would have missed it. If I hadn't been wearing one myself, if I wasn't familiar with the subtle outline, I wouldn't have noticed. But there it was, the faint suggestion of an identical side lacer to the one I was wearing. The thick straps at the shoulder, the scribble of crossing strings on each side of the rib cage. There was the shadow of the fastening, one more unassuming contour of his undershirt, like the fitted hem of the sleeve or the trio of buttons leading up to the collar. One of the buttons had come undone, and he seemed like someone who'd be so careful about such things that I thought of telling him. But I still hadn't found my voice.

This boy had the money to gild a garden in strings of tinted lights. He was as beautiful as the tinsel caught in his hair. And he had allowed me this glimpse of him. It set off a flare in my chest, bright enough to burn through my own shirt.

"You're . . . ," I blurted out, but stopped myself, so the single word hung in the juniper-scented air.

Gatsby put on another shirt, a brown one that gleamed like bronze.

The fizzing hope of meeting another boy like me sank when I realized something else. He wouldn't have risked me noticing what was beneath his undershirt if he couldn't guess what was under mine. I had erred in some way that made it obvious. A lapse in how low I held my voice, or a nervous laugh pitched the wrong way, or a gesture that was perhaps familiar to him because he'd had to train himself out of it.

"How did you know that I was . . ." Another half-finished sentence, lank in the air like a cast-off shirt. "How could you tell? What did I get wrong?"

"No, it was nothing like that." Gatsby looked at me like I was worth all the faith in the world. "You didn't get anything wrong."

For the minute he cast his reassuring smile on me, I believed in the absolute truth of the boy I had made of myself in Wisconsin, and the shimmering possibility of the man I would make of myself in New York.

As he shrugged back into his suspenders, I waited for him to ask me not to tell anyone, something I was about to ask him for. But I wanted him to bring it up first.

He didn't. It seemed a matter of unspoken, infinite trust, like he knew his confidence was as safe with me as mine was with his.

I put on the green shirt, knowing the shadow of my own side lacer was nothing much of note to Jay Gatsby.

"I think we just recognize each other." He fastened the buttons on the gleaming brown shirt. "Boys like us always know one another about a thousand years before anyone else knows us, don't we?"

CHAPTER VII

Before I'd left Wisconsin, my mother bought me a few leaves of stationery and ink. She said I'd need it in New York, that that's how you showed manners, a handwritten note rather than a basket of tomatoes or tortillas.

I planned to leave the note in the wrought-iron box. But Gatsby appeared from the lemon-hued early light in morning slacks and a sweater, as though the carefully shaped hedges had floated him forward.

He looked as fresh as the grounds themselves, already cleared of citrus husks and discarded glasses. All that remained were sprinklings of hairpins and lost pearls. A few necklaces and bracelets had been draped on tree branches and forgotten, a few coats tossed over hedges. Bits of tinsel streaked the grass like falling stars.

"You've got to teach me how you do it," I told him.

He smiled. "Do what?"

"How you drink at a party and look so clear the next morning," I said.

"No secret to it," he said. "I don't drink."

"Then why bring it in?" I asked.

He shrugged. "Everyone else likes it."

I handed him the envelope. "I'll bring the shirt back too. I was just going to have it cleaned."

"Oh, don't, please," Gatsby said. "Keep it. You'd be doing me a favor. The fabric was a such a lovely color on the bolt, but the moment I put it on I knew it was a mistake. I can't carry off that green. It looks right on you though. I think maybe it was meant to be yours. Would you like to come in? I was just fixing breakfast for a friend, and we'd be happy for a third. You two would get on, I think."

"No," I said. "That's all right."

"Then how about a tour?" he asked. "I can show you the grounds."

"What about your guest?" I asked.

"Most likely on the telephone for the next half hour," Gatsby said. "There's always something to attend to. I've learned to make dishes that can keep."

It was early enough that I couldn't make a convincing show of having to catch the next train. So I followed along the stone path with Gatsby.

"The truth is, I'm glad to have a chance to talk with you when we can properly hear each other," he said. "It's as loud as Fifth Avenue whenever a good party gets going, isn't it?"

The men working at the garden looked at us as though we were interrupting a portrait session.

"It's going to be a sight to melt a heart of snow," one of them said, with an Irish accent. "So long as you don't keep changing your mind about it."

Gatsby gave an apologetic dip of his head. "I leave the artists to it."

The men returned their attention to the earth.

I couldn't imagine improving upon anything. Lemon and olive trees filtered the silver off the bay, and pines grasped at the sky above the mansion. A bright lawn sloped down toward the dark blue of the swimming pool and a gray-green pond, broken by bright islands of flower beds.

I bent down to the dahlias, studying the fractal pattern of the petals.

"Are you a botany enthusiast?" Gatsby asked.

"More of the math in the flowers than the flowers themselves," I said.

"What do you mean the math in the flowers?" he asked.

"There's math under everything." I stood up. "Everything can be broken down into numbers."

He smiled. "Can it?"

I felt the stuttering urgency to explain. Not just the geometry of flowers but the golden mean, the math of planets and of music and of the texture on his wallpaper.

"Every beautiful thing can be broken down into math," I said. "There are numbers under all of it."

"Isn't that a little cold?" he asked.

"No," I said. "It's comforting. It means that underneath

everything that's ever moved you or that you've ever loved, there's something real and irrefutable. There's a lattice of numbers proving that it's true, that it's really there, that you didn't just imagine all of it."

He looked at me so strangely then. It was such a queer, enraptured look that I thought he might be about to kiss me, but what a thought that was. Boys like Gatsby didn't kiss boys like me, if they ever kissed boys at all.

But then he said, "Tell me how something beautiful is math."

I thought about it. "Did you know that there are no green or purple stars?"

"What's that got to do with math?" he asked.

"It's all math," I said. "It's the physics of how light travels through space, atmospheric composition, how the human eye perceives color, the angles of our vantage points here on Earth. And the electromagnetic spectrum, that's math too. Green is in the middle of the visible light spectrum, so if a star emits peak radiation at a green wavelength, it's going to emit a lot of other colors too, so it'll look more white than green. And with purple, humans tend to be more sensitive to blue than purple, so a star emitting peak radiation at a violet wavelength is going to look more blue to us."

Gatsby turned to the corner of the sky that still held a little of the blue hour. The last few stars clung to the horizon, and Gatsby gazed at them so intently I thought he might be trying to prove me wrong.

"That doesn't mean they don't exist," he said.

"What do you mean?" I asked.

"Well, think about it," he said. "Standing here on Earth, we might think there are no green or purple stars anywhere in the universe simply because we can't detect them. But they could be there. Whether we detect them or not."

"Jay." A woman's voice, low and clear as a radio actress's, rang out into the gardens. "Where did you get off to?"

Gatsby's face broke into an embarrassed smile. "It isn't what you think. Martha is a good friend and a business partner, but not . . ."

"Not in a million years." The woman appeared and slid a hand onto Gatsby's shoulder.

She wore the kind of menswear-inspired clothes Daisy had shown me in catalogs. Wider-legged trousers. A button-down shirt under a vest. They were so well tailored to her shape that the overall effect was to make her look more feminine. She looked out from under the brim of an angled hat adorned with a jeweled pin. Her lips were painted an orange pink that brightened the contrast between the blue of her eyes and the medium brown of her hair. She had the aura of a film star, and it seemed too bright for daylight.

"I mean"—Martha looked at Gatsby as though reconsidering—"he's handsome enough, but a thousand miles from my type."

"This is my neighbor, Nicolás Caraveo," Gatsby said.

Martha extended her hand. She shook as firmly as any

man, but her hands were soft as plums, the nails varnished a melon pink with that moon of cuticle unpolished at the base.

"Martha Wolf," she said. "And I assure you I find you just as handsome, but alas"—she gave us both airs of regret—"neither of you will ever win my heart on account of being men, so please do give up all hope now."

I almost caught her meaning, but I was too slow to stop myself from saying, "I'm sorry?"

"Women, my dear," she said. "I like women."

With a fizzing mix of delight and nerves, I let out a laugh.

"Have I shocked you?" she asked.

It wasn't that there weren't women sharing their lives with women in Wisconsin. But I'd never heard any refer to the fact so plainly. I'd been on West Egg a single weekend, and I'd already met another boy like me and a woman who spoke, easily and out loud, of liking other women.

"Nick, you've just met the woman with the most distinguished palate ever known to New York," Gatsby said. "Martha can taste anything."

Martha and I both started laughing, though she did more openly, while I was trying so hard to stop myself that I started coughing.

"I didn't mean it that way," Gatsby said. His own laugh sounded reluctant for only a moment before it bloomed full. "I meant she's a connoisseur. A gourmet. You give her the most complicated cocktail, she can tell you what's it in. A cup of tea, she'll name every herb and leaf. Pour her a glass of champagne, she'll tell you what was growing in the fields near the grapes. She's famous for it, the envy of every collector and every show-off with a wine cellar."

Martha nodded at the compliment, but she was still coming down from her laugh, and I was still stifling mine.

"That took all of"—Gatsby examined his watch—"two minutes for you both to start." Then he looked at me. "Didn't I say you would get on?"

"Pleased to meet you, Nicolás Caraveo." Martha touched her wrist just under the cuff of her sleeve. I thought she might be checking a watch for the time. But the way she did it, so carefully, made me sure this was something else, like touching a charm bracelet from a lover.

A telephone inside gave a metallic ring.

Martha sighed. "They're all going to start thinking this is my office."

This seemed my best chance for a graceful exit.

"Thank you," I told Gatsby. "For the party. And the shirt. I guess I don't understand the dress code. Or anything around here, really."

"I could teach you a few things," Gatsby said. "If you'd like."

"You'd do that?" I asked.

"I had to study all of it myself," he said. "Someone else might as well benefit."

"You did?" I asked.

"Sure," he said. "The finger bowls with the petals in them? I thought they were artistic flower arrangements. I had to learn all of it. Come over after work. I'll tell you more ridiculous things than you ever wanted to know."

I smiled before I could help it. "Thank you." I turned in the direction of the cottage.

"Good to see you, Nicolás," Gatsby called when I was halfway across the lawn.

I turned back. The last of the stars twinkled out over Gatsby's head.

"Nick," I said. "It's just Nick."

CHAPTER VIII

"Now don't let all the noise scare you," Mr. Benson said, leading me through the fray of men shouting about fire sales and futures.

"We're behind the eight ball on this one!"

"Even money on whether it'll be silver or gold first!"

Each yell added to the pounding in my head, this time not from wine but from how little sleep I'd gotten. The bright whir of Gatsby's party was as intoxicating as cordial, and I was still stumbling out of it.

"No dice! It'll go bust in a month, you mark my words!"

"Buzz your bright-idea man. He got us into this mess!"

"Just ignore them," Mr. Benson said. "That's the thing you're here for, to take the emotion out of it."

A man loosened his necktie with one hand, and with another, held a sheet of paper. He studied it for about a half a second, threw it on the floor, and unleashed a flurry of profanities that would scandalize a longshoreman.

"Oh good, he's come early," one of the neat-haired young men said. "I'll take a sardolive and egg right at noon."

Two more men who looked just like him broke out laughing.

I kept my face still.

"He's not your sandwich boy, Lockhart," Mr. Benson said. "You'll be taking his order before you know it. Especially if you don't get me those numbers I asked for during the last ice age."

Mr. Benson led me to a desk squeezed between two file cabinets. It took me a minute to even recognize the thing as a desk underneath the piles of paper.

"Hexton'll have his own ideas about what to do with you," Mr. Benson said. "But just remember, *I* found you in Minnesota, not him."

"Wisconsin," I said.

"Didn't I say Wisconsin?" Mr. Benson ran a hand over his head, where so much brilliantine had left his hair as shined and motionless as patent leather. "Point is, I hired you, and I say you're helping forecast the price of commodities." He threw the file in his hand on top of the heap. "Now, first-day quiz. What are the top four industries in our great country?"

"Steel," I said.

"He's quick," Mr. Benson said. "And the second?"

"Railroads?" I said.

"Don't ask it, say it. Yes, railroads. And?"

"Automobiles." I almost made that one a question too but stopped myself.

"Three of four." Mr. Benson nodded. "Last one."

I stalled a second too long, and Mr. Benson leaped in with "Movies! It's all about silver and cellulose these days! The dreams of millions are wound up in those reel tins. There's more money in selling dreams than in all the wheat futures in the world. Never forget that, Carraway."

"It's Caraveo," I said.

"I'm doing you a favor here," he said. "Back in Michigan, you be whoever you want. But here, you forget the family name. You're Nick Carraway."

CHAPTER IX

"Now this might seem like a small thing. But it's important if you don't want everyone to know you grew up on a county road." Gatsby set a wooden cutting board down on a garden table. "Try not to stare at women's stockings. They'll tease you forever, and they'll know you're not from New York or Chicago or any big city."

I doubted that would be a problem. The women back home could barely get me to dance with the girls at the church halls.

Gatsby halved a grapefruit. "It's not because I think you make a habit of staring in general. It's because the stockings here are probably a little different from what you're used to seeing."

"Has the mechanism changed greatly?" I asked. I had girl cousins and therefore knew more about ladies' clothing than I ever wanted to. "They use garters to hold them up during the day. They roll them down over the garters at night."

"I didn't mean how they work." Gatsby halved another

grapefruit. "I meant the style. Everything from ribbing to embroidery to prints of Rudolph Valentino's face."

"You're joking about that last one," I said.

"Oh, not at all," Gatsby said. "Martha gave a lady friend a pair of those, and she just went wild for them." He started the first grapefruit half on a ceramic juicer.

"Need a hand?" I asked.

He shook his head. "It's nothing, truly."

With a few twists, he hollowed the juice and pulp from the half.

"And speaking of lady friends," he said. "If you hear a woman telling her boyfriend 'Bank's closed,' it means she's not going to kiss him anymore just then. Usually because she's annoyed with him. Usually because he's given her good reason to be."

He moved to the next half, clearing it out with a few more turns of his wrist.

"And something else about the clothing," he said. "Most gowns you'll see around here don't have fastenings. They're simply slipped on. So if a girl pulls you into a closet and you notice there aren't any hook-and-eye closures, don't worry, she hasn't suddenly torn off her gown. That's not her slip. It's her actual dress."

"Why do you keep giving me advice on girls?" I asked. "Is there someone you and Jordan plan to fling me at?"

In a rare moment of Gatsby looking something other than at ease with himself, he couldn't meet my eyes. He seemed to offer a shrug as a kind of substitute. "You're a handsome sort, that's all. If you wanted to find yourself in need of such practical knowledge, it wouldn't take much."

It was a compliment. That was all it was. It didn't mean anything beyond that, and I knew it. But if he'd meant to make me as uncomfortable as he seemed, he'd succeeded.

He juiced another grapefruit half, and it sweetened and sharpened the air. "Next we've got to talk about Mondrian," he said.

"Who?" I asked.

"He's a painter," Gatsby said. "Abstract forms. You'll see a hundred forgeries of *Tableau I* by the time the summer's through. But what you need to know is the colors. The black and white, scarlet red, blue, yellow. Primary colors are everywhere this year, and that's part of why."

I thought back to the party. It was true about the primary colors, but they'd also been alongside faded peach, rose beige, acorn brown, deep brown, soft colors sparkling with beads and paillettes. So I asked about this.

"Right," Gatsby said. "It seems like everything at once, doesn't it? Subtle colors alongside bright ones. But if you look at everyone at once, there's a logic to it. It's like a painting. Everyone sort of helps everyone else stand out."

I pictured it that way, the faint contrast of sage green and silver, the brilliance of black and gold. There were a thousand things I needed to learn, but this—knowing how best to view the artwork of a New York society party—this was a start.

Gatsby poured the grapefruit juice into glasses and handed one to me. "People drink orange juice in the morning, but there's a kind of magic about drinking something the same color as the sky, don't you think?" He lifted his glass toward the pink clouds over the sound.

I did the same. "¡Salud!"

"Good," he said. "I thought you were going to say cheers."

"What's wrong with *cheers*?" I asked.

"Nothing so far as I'm concerned," he said. "But apparently around here it's *good health*, not *cheers*."

I drank from the glass, the pink sugar a little bitter, like tasting those clouds alongside the bite of the sea.

"What am I ever going to do for you?" I asked.

He drank from his glass. "What do you mean?"

"How am I ever going to repay you for what you're teaching me?" I asked.

"Why do you have to repay it?" he asked.

"I don't know," I said. "I guess I don't like thinking that there's so much you're doing for me and that there's nothing I can do for you."

An odd look passed over his face.

"What is it?" I asked.

"What's what?" he asked.

"There's something you don't want to ask me for," I said. "What is it?"

"You've just answered your own question," he said. "I don't want to tell you."

"Why not?" I asked.

"Because you'll laugh," he said. "Or you'll think it's why I invited you to my party in the first place, and it wasn't."

"Well, now you have to tell me," I said.

"What you have to understand is," he said, "I didn't even know you knew Daisy until Jordan said something."

I tapped the basin of the juicer, where grapefruit seeds rested on the damp ceramic. "If you keep stalling, these are going to sprout."

When he took another drink, I thought he was delaying further, but it turned out he was shoring himself up.

"I met Daisy a long time ago," Gatsby said. "Before I left for the war."

"Left for the war?" I asked. "How old are you?"

I wanted to snatch the question back, and my rudeness with it. But Gatsby said, easily, "Nineteen."

That meant he couldn't have been older than fourteen or fifteen when he was in the war.

"Then how did you"—I stopped and tried again—"I mean, weren't you too young?"

"Old enough to sell them on the lie," he said. "And old enough to get into the dances, which was where I met Daisy."

He said her name like a pale gold breath.

Then Gatsby told me the story of him and the girl he did not know was my cousin. He told me of recognizing each other, not from having met before but because they each noticed things in the other that made them the same. They were both dream-filled, acting at being older and moneyed, her speaking casually of a cream-finished car she did not own, and he of a prep school he did not attend. They were a boy and a girl from corners of the earth so distant, New York wouldn't cast its glittering gaze that far west.

"I remember all of it, right back to that first night," Gatsby said. "When she laughed, it was like the inside of her was a church echoing the sound everywhere, like that was the perfect noise of the whole world. And the way she moved her hands . . . it was birds taking flight, that first moment of them on the air, every time. And I could see a life with her, this glorious kind of life I never imagined for myself. One I thought I could never have."

I wondered what it took to maintain such a sense of romance.

"Even back then, I could tell what kind of woman she'd be," Gatsby said. "She had that idea of who she was turning into already. You could see it in how she arranged her hair, in the way she lifted the hem of her dress to go upstairs. I knew what I'd have to do to become a man worthy of that woman she was going to be. And I thought, if I could ever be the kind of man that a woman like that would want to share a life with, then I would have gotten it right."

I could picture them under the salt of summer stars, imagining the radiant people they would make of themselves.

"And when I realized that I cared for her," Gatsby said, "I told her so, and I almost hoped she'd tell me she didn't care for me so I could let the whole thing go. But she did, so that was that."

That was that, at least, until the war he was too young to fight took him across an ocean. The last time they saw each other was in the wet chill of the coming autumn, firelight held between their lips.

"How long were you two . . ." Another of my unfinished thoughts. Every time I talked to Gatsby, I littered them across the grass.

"A month," he told me.

A map of the bay resolved in my mind.

A young man happened to buy a house in West Egg, just across the water from where a young woman, dazzling as yellow diamonds, was staying at the Buchanans' East Egg estate.

A young man in West Egg stared out toward one particular point on the opposite shore.

None of it had been coincidence. Gatsby had bought this mansion—and created the lavish grandeur of these parties—to pull at Daisy's heart from across the bay and to show her, in brilliant gardens and brass bands, what he'd made of himself. He'd been by the dock the night I stumbled off Tom's motor cruiser because he'd been watching the point on this earth where Daisy was.

Daisy had been so understanding when I told her I was a boy. And now I wondered if Jay Gatsby might have been her first introduction to the truth that some boys were thought to be girls at birth, and that we then faced the task of making ourselves.

"You know she's with Tom," I said.

Gatsby nodded to the sheered grass. "I wasn't quick enough." He said it not with bitterness but as a fact I needed to know. "I didn't have anything to offer a girl like her back when we met. I thought I could though, one day. But while I was gone, she got too far ahead of me. She became that girl, that woman, she always dreamed of being, and I hadn't gotten all the way to being that man. It took me too long to catch up. It took too long for the war to be over and for me to get back, and by the time I did, I still wasn't that man even though she was that woman. I didn't want to find her again until I had a version of myself worth showing her."

Gatsby told me, in a near mumble, how he'd heard about it all after the fact, how in the intervening time, Daisy had wanted her life settled and decided. In that window of her restlessness, Tom Buchanan had appeared.

The light on Gatsby's face shifted, as though he was coming back to the present day. And in the present day, my cousin wore an emerald ring that winked across the bay like a second dock light.

"And what happened on that boat." Gatsby's voice tightened. "I'd never have let that happen to her."

That stirred me toward Gatsby more than any romantic story. I wanted Daisy to be with someone who'd look out for her. Just because she was a good enough swimmer to drag herself to shore didn't mean I wanted her to have to.

"Anyway," Gatsby said. "I was wondering if you might invite Daisy over some afternoon and have me around at the same time."

The shy request made me hesitate.

Tom didn't seem the kind of man who'd take such a reunion well. Thanks to Daisy's lies, he already thought I was unrelated to her. Inviting her over alone might cast the sight of her hands on my forearms in a different light, even if Tom knew nothing about Gatsby.

"If you'd just think on it, Nick," Gatsby said. "Even if you decide you won't do it, I'd appreciate you thinking on it more than I can tell you."

CHAPTER X

I soon learned the purpose of the second file cabinet, which was to keep the stock room door from causing me injury every time it flew open.

The numbers swam in front of my eyes, and I blinked to get them still. But as I compared each set to the next, the first wisps of patterns emerged, the geometry of how production predicted price, how prices rose and fell in rhythm with one another. It was all a dance to the time signatures of linear algebra. It was the beautiful chaos of what happened to certain differential equations over time.

By the time the day was over, the throbbing in my head had eased, letting in those mathematical songs. It was a thrill not unlike being in Gatsby's house, in his room with all those shirts in so many colors.

The revolving door in the lobby spun men out from the building, but I wasn't getting near that thing. The side door that swung on a hinge did just fine for sending me into the city evening.

Home had been all fields stretching toward the horizon, but New York was all about height. It was the white marble of the library, the iron and rust of the elevated railways, the theaters blowing the smell of magnesium lighting out their doors. Passing traffic at Fifth and Twenty-Third rustled skirts enough to show ankles, and the Flatiron Building cut the sky above me in two.

I was still looking up when a hand landed on my shoulder. I whirled around, and might have shoved the stranger away if I hadn't recognized the grinning face of Tom Buchanan.

"How was our go-getter's first week?" He clapped me on the back. "Come on, we're celebrating."

"I was just heading for the train," I said.

"For a thrilling evening of clock-watching?" Tom asked. "I refuse to accept it. A friend's having a party, and we're going."

Tom set the weight of his hand between my shoulder blades. He shoved me into a cab, and then out of the cab and up toward a sixth-floor apartment. The walls were papered in lipstick red until about halfway, and then to the ceiling in silver. In the dim lighting, the chandeliers bounced their glitter off the metallic paper.

A young woman in lime green rushed to the door and threw her arms around Tom. Her hair was the red of winter wheat, and she had the kind of figure Daisy had once, and might still have under the lacers and girdles.

"And who is this?" The woman extended her hand, not

like I was supposed to shake it, more tilted forward, like a lady in an old novel. And because I didn't know what else to do, I grasped her fingers and set an awkward kiss on the back of that pale hand.

The woman shrieked out a laugh. "I like this one, Tommy!"

"I told you," Tom said. "Cathryn'll like him, don't you think?"

The woman spun her head toward Tom, pinned curls catching the light from the trio of chandeliers, then back to me. "Myrtle Wilson. Pleasure to meet you. Make my home your home."

Another woman strolled up, her eyes taking the measure of my shirt and suspenders. "Oh, he's adorable." She was taller and more angled than Myrtle but had hair that same wheat red. "Don't you want to just dress him in a sailor's uniform?"

"Please don't," I said.

"This is my sister, Cathryn," Myrtle said.

"Call me Trinette. It suits me better, don't you think?" She turned toward the women draped over the furniture, laughing with upturned cigarettes. "Don't you all agree it suits me better?"

Tom paused alongside me. "If you can manage to talk about something other than your math books, you won't go home alone tonight." He looked from the women's skirts, hems pooling alongside chaises, to me. "You're welcome."

Before I could understand the favor Tom thought he was doing me, he went into the bedroom with Myrtle.

No wonder Tom left the East Egg estate to Daisy while he stayed in the city. It was the easiest gallantry in the world.

Trinette pushed me down onto a chair. "Mingle, will you?"

The women didn't say anything to me at first, and that let me study them in the way I often found myself studying girls. They each had a kind of beauty made severe through winnowing down and then building back up. Some had shaved off their eyebrows and penciled them on again. A few wore eyeshadow from the lash line up to the brow, in deep purples and greens, charcoal and indigo blue.

Trinette shoved my shoulder. "It's cold cream."

"What is?" I asked.

"Why they're so pale. They use cold cream as foundation."

"You're joking," I said.

"And white powder," Trinette said. "Can I get you a drink?"

"No, thank you," I said.

"That's disgusting," one woman said to another.

"Well, how else are you going to get it started?"

"By wetting it from the tap, Dora, not spitting on it."

"What if I'm not near a tap?" Dora said.

The first woman noted my confusion. "You never heard of cake mascara? Don't you know anything about women?"

"Not much," I said.

"It's soap and coloring," Dora said. "And you have to activate it."

"But not by sticking your tongue on it."

Above us, sparkling, uneven strands dipped down from the chandeliers. Jewelry, I realized. Both costume pieces and real pearls served as garlands, with the occasional hat shading a bulb.

"Do you know the fiancée?" a woman in purple silk asked.

"Whose fiancée?" I asked.

"Girlfriend, not fiancée." Trinette handed me a glass of water. "Nothing final in the eyes of God or the law or even De Beers."

The woman in purple silk tilted her chin toward the closed bedroom door. "Well, do you know her?" she asked me again. "Tom's girl."

"Yeah," I said. "I know her."

"Is she as dreadful as she sounds?" Dora asked.

I watched the bedroom door, waiting for either Tom or Myrtle to emerge, or for one of them to come out of a different door altogether, like a magician's trick. I wanted proof that Tom wasn't alone in a room with someone who wasn't Daisy. I wanted proof that he hadn't brought me here either to flaunt it or to make me his cover.

Trinette propped up her feet. "My sister deserves a good man to take her out of that awful place."

"What awful place?" I asked.

"The Ash Heaps," Dora whispered. "She was always made for better stuff than her brothers' service garage."

My cousin's name sounded through the wall, a chorus of *Daisy, Daisy*.

The conversation stopped, all attention pricking toward the bedroom.

Tom's bellowing voice followed. "Now don't you start with that—"

"Daisy, Daisy, Daisy." The name turned mincing on Myrtle's tongue.

"You want to ruin a nice night?"

"If her name ruins a nice night, why are you with her?"

"Enough, Myrtle."

"Daisy, Daisy, Daisy!"

Maybe she was the cousin who pretended we didn't belong to the same family, but she was still my cousin, and that was still her name. By the next repetition I was at the door, and by the one after, I'd thrown it open.

Myrtle was still in her wheedling song, "Daisy, Daisy, Daisy," and Tom was still in this room with a woman who wasn't my cousin. I reached out to grab his arm, as though pulling him out of the room might pull him out of ever having gone in.

Tom jerked around. "You goddamn bell polisher, are you ever going to mind your own business?"

The point of his elbow caught my upper lip so precisely that my own tooth sliced it open.

"Oh, for God's sake, Nick." Tom pulled back with equal

parts horror and annoyance. "Oh, Nick. I thought you were McKee."

I pressed my hand to my lip, the taste of salt and metal rushing into my mouth.

"This photographer Trinette brings around sometimes." Tom sounded more apologetic than I thought a man like him knew how to be.

But my lip was still split open, and the woman Tom was with instead of my cousin was watching, arms folded.

"He's always trying to play armchair psychoanalyst with Myrtle and me. I didn't know it was you, honest to goodness. Myrtle, get some salt water."

I waved him off and left the room.

Outside the door, Trinette said something to me, but I didn't catch it. I mumbled a goodbye on my way out.

Was this why Tom hadn't seen Daisy fall off that yacht? Was this why someone else had had to ask where she was, because Tom was off in some corner of the yacht with some other girl? If he hadn't been, would Daisy have fallen in the first place?

She couldn't marry him. Daisy couldn't marry someone so careless with her heart and body.

But I couldn't tell Daisy about Tom and Myrtle. It would tear her into pieces like a rend in a dress. She would fold in on herself along with all her cut-crystal dreams of New York. Then, if Gatsby offered her the neat rose of his love, it wouldn't be her but her broken heart making the choice. That would be fair to neither her nor Gatsby.

But there might be another way.

I caught the next train to West Egg and then a taxi from the station to the paver-and-grass drive of Jay Gatsby's mansion.

He answered the door himself, top button of his starched shirt undone in what must have been his idea of lounge attire.

"Nick." His delight turned to worry as he saw the blood on my face and shirt. "What happened? Come in. Let's get you cleaned up."

I shook my head. "I'll do it."

Gatsby stared, uncomprehending.

I let my hand drop from my mouth. "I'll do it." Each breath threaded the sting of air through the gash on my lip. "I'll help you with Daisy."

Before Gatsby could rush out his thanks, before I could even witness the hope dawning over his face, I turned for the cottage.

Daisy had saved me once. She had seen me crumbling inside the shell of a girl I could not be, and she pushed me, letter after relentless letter, to tell my family I was a boy. She had saved me, and now I needed to do the same for her. If she got engaged to Tom and then married him, or worse, became his hidden-away mistress like Myrtle, we would lose her for good, and she would lose herself.

My cousin needed to get away from Tom Buchanan.

And if Jay Gatsby was the best chance to change her mind,
I'd do anything he asked.

———————— •◦• ————————

Mr. Nicolás Caraveo
West Egg, New York

Dearest Nicolás,

*How darling of you to invite me to tea! And how lovely to
pass an afternoon with you at the cottage.*

*Now you must let me tend to those roses. They like me,
you see. They whisper to me where they'd like to be pruned
back. Perhaps I'll make us both crowns of blooms!*

*Nicky, are you all right? Tom told me some ridiculous
story about a row you got into, and I didn't believe him for
a second, but he said I'd see for myself, that you had the
split lip to prove it. He said some Harvard boy in town with
his friends made a lewd comment to some pretty young nun
(Truly? To a nun? There are next to no good men left to be
had in this whole city, are there?) but that you put him in his
place so handily it came to blows.*

*Tom said he knew you were a good one. And how could
anyone argue with you defending the honor of a postulant?
But really, Nicky, a fight in the middle of Grand Central?
What would you have done if Tom hadn't been there to
smooth things over?*

Oh, you know how I hate sounding like some fretting aunt. But I worry about you, and I promised your mother and father that if they let you come east I'd look after you. So please, no more fisticuffs? For me?

Now, with all that business through, I'm off to choose something smart to wear for my visit. What shall I bring? Why don't you leave dessert to me? You steep the tea, I'll bring something sweet.

Yours, in hopes that you don't now
think of me as dreadfully dull and serious and
ruining all your boyish antics,

Daisy

CHAPTER XI

I came off a dizzying day at work to find a white man in a pale checkered suit at the cottage. He had on a straw boater hat, and emitted a sense of leisure that matched it. He had the kind of magazine-advertisement good looks that made it difficult to tell him from so many other moneyed men, down to the eyes that seemed to have been hand-tinted bright blue.

"You've got the wrong address," I said.

He held out his hand. "Elmer Dechert."

I didn't take it. After the headache of trying to explain my graphs—and by extension, myself—to Hexton, I was in no mood.

Dreary stuff, Carraway, Hexton had said. *Benson didn't hire a prophet of disaster. Tell us what to buy, not what to stay away from.*

"I'm from Port Roosevelt Limited," Elmer Dechert said. At my silent incomprehension, he added, "Insurance."

"I'm not interested," I said. Even if I had been, I didn't have anything to insure.

"I'm only here to ask you a few questions, Mr. Caraveo."

The sound of my name stopped me, my key half in the door.

"It won't take a minute," he said.

In an instant, I knew what he did for Port Roosevelt Limited.

In the same instant, I wondered how he managed to be taken seriously as an investigator looking like a member of the Whiffenpoofs. But I guessed that was the point—to seem at home along these shores.

"I was wondering if you knew anything about an incident earlier this summer," he said. "Involving a young lady and a yacht."

"Why are you asking me?" I said, a little too quickly.

"You're a friend of Miss Fay's," he said, "aren't you?"

"She's got a lot of friends," I said. "And if you want to know about what happened, why don't you ask someone who was on the yacht? It all happened before I got here."

"Did it?" Elmer Dechert asked.

"What is it you want, Mr. Dechert?" I asked.

"I'm just being thorough." He lit a cigarette, and I hoped it wasn't a sign of him making himself comfortable. "When a company finds itself in the position to pay out several hundred thousand dollars for a lost necklace, there's going to be a little digging around. You understand."

"Have you sent divers after it?" I asked. "That thing had to be the size of a jellyfish."

Dechert laughed. "You don't fit in here, do you?"

I turned toward my door.

He came forward, as though he meant to pat me on the back. "It's a compliment."

I shrank away from his arm.

"The thing is," he said, "I'm not so sure it ever ended up in the water."

I pretended that unlocking my door took the skill and focus of relating line integrals to surface integrals.

"Your friend Daisy," Dechert said, "she can't remember falling off the boat. She says the necklace came off her, but I think she wants to believe what she wants to believe. It makes a better story if the thing comes loose and she swims for her life. But I don't believe in angels or mermaids, and I think your friend was lucky to live."

"She was," I said, hoping I'd prove boring enough to leave alone.

Dechert kept talking. "From what I hear, she would have been too drunk to unfasten it on dry land, forget in the middle of a swell. I don't think she wants to consider that anyone had anything to do with sending her over. But it makes me wonder who might have had motive to take the thing."

A chilling image came into my head. My cousin stumbling around a yacht. Any number of thieves—none of whom would be suspected because they were all from such storied families—carefully unhitching the clasps and then guiding her toward the edge. *You've had a lot to drink. Let's get you somewhere you can lie down; how about over here . . .*

"Now, I've been through the staff on the yacht," he said. "They were the first interviewed."

"Of course they were," I said under my breath.

"So now I'm on to the guests," he said. "And I'm wondering if Miss Fay has said anything to you that she might be afraid to say to me. The kind of thing a proper lady wouldn't want to tell a stranger. Anything or anybody she was tangled up with. Any catfights. Any flings."

My protectiveness toward my cousin flared.

"I think you'd better leave," I said.

He lifted his hands. "I didn't mean anything by it. I'd think you'd want to figure out who may have wanted to do the young lady harm." He handed me a plain card lettered on one side with PORT ROOSEVELT LIMITED and his contact information on the other. "If you think of anything she's said to you, anything at all, I'd appreciate it."

The man who looked less like an investigator and more like one of Tom Buchanan's college friends strolled toward his parked car.

The printed card grew heavy between my fingers the longer I stood there.

Had someone stolen hundreds of thousands of dollars of pearls off my cousin's neck?

Had someone wanted to cover it up enough to want her dead?

CHAPTER XII

"You don't mind if I bring a few things over on the day of, do you, Nick?"

I answered Gatsby's harmless-enough question with what I thought was a harmless-enough answer: "Sure, of course."

To be accurate, first I answered with "Por supuesto." Then I remembered that I shouldn't speak Spanish on either Egg, East or West. So I pretended I'd been clearing my throat, then answered again in English. Gatsby had a way of making my tongue forget what it was supposed to be doing.

The morning of Daisy's arrival, I had to dodge out of the way of a woman in a cream skirt suit, her expression thoughtful and serious as she directed three equally thoughtful and serious arrangers. By the time they left, the air was thick with the smell of sugar and leaves. Scrolled silver vases burst with peonies and lilacs. Pewter bowls spilled over with lipstick-deep roses and two-tone sweet peas. Blue hyacinth crowded together with gold and pink freesias. Yellow laburnum and purple wisteria dripped down like the crown molding was growing it.

At least I'd told him Daisy was bringing dessert. Otherwise he might have produced an iced gingerbread house the size of the cottage.

Gatsby paced the rug in the sitting area, the robin's-egg of his suit picking up the blue of the water through the glass doors. His eyes wandered between the clock on the mantel and the bank of silver clouds over East Egg.

"It's going to rain," he said.

I couldn't tell if he was raising a concern or making conversation.

With another glance at the clock, Gatsby said, "She's not coming."

"It's four minutes past," I said.

"And you're sure I shouldn't have gotten more tea?" he asked.

With great deliberation, Gatsby had selected a variety laced with blood orange. If we started over, we'd be here until September.

"It's perfect," I said.

Gatsby's eyes left their orbit between clock and sea. Now they drifted toward the door. "This was a mistake."

A rumble of distant thunder sounded. Gatsby's face fell, as though the sky was in agreement.

"I should have brought different kinds." Gatsby turned away from the clock. "I should have choices on hand. I bet he never gives her choices."

"She'll love the tea," I said. "She'll love all of it. How could she not?"

What I'd thought was thunder settled into the soft growl of a car's engine. After the three-note trill of the horn, the bell of my cousin's voice rang out. "Nicky!"

A mix of fear and enchantment brightened the green of Gatsby's eyes. They glowed with memories I could only guess at. Maybe her combing his hair out of his face with her cream-softened hands. The film of her skirt fluttering against the ironed seam of his trousers. The smell of her powder and matching perfume, the wildflower breath of As the Petals, before Daisy learned that wearing talcum and eau de parfum in the same scent was a sign of a girl trying too hard.

"I'll bring her in," I said.

Before I saw Daisy's face, I saw her lavender hat and the gleam of the pearl buttons on her dress. The moment I was within grabbing distance, she pulled me into a hug.

"You look nice," I said.

"Do you like it? I've almost gotten the knack of my hair-waving iron. It took me ages to perfect my Elizabeth Arden face." She had paled her complexion with makeup so thick it looked like a doll's porcelain.

Her expression changed from bright to pitying. "Oh, Nicky."

She touched my mouth, and a slash of pain stuck my lip. I'd almost forgotten it.

"It's closed over," I said. "It doesn't hurt anymore. Not unless I suck on a lemon."

She laughed to the tune of the sea.

"Daisy, I've got to talk to you," I said.

"I might have gone a little mad at the patisserie!" She turned back to the car. Not the blue-gray pearl roadster she'd been in when she came for me at the station. This one was citrine yellow. How many cars did the Buchanans have?

"But you're a bachelor," Daisy said, "and I don't want you starving just because you don't know how to turn on an oven."

"I help my mother with the cooking all the time," I said. "I didn't just stop when I changed my name and my clothes. Please, will you listen for a minute? Please?"

The second *please* slowed her.

"Why didn't you tell me about the yacht?" I asked.

She sighed. "I knew you'd ask eventually. It's all so horribly embarrassing."

"Don't pretend at that with me," I said. "I know you. You like everyone talking about you."

She gave a guilty smile. "Of course I do. But I didn't mean that part." The smile evaporated. "I mean, the truth is, I was so drunk, I don't remember any of it. I only had champagne, a glass or two, maybe three at the outside, but the trouble was I'd hardly eaten a thing. I was just too excited over everything, so it all went straight to my head. I barely remember anything. Until I felt the water pulling me under." She dipped her head so low that the hat brim hid her face.

"That must have been terrifying," I said.

"It was," she said. "But only until I realized that swimming was what I had to do. Once I knew what to do, I wasn't scared anymore. The frightening part is not knowing how I got there."

I leaned against the car alongside her. "Why didn't you tell me?"

"Oh, I couldn't talk about it with anyone," she said. "I could smile for all the pictures, but when anyone asked me about it, I just told them about the swimming and the getting to shore at dawn. That's all they wanted to hear about anyway. I couldn't talk about all of it, because then who am I? Daisy the drunk who fell off a boat."

She stayed in the shadow of her hat brim, but I could hear the shame in her voice.

To everyone else, Daisy had been some luminous mermaid swimming toward shore. Their vision of her was set among a fortune of Riviera pearls snapping off their strands and floating to every ocean in the world.

To herself, she was a newcomer to East Egg who'd made a sloppy and clumsy display.

"It could happen to anyone," I said. "I probably would've fallen off the dock into the water the other night if it wasn't for—" I stopped myself. Telling her about how I'd met Gatsby seemed like giving something away, revealing too early the possibility of the boy waiting for her.

"Does your mother know about what happened?" I asked instead.

"Nicky, no," she said. "Why do you think I didn't tell you? She'd be worried sick. She would have sent my father and sisters right here to bring me back."

A few minutes ago, I'd wanted every answer Daisy had to give. But now I wanted nothing more than to help her forget it all.

"What did you bring?" I asked.

Daisy came back to life. "Wait until you see."

She stacked boxes into my arms, and with each one she inventoried the land of sweets she'd brought along. Lattice-topped Linzer tortes. Sugary squares of dried fruits and nuts ("They call them honeybees!"). Cookies frosted in chocolate and vanilla and mint fondant. Lemon cake drizzled with icing the exact yellow of Daisy's car.

I searched her face for any sign that this made her even a little sad, all these things our families couldn't have had back home. I wanted to package it all up and send it to Wisconsin, and the closest I could get was sending them money. Maybe this was what drove Daisy forward, outrunning that sadness, fending it off with everything she wired home.

"And let's not forget." She showed off a box of miniature upside-down cakes. Each rounded, shining top had a candied cherry at the center.

"Is it my imagination," I said when she tipped the box lid up, "or do those look like . . ." I cut myself off before I could say *tetas*, or *breasts* in any language.

I thought Daisy might tell me that I was seventeen and in New York now, and what's more, working in the city. That I needed to act like a man and not a little boy, laughing and scandalized by anything that was the right kind of round.

But my cousin gave me her soap-bubble giggle, the same one as when she stuffed a snowball in the bed of her meanest sister.

She knew exactly what they looked like. She'd probably bought them to see if I'd notice.

"Do you do everything to such excess?" I asked as she set another box in my arms.

"Whenever I can, to whatever extent I have the means for," she said. "You see, I live with this sort of faith that life can be as we dream it. With the light just so." She spun under the lilacs, and I had to dodge to keep clear. "All gold and purple."

"Like those paintings," I said.

"Yes!" She rounded on me, face glowing. "Parrish and Hughes!"

Now that I thought of it, once she took off the hat, she'd look a lot like the girl in her favorite Hughes. Her dress was antique gold, sleeveless and textured with lace and embroidery and pink roses. It dropped gently but straight, without the bell of a full skirt. Anyone could imagine her gathering the hem in her hands on a midsummer night, surrounded by a glowing fairy circle.

"Don't you just love their paintings?" she asked.

"I thought they were a little cloying," I said.

"I forgot you don't have a stitch of romance in you," she said. "No sentimentality at all."

"You say that like it's a bad thing," I said.

"Not bad, just a little despairing," she said. "Don't you want to live? To fall in love?"

Was this what Gatsby had so loved about her? She was all the romance of a girl in a painting, adorned in sunset chiffon, standing against a sapphire-and-emerald night and reaching for the moon. She had been this way since we were growing up, always making flourishes out of wildflowers, setting the buñuelos in arrangements as intricate as houses of cards.

"Don't you want to have wild adventures?" she asked.

"I want to survive, Daisy," I said. "I want to have a decent life. A quiet one."

"Oh." She sounded like I'd pricked the fragile balloon of her very soul. "Aren't your dreams any loftier than that?"

"You know all about me," I said. "A quiet life is a lofty dream in itself."

"Oh, but you deserve so much more," she said.

"I don't want to get so distracted with what I might deserve that I miss what I might actually be able to have," I said.

Gatsby and Daisy were so perfect for each other, believing in the filmy possibilities of love and violet stars. It was a good thing Gatsby was in love with her instead of me, because in all such things, I would only prove a disappointment. I was as different from Daisy as the coveralls I wore at home were from a pair of engraved cuff links.

The glossed pastry boxes were high enough that I had to tilt my head to see over them, so Daisy guided me toward the cottage.

"You devious thing." She lightly slapped my arm, and I held my center to keep the boxes from toppling. "You didn't tell me you put in a tulip border."

The toes of her lavender shoes skipped over the flagstones. The damp grass and the newly planted tulips shivered at Daisy's arrival.

She floated toward the open door, a few steps ahead of me. I tried catching up, but she was in before I'd gotten to the front step.

From inside she called out, "Oh, Nicky, what have you done?" and I nearly dropped the stack of boxes.

She'd seen him. She'd met the sight of him not with delight but with a demand that I explain.

I staggered inside and eased the boxes onto a side table.

I braced for tears glittering in Daisy's eyes, a look of shock or betrayal that I'd done this without warning her.

But her face reflected back all the silver of the sound.

"Oh, it's a garden." Daisy spun, her fingers tracing roses and freesia. "An Eden." She bent her face to the peonies.

"Did you roam the earth for all these flowers? Just for me?"

Jay Gatsby was nowhere to be found.

CHAPTER XIII

Daisy was in a fine mood to arrange a tower of macarons, humming as she placed the rounds of green and violet and candy pink.

And I was in a fine mood to kick the ass of the boy who had talked me into this only to run off.

"Excuse me," I said, ironing my voice into something more polite than I felt.

Thanks to Jay Gatsby, the cottage had become an arboretum. My cousin had brought over enough sugar that the air smelled as much like icing as flowers. And I had gotten my hopes up that Daisy might hesitate about marrying a polo mallet of a man called Tom Buchanan.

It was raining now. I went out into the downpour without a hat or umbrella, set to storm across the grass to the mansion.

Then the shape of Gatsby came to me, a specter cowering under an eave.

He had pulled into himself, hiding beneath the dripping

lilac trees. His soaked hair stuck to his forehead, the pieces shifting in time with the speed of his breath.

"What are you doing?" I asked.

"I can't go in," Gatsby said.

I came close enough that we could both whisper. "After all this?"

"She's not going to want to see me," Gatsby said.

I set my hands on his upper arms. "Get ahold of yourself."

I felt the strength of the muscle under the robin's-egg blue of the fabric. Every sinew beneath my palms seemed tensed.

"Anybody would be happy to see you," I said.

His smile was a needle of sun piercing a gray scrim of clouds. And perhaps it was this, how he could be touched by so small a compliment, that made me understand all he'd stored up in his heart.

This boy whose shoulders I held in my hands, I wanted him to have the shimmer of the whole world. And for him, it was all held in the dark honey of Daisy's eyes.

Gatsby's fingers grazed my waist. My breath sharpened with the anticipation of his palm landing there. But his hand moved to my back. He patted my shirt with what would have been the casual affection of friends, except that his hand stayed. His fingers spread out, thumb contouring to the lower point of my shoulder blade.

My breath caught up to his, quick and shallow. I thought of kissing him in the way I imagined everyone must think of kissing someone who was this close and this beautiful. It was the way I should have thought of kissing girls but only did if I put my mind to it. But there was no putting my mind to this. Kissing Gatsby was a thought that slipped in like that knife of sun, sudden and bright.

I was just like everyone else in those gardens, entranced by the brilliant enigma that was Jay Gatsby. I was no different from the party guests speculating that he'd made his fortune in the Nevada silver fields or in Montana copper or contraband gin.

I let go of him. I stepped back.

His face fell in the same moment his hand fell from my back.

"This is your chance," I said. "Do you want it, or not?"

I brought Gatsby inside, expecting Daisy's usual burst of delight to reassure him.

But when she saw him, she was quiet. The shine of her in that moment was not so much dulled as softened.

"Jay."

She breathed his name like a burst of perfume through an atomizer.

That breath surprised him, and he shuddered back. He bumped into a table and knocked a vase of flowers to the floor.

Gatsby knelt to the fallen blooms, shaking his head. "It's

too late," he said, gathering up the soaked petals. "It's ruined. There's no fixing it."

Then Daisy was on the floor next to him, her lace-gloved hands lifting the wet lilacs. "It's never too late." She gathered it all up and him with it. She cupped his face in her damp, rose-scented hands, and he set his palms over those hands, and the intimacy of the whole thing made me want to leave the cottage and West Egg and then maybe the planet altogether.

"I'm going to go out for some"—I grasped for an innocuous item—"milk."

I saw the milk bottle in plain sight, so cold that moisture beaded on the glass.

"Lemons," I corrected myself, then winced. First, at the unappetizing image of milk and lemon together in one of those finely painted teacups (not only was I spoiling the romance of all this with my presence but now with the suggestion of curdling milk). Second, at the gleam of so many pewter bowls overfilled with lemons and oranges and grapefruits. All had been furnished by Gatsby, each piece bright as the fruit brought in by the crate for his parties.

But the boy and the girl staring into each other's eyes didn't notice how pathetic my lies were. I had served my purpose of bringing them together.

I went out, not for milk or lemons, but to the Western Union in West Egg Village, to send my mother and father a portion of my first New York paycheck. It was probably a handful of pennies compared with what Daisy managed to send back to her own family, siphoned from the vast Buchanan fortunes.

But this still had a copper shine to it. I could help the parents who had helped me for so long. My mother and father had not questioned the fact that I was a boy from the day I declared it, and to give them some small appreciation left me more intoxicated than Daisy's forbidden wine. I could understand it now, her draw to money. It let you do things for people you loved.

When I came back, the rain had stopped, leaving the world glossed and shining. I was so keyed up that I had forgotten Daisy and Gatsby were still at the cottage.

They sat on the brocade sofa (Or was it damask? Jacquard? Daisy knew the differences; I didn't, and she was forever trying to teach me). Their hands rested inches from each other. Gatsby's, the one that had mapped the ridge of my shoulder blade, was still on the gleaming fabric. Daisy's fingers trailed across the shining patterns.

When they did notice me, they flinched back from each other, their smiles all mischief and propriety, like an adult had just walked into the room. I was a year younger than Daisy and two younger than Gatsby, but still I felt like their chaperone.

"Jay was just about to show me his house," Daisy said, breathless as the way she'd said his name.

"I won't keep you," I said.

"No, you must come with us." Daisy rose to her feet.

I expected Gatsby to look disappointed, but he echoed her with, "Please, Nick, join us."

He sounded so sincere I almost believed I wasn't spoiling something for them. He nearly convinced me that my presence was for some other purpose than buffering Daisy against scandal.

• • •

My cousin skipped under the hawthorn and plum blossoms, greeting each jonquil as though by name. She tucked roses into Gatsby's hair and her own and tried it with me. When the two of them spun through Gatsby's gardens, sprays of rain flew off the blooms.

"You live here all alone?" Daisy asked as she twirled across the marble floors. Her hands reached to touch everything at once. She smoothed her palms over the lavender and rose silk on the beds. She stroked the gilded pages of books in the library. Her fingertips counted every one of his folded shirts, and he unfurled them like bolts of uncut cloth. Apple green and monogrammed blue and coral flew through the room. Daisy and Gatsby laughed and grabbed at the rainbow they'd made of the air.

"You were always the most beautiful boy," Daisy said, snatching a mauve shirt from above her. "You should have the most beautiful shirts."

With a hitch in my stomach, I thought of being in this room with Gatsby, the crisp fabric of one of his shirts crossing my back.

When the rain started up again, they dashed across the grass. I watched from the windowed doors as they invited the rain onto their bodies, soaking his blue suit and the sheer film of her dress. When they came back inside, they danced, dripping on the gramophone each time they changed the song.

They were beautiful, the two of them, as well matched as the pink clouds and the first pepper of evening stars. When I left, I wondered how many songs and shirts it would be before they noticed I was gone.

Mr. Nicolás Caraveo
West Egg, New York

Dearest Nick,

I feel as though I owe you something of an explanation. Oh, how terribly you must think of me.

I met Jay when I was in Chicago, when I was making bandages with the Red Cross and going to all those patriotic dances, the ones the civic organizations put on for the soldiers' morale.

There's no use in denying that I fell a little bit in love with Jay, at least as much in love as I've ever been with any boy.

You see, Nicky, boys are always falling in love with me, but I don't much fall in love with them. I've always wondered if something was wrong with me, to tell you the truth, but Gloria says that's the best way for things to be, for a boy to love a girl faster and more than the girl loves him. And really, I don't know if I was truly in love with Jay, but I got closer with him than I'd ever been. So maybe that was falling in love? It may not have been the great romance of storybooks, but that feeling of someone seeing into the center of you and recognizing you, what else could that be but love? Don't even best friends have to fall a little in love?

To tell the truth, I never much wanted to get married. But getting married is what girls do, so if I had to suffer the whole affair, I couldn't do that for a poor boy from the Dakotas. I'd need society kinds of money to make it worth it, and I'd come to Chicago for just that. Despise me if you want to. But how else can a girl get anywhere in the world we live in?

I don't suppose you've heard about the party, the one meant to present me to Tom's family and friends like some jewel in a glass case. It seemed so much like an engagement party except no one was willing to call it that, and Tom hadn't summoned the courage to ask me yet (and he won't until I win over his family). Jordan could tell you better than I could, but she's awfully tactful about such things, so I doubt she has. It wasn't one of my finer evenings. I was about three drinks ahead of Jordan. But as far as I remember, she found me hiding in the bathtub. The water had long gone cold. And I'd sat in there so long reading Jay's letters that all the paper was coming to pieces in the bath. It was a little bit beautiful, to tell you the truth. It looked like tiny drifts of snow. But I only think of that now. At the time, I wasn't in much of a state to find anything beautiful, not even that albatross of a pearl necklace.

In my Sauternes-soaked state, I asked Jordan, "Please, tell them I'm not coming. Tell them Daisy Fay's changed her mind, that she's not waltzing out on the arm of Tom nor any Buchanan of any sort."

But Jordan was good enough—and really, she's too good for me—to talk me into being a little quieter. She told me I could always break things off with Tom, but if I didn't show at the party, if I didn't sparkle right alongside those chandeliers and candlesticks, I'd be ruined in city society. She was right, of course.

But a funny thing happened as Jordan got some food into me and me into the dress and under that impossibly long strand of pearls. I thought of my mother and my father and my sisters. I thought of the money I could send them if I married a man like Tom. Jordan knows just what I'm talking about. She sends a good portion of her tournament winnings to her family, did you know that?

Something else happened too. I realized that there was nothing at all wrong with me. The kind of love between a man and a woman has never been any particular dream of *mine, and that was a gift, not a fault. If the storybooks never held much for me, I was uniquely suited to choose a man who could give me what I wanted.*

So I did sparkle under those chandeliers, and I shined like that dreadfully heavy strand of pearls. Daisy Fay was gay again, as gay as ever.

I'm going to marry Tom. I think I'm almost certain that I'm going to marry Tom, soon as he asks me. I just think I need to spend a little time with Jay. Nothing untoward, of course. I'd simply like to know him a bit better now that we have the chance. I've never met a boy who understood so many things about me, who doesn't think I'm silly or fragile as bath bubbles.

Oh, you know I love you, Nicky. But you're not so much the sensitive sort. You were born with that Wisconsin shale right in your bones. There's something softer about Jay, something that I've never found in any other boy.

Jay and I never even got to say proper goodbyes. So perhaps we just need a sort of long goodbye now. You understand. Don't you, Nick?

> *Yours in eternal adoration,*
> *Daisy F.*

CHAPTER XIV

After Daisy had gone, I went back to the mansion and found Gatsby carefully folding the shirts they'd thrown around the room.

When he noticed me, he said, almost apologetically, "Why should anyone else have to do it?"

I worried that, one day, this would be the thing to ruin the dream of Daisy and Gatsby. She reveled in making glamorous messes, and he followed after her, quietly cleaning them up.

"She said she's going to come to one of my parties," Gatsby said.

"Oh?" I picked up a shirt the color of Irish moss. "That's good. That's . . ." I'd heard my cousin use the word *peachy* and considered trying it on, but didn't know if I could carry it off without sounding sarcastic, so I settled on "Great."

"She said it might be a little while before she can get away," Gatsby said.

I buttoned the shirt, folded it, and handed it to him.

"Will you keep coming?" Gatsby asked as he took the shirt. "To my parties, I mean."

He looked at me with a birthday-candle sort of hope, and all I could say was "Of course."

———————— ✦✦✦ ————————

When I went back to the cottage, my least-invited visitor was waiting. I'd have preferred Tom Buchanan dropping by unannounced with a gaggle of his Yale friends.

"Nice place," Dechert said.

What response could I give? Yes, the place was nice, but it wasn't mine, so there was no point in saying thank you.

"You're here courtesy of Mr. Buchanan, aren't you?" Dechert asked.

I stopped on the pavestone path. "Is there something I can help you with?"

"He spends money like it's on fire, doesn't he?" Dechert strolled toward me, not with the menacing air I always imagined of investigators or detectives, but with a casual leisure. It was all the more unsettling, as though he had endless time to get wherever he wanted. "The polo, the bets on the races, the dinners, the hotels, the gifts . . . And it seems he has another girl. At least one. Keeps a whole apartment for her. In high style too."

He seemed disappointed that I wasn't shocked.

"So you can see why he'd have debts all up and down Manhattan and Long Island," Dechert said.

"Debts?" I blurted out the question without meaning to. The Buchanan estate was as big as I'd imagined the manors in Jane Austen novels. Why would he have debts? "How is that even possible?"

"Ah." Dechert seemed pleased he'd gotten me. "That's where it's interesting. You see, Mr. Buchanan's such a spend-thrift that his grandfather insisted the family put him on an allowance. And he torches it fast every month."

My stomach felt heavy as cast iron.

"A man might do some funny stuff to get out from under his family's thumb," Dechert said.

"And what are you telling me this for?" I asked.

"Miss Fay hasn't been very forthcoming," Dechert said. "And I got to thinking that maybe she's trying to protect her beau. But maybe she doesn't know everything about him. Maybe there's some pieces she's not putting together. So, if you really are her friend, I'd see if you could get her talking. For her sake."

CHAPTER XV

"Put me out of my misery," one of the men at the office groaned as I came in.

"What's the matter with him?" I asked.

"He overdid it on the veronal last night," another man said, the one I knew as Princeton. (I knew this but not his name because he mentioned Princeton more often than his name.)

Now he was holding his necktie forward. "The lady bought me this for my birthday," he said, and the bar of gold clipping the fabric caught the light. "Do we like it, or do we think it's too much?"

"As if I have a care for your tie bar," the first man said. "I have that big presentation with Benson." He rested his head against the wall. "I needed to sleep well last night so I didn't flub it this morning, so I thought I'd get a little help."

"Fine way that turned out for you," Princeton said.

I reviewed the new papers on my desk. "What's veronal?" I asked.

"Barbiturates," the first man lamented.

"Don't they teach anything in Wisconsin?" Princeton asked.

"You took barbiturates the night before a hectic day at work?" I asked. "Real slick."

Princeton and even his groggy companion perked up. Who knew that a couple of well-thrown-in words could make me seem at home among these men? It turned out Gatsby had known. He'd told me to use *hectic* instead of *busy*, *slick* instead of *clever* or *smart*. He'd taught me how to seem at ease among men who said the word *white* so meticulously it carried an extra breath.

"Carraway!" Hexton yelled. "Get in here!"

Princeton whistled softly. "Bon voyage."

Once I was in his office, Hexton was oddly quiet, looking over papers I could tell were in my handwriting. He was the half of Benson & Hexton I knew less, so I thought it better to match his silence.

When he finally looked up, he asked, brandishing a sheaf, "You think we should buy on this one?"

I nodded.

"Tell me why," he said, looking down as though consulting his tiepin.

"The price seems to rise and fall with wheat, with a slight lag," I said. "Wheat's on the upswing, so there's a chance it'll follow."

"Are you sure?" he asked.

"No one can be sure," I said. "Anyone who says that in this business is a fool or a liar."

Hexton gave me a smile more unnerving than his grimace. "Right answer."

———————— ·◉· ————————

Every weekend, the smell of fruit and flowers and cocktails drenched the gardens. Every weekend, guests soaked themselves in liquor Gatsby never drank, and their speculations continued.

Did you hear that he has no fingerprints?

I heard he's the second cousin to the devil.

Well, that would make sense, wouldn't it? The devil doesn't have fingerprints either.

I became as much a fixture at Gatsby's parties as the strands of blue lights. I helped him look for Daisy, who every week said she'd try to make it to West Egg. And every week Gatsby's parties took on more of a shine, as though the gilded air might draw her across the water. Stars drifted out of catering baskets. The moon dipped low for sips of champagne.

Each week, Gatsby rethought what might delight Daisy. One Saturday the grounds sprouted ice sculptures. The next, the lamps all had tinted bulbs, spilling rose honey over the hedges and blooms. Then banners and tents as blue as the Mediterranean unfurled through the air, rivaling the sky.

"Do you think she's coming tonight?" Gatsby asked each time.

Each time I said, "She might."

When I ran into Martha, it was clear she knew about Daisy.

"I worry about him," Martha said. "He's good about not getting his hopes up about things in business. He's objective, neutral. But about the rest of his life, that hope is so active, it's as though his heart is carbonated."

"He seems to be keeping up his morale," I said. "All these parties for one girl? I couldn't do it."

Martha gave me a strange look. "The parties aren't just for her."

"Aren't they?" I asked.

"They're as much for business as love," she said. "Sure, the ice sculptures and the flower arrangements the size of ponies, those are for Daisy. But the parties are a good part of our work. These little get-togethers are where we find half our new customers."

"You and Gatsby work together?" I asked.

"Didn't you know?" she asked. "There's a whole group of us who work together. We're purveyors of difficult-to-find luxury items."

"French perfume and Belgian chocolates, I'm guessing," I said.

Martha smiled. "I've decided you can stay." She looked for Gatsby in the crowd and nodded in his direction. "Jay has the distinction of being one of the few men I work with on a regular basis. Has he told you that?"

I shook my head.

"Well," Martha said. "He's discreet in all things, so I shouldn't be surprised. That's the way I like my friends. The only downside to discretion is that it leaves so much room for assumptions. And a lot of people assume that because I'm Jewish, I must be the one making all the business decisions, and that all my business connections must be men I've known my whole life. But most of my associates are more recent acquaintances, and most of them are women."

"Are they—" I cut off my own rude question before I could finish it.

But Martha said, "Yes, Nick. They're also lesbians." She laughed. "Look at your face."

"I'm sorry," I said. "I'm not used to people saying a word like *lesbian* without whispering it."

"Would you rather I whisper it?" Martha asked.

"No," I said. "I like being around people who speak who they are instead of whispering it."

Martha touched that place just under her sleeve, like she had the first time we met. Now I was even surer that whatever she wore on her wrist wasn't a timepiece. Or, if it was, it was more for sentiment than function. There was such care to how her fingers slipped under the cuff of her shirt, as though checking that something was still there and hadn't slipped off and gotten lost. Maybe a piece of jewelry inherited from a great-grandmother. But the gesture was so quick that there was no natural way to ask.

Gatsby's gardens were a place of ecstatic dancing, in which the whole world seemed to be having a gay time. The women had French bobs, and blush rounded the apples of their cheeks. The men flirted through pocket doors between green and gold rooms. Fingernails shined with paintings of butterflies and stars. The dresses were loose, the waists set low. But there was something daring about how many were sleeveless, how filmy the fabrics were, how many were shades of pink or beige or brown that nearly matched the skin. No one blinked at hems high enough to show all of the ankle, right up to the middle of the calf (back home that was either the sign of a secondhand dress or of a girl I was warned not to be seen with). Names like Lanvin and Gustave Beer were thrown back and forth as though everyone knew them personally.

"Who's Balenciaga?" I asked Jordan one night.

She blinked her mascaraed eyes at me.

"Everyone keeps talking about him," I said.

Jordan threw her head back and roared a laugh to rival the band. "Oh, Nick, sometimes you're so sweet it makes my teeth hurt."

I leaned toward Jordan. "Do you think Daisy's ever gonna show up?"

"Patience," she said. "She's been trying up, down, and sideways to talk Tom's family into throwing her a debut, and that means she runs all over town working on her mother-in-law's little pet projects. The Ladies Auxiliary. Modeling dresses for some charity fashion show."

Jordan took my arm. "Come on. I need air and to see the stars."

She led me out onto a terrace, where we stood near what Gatsby had taught me was either a balustrade or baluster. I couldn't remember which.

"Enough about Daisy." Jordan leaned against the chilled stone. "Tell me about yourself."

"I never do know what to say to that," I said.

"Fine. Then tell me something about your family. The first thing to come to mind."

"Well," I stalled. "When my mother was growing up, she always dreamed about having blue window boxes. So my father asked her to marry him by making her the window boxes himself. They didn't have a house yet, so they didn't have any place to put them. And he left them unfinished, just the raw wood, because they couldn't afford the blue paint yet, and because he said he wanted her to choose it. So that when they had the house, and when they could get the paint, it'd be exactly the blue she'd imagined."

"That's very sweet, isn't it?" Jordan said.

I searched for any trace of sarcasm. I waited for her to make fun of me and my family and the whole state of Wisconsin. But she looked charmed, wistful, as though she'd just finished a romantic novel.

"Did she ever get someplace to put them?" she asked.

"She did," I said. "They're still up. She grows everything in them. Marigolds, rosemary, sage. My father repaints them when they need it."

"What's he like?" Jordan asked. "Your father."

I thought of the carved wooden knight. "Better at chess than I'll ever be," I said. "He loves it. He'll play with anyone he can talk into sitting down with him."

"What is it about fathers and drawn-out games?" Jordan asked. "My father plays the most complicated variations on solitaire. Just sitting there with the cards, in this concentrating silence."

"My father's the same," I said. "He doesn't talk during chess."

"It's unnerving, isn't it?" Jordan asked, though her laugh was fond and remembering in a way that made me miss my own father. "And what's more, he seems to truly enjoy it. À chacun son goût."

"You lost me at the end there," I said.

"It's French for 'to each his own,'" Jordan said. "And I'm sure my brother would wince if he heard how I just pronounced it."

"You have a brother?" I asked.

Jordan nodded. "He's a little older than I am."

I wavered between whether it was ruder to ask the obvious question or to let it go unspoken.

"Was he in the war?" I asked.

She nodded again. "Infantry. The Sixty-Fifth."

Sixty-Fifth. I knew that number but couldn't remember where from. Had a family friend mentioned it? Had Gatsby?

I hesitated before another question that seemed rude to ask or leave unasked. "Is he all right?"

"How all right is anybody after a thing like that?" she asked. I knew she wanted to drop the subject when her tone changed, a willful brightening. "And I meant it about my pronunciation. He speaks perfect French, Spanish, a bit of Italian. He picks things up very quickly."

"Like card games?" I asked.

Jordan smiled. "He knows them but never took to them like my father. Though my mother has been known to join my father from time to time. It's really something to see people who are that comfortable being quiet around each other. I hope I have that with someone when I'm their age."

"What's your mother like?" I asked.

"She does everything beautifully," Jordan said, "from trimming a Christmas tree to putting on lipstick. Without her, I never would have bothered to make sure my dress was neat as a pin. I was too distracted reading. My father loves books. It's half of what we talk about, in person and in letters. Right now we're reading *Madame Bovary* together, and I know the next I hear from him will be all about how it's nothing but a story about shopping, though that sounds like a splendid book if you ask me."

"I think Daisy would agree with you," I said.

"Oh, I know she would." Jordan looked around, as though checking that we still had the balustrade to ourselves. "My mother loves books too, but she'll put down her book and talk to someone who's in front of her. She loves meeting people. My father, he's a wonderful conversationalist if you can get him talking, but if he's the middle of a good book, he'll forget you're there entirely. I was the same way growing up. But I needed these enormous spectacles to read anything. I still need them when I'm reading small print."

Jordan turned toward the bay. "My friends and everyone else made fun of me for those glasses, and I got tired of being made fun of. So I started listening to my mother. She taught me all about mascara, and how to carry myself, and never to leave the house unless I looked my best. And I found what she already knew and what I knew too but hadn't wanted to think too much about. I learned it was to my benefit to look a certain way. People treat a girl very differently depending on how she looks. Doors open that you didn't even know could be doors because they always looked like walls."

Jordan gazed out over the water, and the wind coming from East Egg to West skimmed our faces.

"And it turned out a beauty could get away with wearing any glasses at all," Jordan said. "Who knew?"

"Your mother," I said.

Jordan laughed. "Yes, that's right. My mother. They always

do know, don't they?" She glanced at the lit windows. "We'd better go in before they all start saying we're lovers."

She led me back inside. "Doubtless Daisy will be around here somewhere. She always makes her entrance at the height of any party."

As though summoned by Jordan, Daisy appeared. The gold of her hair emerged through a flurry of petals and bright paper. The same wind that bore confetti to the bay rustled her dress. The blush satin was so soft at the hem and ruffled sleeves that it seemed spun from the pink clouds overhead.

"Don't you both look lovely!" Daisy took us in first with her eyes and then with her arms. "Oh, Nicky, that shirt's such a perfect blue on you. And Jordan"—she reached for her friend's hands—"in coral ruffles you look like a field of anemones. I could lie down in your skirt and fall asleep for a hundred years."

"My sleeping beauty." Jordan kissed the air alongside each of her cheeks.

"Decided you couldn't beat the awful parties so you joined them, Nick?" It was only as Tom Buchanan leaned close enough to share his joke that I realized Daisy hadn't come alone.

Her not-quite-fiancé had come with her.

CHAPTER XVI

"Daisy, I need to talk to you." I tried to pull my cousin away enough that we wouldn't attract Tom's attention, but it stayed trained on us.

"How's business, Nick?" Tom asked.

"A whirlwind," I said, forcing the sound of enthusiasm.

Where was Gatsby? Was he changing his suit for the hundredth time? Had he seen Daisy and run for his wardrobe, debating between the merits of a gold tie versus one that matched the color of the bay through his window?

"Numbers fly back and forth like hornets," I added. "Futures go down and suddenly it's 'sell three dozen contracts!'"

Tom chuckled. "You'll get used to it."

I had learned that so long as I acted as though he had something to teach me, Tom Buchanan liked me. I hadn't told Daisy about Myrtle, and that probably didn't hurt either. He likely assumed it was out of some great loyalty to him.

"The other day, I was sent to fetch a man from the bathroom," I said. "They told me 'Get him back here now, it's down thirty points!'"

Tom's chuckle turned into a full laugh. "Don't get caught between Benson and Hexton. Whenever you have a bull partner who wants to stick with things to the end and another who's more careful, you don't want to end up in the middle. That reminds me, Nick, I have a joke for you."

"Oh, please, let's don't," Daisy said.

"He wants to hear the joke," Tom said. "Don't you, Nick? It goes: How do you spot an extroverted mathematician?"

"I don't know," I said.

"The extroverted mathematician is staring at your shoes instead of his own," Tom said.

I set my mouth in a grim smile and hummed a laugh through my teeth.

Tom looked to Jordan. "Can we expect another triumph at your next tournament?"

"I never expect anything on the course," Jordan said. "She doesn't like you coming in with expectations. I just bring her the best I have."

"I've got a question for you about a brassie I'm considering buying," Tom said.

I took their conversation about golf clubs as a chance to draw Daisy away. I put a few people between us and Tom, and their voices shielded ours.

"I've been trying to reach you," I said.

"Oh, I know," she said. "It's the season. Never a moment of rest. Try me again in August." She clasped my hands. "Everyone's gone. We'll spend the whole month together."

"I've got to talk to you now." I took her hand in one of

mine and set the other on her waist, so we'd at least look like we were having a good time.

"Nicky, if you needed someone to practice your dancing with, you should have told me," she said. "I would've been right over."

I led her in time with the music.

"You're shocked to see me in so much makeup, aren't you?" Daisy asked. "Don't tell my mother. She'll wonder if I mean to become an actress." She laughed. "Quelle horreur, n'est-ce pas?"

"Daisy," I said.

"She doesn't realize actresses are goddesses now," Daisy said. "The makeup companies even hire them for advertisements. Everyone these days wants a cupid's bow like a screen siren."

"Daisy," I said.

"Did you know they're the ones we can thank for all this?" She pursed her wine-dark lips as if posing for *Photoplay*. "Lighter lipstick reads gray on-screen. And then the arched eyebrows. Everyone wants to be a film star even in real life. Talking with our faces as though we're on a silent reel."

"Listen to me for a minute, will you?" I asked.

She leaned in. "Why? Do you have a delicious secret to tell me?"

"I don't like you with Tom," I said.

"So protective," she teased.

"I mean it," I said. "I don't trust him."

"I think he has more reason to be worried about me, don't you?" She quirked her lips, shining with lipstick. "He did give me that beautiful little pistol. And to think, he's convinced I need a big strong man to teach me to use it."

"You have to get away from him," I said.

"Where is all this worry coming from?" she asked.

"Did you ever wonder if there's more to how you fell off that yacht?"

"We talked about this." The agitation of her whisper gave it the sound of rushing water. "I was having champagne, and I'd just as soon rather not discuss it further."

"What if he needs the money?"

"What money?" she asked. "Money for what? The Buchanans couldn't count all their dollars if you gave them the rest of their lives."

"But they have him on an allowance," I said. "And he's burning it up. It's not enough for him."

"Well, he'll get more when we're married," she said. "His grandfather always had concerns about the bachelor lifestyle."

"Except he's not exactly rushing you to the altar, is he?"

I spun her, and she gave a perfect performance of delight at being twirled.

I brought her back in. "You think a man like him wouldn't shove you over the side of a yacht so he could sell a necklace and get an insurance payout? Who do you think does that kind of thing? Not farmers back home, I'll tell you that."

"Are you going mad in that little cottage all by yourself?" she asked. "Now I feel terrible for not visiting more."

"How would that necklace have come off you?" I asked. "I don't believe for a second that a piece like that had a single clasp weak enough to just come undone underwater. Did you ever think that maybe he pulled it off you before you went over?"

"Nicky, do you hear yourself?" she asked.

I kept us still and caught her gaze. "He either used you, or he was trying to kill you."

Her expression of shock lasted only a few seconds. But it had been there. I had her wondering whether I was right.

She straightened my tie. "You're a dear for worrying about me. But I know what I'm doing."

"Do you?" I asked.

"Daisy." Jordan took my cousin by her lace-gloved hand, the lattice as delicate and blushed as her gown. "What storied venue will be holding the debut of one Daisy Fay? Is every family in Tuxedo Park vying to have you bow at their summer estates?"

Daisy's face fell. The streamer of one perfect curl shaded her right eye.

"Enough with that old chestnut," Tom said. "Girls get these ideas in their heads. Daisy, I want you to meet someone." With a hand on her back, he turned her toward another couple.

"It's disgusting, isn't it?" Jordan whispered.

"What is?" I asked.

She sipped a pastel drink. "He just doesn't want her eligible for anyone else."

"I don't understand," I said.

"Right," she said. "I forget you're a Midwesterner. Do they have debutantes there? Running around with the cows?"

"Hey," I said.

"Here's how it goes," Jordan said. "Debutantes make the best marriages, so as long as Daisy doesn't have a debut, Tom's claim on her is practically unchallenged in New York society. But if she comes out into society, she'd be announcing herself as ready for marriage."

"I think Tom already knows she's ready," I said.

"But a debut would tell everyone she's still looking, that Tom doesn't truly have her," Jordan said. "She could have a dozen proposals before the stroke of midnight. So of course Tom wouldn't want that. Right now he has that claim on her without having to make any kind of commitment."

As though written in the paper and petals drifting toward the bay, an idea came to me. By the time it formed, Daisy and Tom had turned their attention back to Jordan and me.

"Will you all excuse me?" I said. "I've got to find somewhere to sit down for a minute. I think I've had a little too much to drink."

"You don't drink at these things any more than Jay does," Jordan whispered as I went by.

"Just keep them here," I whispered back. "Please?"

CHAPTER XVII

I knocked on Gatsby's bedroom door.

"I'll be down in moments," he said. "Just attending to long-overdue correspondence."

He was talking in the overwrought voice he used with people who didn't know him.

"Jay," I said. "It's just me."

"Oh," he said through the door. "Come in."

When I did, I shoved the door shut behind me, pinned in place by the sight of Gatsby in his underclothes.

Covered from collar to mid-thigh, there was nothing particularly naked about him in this moment. He wore an undershirt, thick enough to hide the outline of the side lacer underneath, and boxers that tied at the sides, identical in style to the ones I wore. Far more of him was covered than any swimmer in a bathing costume on his beach. But there was a queer intimacy in how easily he held himself around me.

"Oh." Gatsby paused. "I'm sorry. I should have asked if you were all right seeing me like this."

"No," I said. "I don't mind."

If I thought at all of touching the fastening bows on either of his hips, I knew it didn't mean anything except that I was nervous and wanted something to fiddle with. Yes, I thought this boy in front of me was beautiful, but who wouldn't?

Gatsby pulled on trousers pressed as cleanly as the tide smoothing the shoreline sand.

"Daisy's here," I said.

Gatsby paused while buttoning a spring-green shirt.

"Your shirt is fine." I put my hands over his to stop him from reconsidering his outfit. "I had an idea."

Gatsby looked at me with the hopeful attention I would have wanted for any idea I'd ever have.

"Daisy," I said. "We need to help make her. I mean, we need to help her make herself."

"I don't understand," Gatsby said.

I realized I was still holding his hands where they had stopped buttoning his shirt. I let go. "If we can help make her into the socialite of the whole season, she won't feel like she has to marry Tom to make her way in society. I know Daisy, and if she's given half the chance, she'll go with her heart, and I don't think her heart's with Tom."

"I don't either," Gatsby said. Pain pinched the corners of his eyes as he got to the last few buttons. "But I still don't understand. How do we make her the girl of the year? I don't know anything about that."

"You know enough," I said. "You've been teaching me all about how everything works here, haven't you?"

"I can only teach you what I know," he said. "And there's

a lot I don't. I found out the other day that you're supposed to call a jack in a deck of cards a knave, not a jack, did you know that?"

"What does that have to do with anything?" I asked.

"It has everything to do with *everything*." Gatsby turned through his ties. "They all have this code, and it's all anyone can do to try to keep up. A *mirror* is a *looking glass*, you don't say *perfume*, you say *scent*, *greens* instead of *vegetables*. *Spectacles* instead of *glasses*. But if you say *pass on* or *pleased to meet you*, you're trying too hard. You have to say *die* and *how d'you do?*"

"Stop." I took his hands again. This time, I tried to do it in the reassuring way Jordan and Daisy did with each other. "Just hear my idea."

The way I was holding his hands seemed to be making us both breathe harder, so I stepped back again. "You'll offer to throw her a debut. If she's the socialite everyone's talking about, she'll have her own power, and she can make her own choice. She'll have her standing as top girl, the debutante of the season."

The gold of the sundown outside spilled over Gatsby's face, and with it came so much hope that I knew I had to temper it.

"She still may not choose you," I said. "I can't speak for my"—I stopped myself before I said *my cousin*—"my friend. My friend might not choose you."

"I know," Gatsby said. "I just want her to be happy. I want her to know she has a choice."

"Exactly," I said.

Jordan found us on the way down the stairs, confetti in her hair. "What are you two wallflowers doing up there?" Her dress floated out behind her as she ascended the steps. "What's the point in hosting a party if you're going to hide in a turret?"

"Can we tell her?" Gatsby asked.

"Well, now that you've said that"—Jordan met us halfway up—"you have to."

With a few whispers and an exclaimed "I love it!" Jordan became our coconspirator.

"You don't think we're plotting behind her back?" Gatsby asked.

"Oh, we're absolutely plotting behind her back," Jordan said. "But you know if there were debuts for gentlemen she'd do the same for you." Now Jordan was looking at me.

"I know she would," I said.

"And didn't she practically connive to get you to New York?" Jordan asked. "I think it's time someone plotted behind her back in her favor for once, don't you?"

* * *

The three of us found Daisy and Tom again, and Jordan made use of a pause as skillfully as using the wind for a golf swing.

"Jay," Jordan said, with the light of a sudden idea, "I was

thinking about it, and why don't you throw a little debut for our Daisy?"

Surprise lit up Daisy's face, and Gatsby feigned the same.

"Look at these soirees of yours." Jordan spun, taking in the party. "A ball would be nothing for you."

Tom surveyed the three of them. "Jordan, why would he do a thing like that?"

I looked to Gatsby and realized we hadn't thought up an idea for *why*.

"My sister," Gatsby said. "She'll be coming east to New York in a few years. I'd like to throw her a debut. My family has never been much for it, so they'd never do it themselves. We're Irish, you see, so they're not taking any traditions from the court of St. James or anywhere else in England. But it means a great deal to my sister, and I'd love to learn how to throw a proper one. I think Daisy knows enough to teach me a thing or two for my sister's sake, so throwing Daisy a party would be the least I could do in thanks."

All four of us watched Tom's face. He made a considering sound. "My mother wouldn't like it one bit."

"No, of course not," Daisy said.

"She says the whole tradition's being eroded by new money," Tom said. "All these girls from western families. No offense meant to your sister, Mr. Gatsby."

"None at all," Gatsby said.

"If you ask me," Tom went on, "it's all ridiculous anyway, girls prancing around in white frocks a year or two before they should be getting married. If a girl has to display herself in order to attract a man, what's there to do but feel sorry for her?"

Even if Gatsby didn't feel offense on behalf of his sister, I did.

"But, Daisy," Tom said, "you're already my girl, so no one would take it seriously."

Daisy's face tightened.

"It could be a delightful little farce," Tom said. "A laugh for all our friends. Daisy, you can show them that sense of humor of yours, prancing about like some courtier."

Daisy's smile was as bitter as the twist of lemon pith in Tom's drink.

"And if it helps Mr. Gatsby with his little sister, all the better." Tom clapped his hands together. "This sounds like a real diversion. Daisy, you get your little party; Gatsby, you get to learn all about how to put your little sister in some silly dress and show her off to all the men of West Egg. Everyone gets what they want." Tom slapped Gatsby on the back. "I look forward to it." Then he followed a waiter who held a tray of drinks.

As soon as Tom was out of sight, Daisy brightened. "You three." She lightly swatted Jordan, Gatsby, and me on our upper arms.

"What did I do?" I asked.

"I know intrigue when I hear it," she said. "It's practically my third language. All of you were behind this."

"We couldn't deprive the New York season," Jordan said. "You're going to be the most beautiful debutante that ever graced the stage. With my help, of course."

Daisy turned to Gatsby. "Jay." She breathed his name in that way she had on first seeing him. "Thank you. I can't tell you what this means to me."

The light from the outdoor chandeliers, hanging from the tallest branches, sparkled over their faces.

"Oh, and think of the time we'll spend together planning it," Daisy said. "We'll catch up on everything. It'll be like no time passed at all."

The hope on Gatsby's face could have lit every lamp in the garden.

Daisy took Jordan by the elbow. "Come talk to me about gowns. I don't want to look like some pale little princess from the Gilded Age."

After this ball, Daisy wouldn't need Tom. The season's most beautiful debutante coming out at the site of the season's most famous parties. After this, designers would probably pay her to wear their clothes. Hotels would give her suites just so she'd be seen in their lobbies. Perfumers would offer her unimaginable sums to hold lilac bouquets for advertisements. Whether she chose Gatsby or not, she would have the chance to choose for herself.

Maybe I was using Jay Gatsby to get my cousin away from Tom Buchanan. But Gatsby only had a chance with her if Tom was no longer her patron and protector.

"Are you even Irish?" I asked Gatsby once Daisy and Jordan were out of earshot.

"Yes," he said. "I am."

"Do you even have a sister?" I asked.

"Yes again," he said. "She's nearly forty. Happily married with three children in Ohio."

"So you just made that up?" I asked. "Right now?"

"You know what this is like." Gatsby was close enough now that his arm was against mine. The heat of his body found its way through his shirt and his jacket sleeve and then through my shirtsleeve to my skin. "Boys like us get used to having to lie about everything else just so we can tell the truth about ourselves."

<hr />

Querida Mamá,

I have the most deliriously wonderful news: I'm going to be a true New York debutante. Can you believe it?

I know you've heard things about the blue bloods, and yes, enough of them are awful. But they're not so bad, really, not the ones I keep company with. None of those spoiled sons who've ripped hotel chandeliers from the ceilings and played at sports with crystal.

I haven't yet chosen a dress—I'm considering a Florrie Westwood or a Norman Hartnell. I wish you were here to advise me. You have such a good eye, though I can sense you rolling your eyes right now. Plenty of fashion here is more practical than you might think. And to prove it, I'm buying you a Jean Patou and Maison Schiaparelli, no arguments. You could wear them to church. You'll see.

Oh, and while I'm thinking of it, I must thank you for all the times you made buñuelos when we girls were growing up. My practice eating them helped me pass a test I didn't even know I was taking the other afternoon. I was offered a cream puff covered in powdered sugar, and it seems the way I ate it without making a mess was a sign that Doris and Betty Fishguard can associate with me. (Their oldest sister is the one who convinced me to make eye and brow powder from the ash on fireplace grates, even though she could afford any cosmetic she wants. She's married to a man who probably has a deed to the sun! Don't worry, I haven't tried it since. I'll never forget the rash it gave me.)

Now if I can just remember not to cause a scandal by dipping a wafer into my coffee.

Your daughter in New York,
the center of everything,
Daisy

CHAPTER XVIII

Dechert was waiting for me again. He lounged in his car, admiring the blossoming trees and the lights of Gatsby's mansion.

"How's the bash?" he said.

I walked right by him. "If you're hoping I'm drunk and feeling talkative," I said, "I'm neither."

"Too bad," he said. "Whatever you got paid for all this, it's not enough to keep quiet. Certainly not enough to take the fall."

I turned so that he wouldn't see the muscle in my neck pinch.

"Like I told you the first time you came around," I said, "I wasn't even in New York when everything happened. I can show you the train ticket if you want."

"Funny thing about things like that," Dechert said. "People see it and think it's proof of something. They don't realize how easy it is to fake."

He thought I might be so devious as to stage my own train travel?

Of course he did.

There was a missing fortune in pearls, and I was the most conveniently in-reach brown person to blame.

But I acted as though I had no care except to stumble toward my bed.

Dechert got out of his car. "You can't afford to be mixed up in something like this, Nick. It'll land on you eventually."

I put my key in the door. "Puedo seguir los manos."

Dechert shook his head. "What?"

I kept my hand on the key but turned to look at him. "It's something my mother says."

"Fine," he said. "What does it mean?"

"It means I can follow the hands," I said. "I'm not stupid. Things like that don't just happen. It's because people like you do things. So if this lands on me"—I unlocked the door—"it's because you put it there."

———— • • • ————

Gatsby knocked on the cottage door the next afternoon as the sun was tilting low. He stood with his hands in his pockets, the light making a gilded outline of him. His shirt matched the late lilacs.

"Are you all right?" Gatsby asked.

"I'm fine." I looked worn, and I knew it. I had been up

most of the night trying to work out all the potential ways Tom or Dechert or Port Roosevelt Limited might blame me for the necklace. It was a math problem I kept getting stuck on. Too many variables.

"I'm just a little tired," I said. "What time does she get here?"

A question formed on Gatsby's face.

"Daisy." In a few hours it would be dark, and Daisy and Gatsby would need the cover of a chaperone. "She's coming over, isn't she?"

It was the summer solstice today, when the light would last the longest and the gold stayed until dark. It was one of my cousin's favorite days of the year, even though she usually forgot it was coming. *I wait through the winter and spring for all that light, and then I miss it.*

"Why do you think I'm here about Daisy?" Gatsby asked.

I shrugged my suspenders onto my shoulders. "I imagine you all have a lot of plans to get started on."

"No," Gatsby said, and now the angle let me see the color of his suit, a blue that was almost lavender. "I had something else in mind. It is your birthday, isn't it?"

My heart gave a hollow flinch.

"How did you know that?" I asked.

"Daisy told me," Gatsby said.

"Why would she tell you that?"

"I asked," Gatsby said. "I was asking about you."

"Why?" I said.

"She's known you for a long time, hasn't she?" he asked.

Why would he spend his time with Daisy talking about me?

Worry crossed his face. "Would you rather I hadn't?"

"No," I said. "It's fine."

"Good." Gatsby handed me a tie as purple as a summer plum. "Because they're waiting for us."

"Who?" I asked.

He was already halfway to his car, parked on the path between the cottage and his grounds. The finish was a dusk lavender a little cooler than his suit.

"Who's waiting for us?" I asked. "Where are we going?"

Gatsby looked back at me how any boy in the world would want to be looked at—as though there was such infinite possibility in me, such infinite light, that I was one endless, longest day of the year.

"Come on," Gatsby said, and so I did.

CHAPTER XIX

Once we got into the city, Gatsby led me through a flower shop with a gold-lettered window. But he didn't stop at the counter, or at any of the clouds of pastel blooms, or even at the chandeliers of dripping blossoms that looked like the arrangements he'd brought into the cottage.

"Frank," Gatsby greeted a white man arranging flowers.

The stems stood twice as tall as the vase that held them. Frank nodded back, shaking the stalks into place.

"What are we doing here?" I asked.

Gatsby turned back, his head haloed in blooms. "You'll see."

"Jay." A Black woman with her nails done in that half-moon manicure stopped Gatsby with a touch on his arm. She wore glasses in the oval shape I now knew to be this season's fashion—I then corrected myself to thinking *spectacles*, not *glasses*—and a hat the same pink as the flowers she was studying.

"And how're the season's brides treating you, Irene?" Gatsby asked.

"There's one who's demanding the moon," Irene said. "And one who doesn't know what she wants, so everything takes twice as long. I don't know who's giving me the greater headache."

"At least June's close to over," Gatsby said.

"And when it is, Belle and I are taking a vacation somewhere no one can ask me about trailing bouquets," Irene said.

Belle? She'd just said a woman's name with the affection of a lover, in earshot of Frank and two other florists. I wanted to know Irene in the way I wanted to know Martha, but at the same time, I worried for her, saying another woman's name so fondly. Would she lose her job if anyone noticed?

Irene handed two tiny bunches of flowers to Gatsby, each stuck with a pin.

"Have fun, you two," she said, and then was gone in a mist of blossoms.

Gatsby took one of the tiny bunches of flowers and pinned it to one of my suspender bands. I tensed so I wouldn't shudder at his fingertips against my shirt.

"Did you know these are called amnesia roses?" Gatsby said, touching the lilac petals. "The story goes that if you smell them, you forget the heartbreak of the past."

"I imagine gin has roughly the same result," I said.

Gatsby laughed. "But for a night instead of forever." He pinned on his own and then slipped behind a wall of flowering branches.

"Where are we?" I asked.

"The gayest place in New York." Gatsby pushed on a wood panel that turned into a door. "In more ways than one."

The door opened onto a space wider than the flower shop itself. The hum of music warmed the air, and the first person I recognized was Martha, leaning against a deep-finished bar. She looked straight out of a B. Altman catalog, wearing a three-piece skirt suit with a high-collared shirt and a row of cloth-covered buttons down the center. She was talking with a Black woman wearing a tuxedo, and I couldn't remember what the lapels on her tuxedo jacket were called—though Gatsby had told me the difference between notched and peaked, I couldn't keep them straight—but the lapel fabric shined like glass. From their expressions and gestures, she and Martha seemed to be complimenting each other's clothing and discussing tailoring.

The shimmer of beads adorned loose dresses. I noticed a woman I'd seen the first time I'd gone to one of Gatsby's parties, the one who'd been holding a tube of orange lipstick. I'd since learned that the man who'd told me she was Chinese American had been right, which made me hope and wonder if maybe white New Yorkers made fewer assumptions, though I doubted it. The woman now shared laughter as glittering as her necklace with the woman she'd been showing the lipstick to. They touched hands every time they reached for their drinks. (Had they been this obviously enamored of each other at Gatsby's? Had I simply missed it?) Patrons who—as the kind of boy I was, I couldn't help noticing such things—seemed as though they might have been called boys at birth wore paillette-adorned gowns, thin brows, and dark lipstick.

Gatsby stopped at a table where two women sat more next to each other than across from each other. They both had brown skin, and one looked a little like my mother in old photographs, and neither was trying to hide her adoration for the other. They held champagne flutes, and they laughed in that intimate way that created gravity, pulling them closer. They had on skirt suits restrained enough to make me wonder where they'd been before coming here. But they also had purple flowers tucked around their low buns, and I was nearly sure they'd put them in upon arriving.

"Nick," Gatsby said, "Helen and Frances, two of my first friends here."

"Jay, how did you manage to send this to our table before you even got here?" Helen lifted her flute.

"Yes, have you been hiding in the flower shop this whole time?" Frances asked. "And who's your friend?"

"Nick is my neighbor," Gatsby said, "and hopefully still friend by the time today's over."

"What?" I asked. "Why?"

Gatsby touched the table. "Happy anniversary, you two."

"Three years, can you believe it?" the women said almost in unison, and then collapsed into laughter. With that laugh, Gatsby and I didn't exist anymore, and neither did the rest of the world. It gave me a hope as buoyant as the bubbles rising in their glasses.

These women had just admitted to being together. *Together* in a way that could be pinned to an anniversary. How had they counted? From the moment they first smiled at each other? From the first time they both breathed the same jasmine-scented air?

As Gatsby and I left them to their sparkling world, I leaned close enough to say, "They just said that out loud."

"That's the point here," Gatsby said. "Everyone gets to be a little more themselves. Remind me to introduce you to their husbands."

"Their husbands?" I asked.

Gatsby indicated a table where two men looked as enthralled with each other as the women did. "Have you ever heard of a lavender marriage?"

"No," I said, though I could now guess.

"They're very chic in the Hollywood sewing circles," Gatsby said. "Marrying for appearances is much easier when both husband and wife are equally fond of and uninterested in each other. I heard rumors that Alla Nazimova arranged both of Valentino's. Do you want a drink?"

"Seltzer, same as you," I said. "You saw me drunk. I'm not planning a repeat performance."

So Gatsby and I drank soda water among the highballs and

rose martinis. The microphone switched hands every couple of minutes, a new song each time. First the woman in the tuxedo, who then tried to hand it to Martha after, but Martha refused. The knowing shake of her head—the look of *Oh no, you're not talking me into this again*—told me how often she must have come here, how many people knew her. Then came a laughing duet between two girls in beaded skirts.

The air smelled like smoke and cedar and the dark pencil of eyeliner. Everyone's sentences were peppered with phrases I didn't know. *Blue ruin. Bell polisher. To the gills.* But unlike Gatsby's parties, where I felt like a hayseed, everyone here had a generous air to them, like we'd all come in out of the rain together.

A group pushed a laughing woman in a white lace dress toward the front of the room. She must have been thirty, maybe thirty-five, and tinier than anyone else here. Her large eyes and heart-shaped face looked as fresh as the flowers they thrust into her hands.

Celebrants in sequin dresses flanked her.

"We have a debutante tonight!" one exclaimed.

"And she's coming out in style!" the second one said with a wave of her arm.

They rained flower petals down on the woman.

"What are they doing?" I asked Gatsby.

"A coming-out ball," Gatsby said. "When you figure something out about yourself, it's worth marking the occasion. This is how everyone here does it."

The petal-crowned debutante danced with Martha, and then with the woman in the tuxedo. Men who seemed generally more interested in each other greeted her with the enthusiasm of waltzing with a bride at a wedding. Next she danced with young men who, I thought, were maybe the same kind of boys Gatsby and I were.

"And if I'm not mistaken," a woman in a beaded dress said, "we have a birthday boy here."

I looked at Gatsby. "You didn't."

Gatsby grinned.

When a group came over to us, I grabbed Gatsby's arm. "Oh, no you don't. If I'm going, you're coming with me."

I pulled him along as we were gathered into the center of the group. One woman said my birthday made me a summer boy, and a sequined dress chorus said that was my name now. Hands with polished nails rained flowers down on us. Men who seemed like older versions of boys like Gatsby and me patted us both on the back, and it felt like a world of pride away from how Tom Buchanan did it.

The music grew louder, and then half the group was dancing, the room shuddering with frantic joy.

Gatsby held on to me, and I was too happy to think too hard about how his arm felt.

"Are you all right with all this?" he asked.

I shut my eyes as tiny petals caught on my eyelashes, laughing as I said, "I'm having the gayest time."

The celebratory fever around us was the only explanation

I had for why I kissed him. And it was the only explanation I could come up with for why he kissed me back.

It all felt friendly and casual, more like a greeting than an overture. The cheers of our fellow revelers spurred us on, his mouth hot on mine as he kissed me harder.

But when we stopped, he laughed, like we'd thrown tinsel or sprayed champagne fluff everywhere.

That was how I knew it was nothing but fun to him. That was how I knew I didn't have to think about it too much. We'd gotten swept up in the impossible magic of so many hearts being fearlessly themselves.

That was all.

Querido Papá,

I haven't heard from Mamá, so I will bore you next.

Do you remember telling me growing up how things are always interesting when you're paying attention? Well, today I paid attention to every taxicab I saw. Just in an afternoon, I spotted gray, green, midnight blue (at Grand Central Terminal), purple (near the library), even a checkered one (outside the old Putnam Building on Forty-Third and Forty-Fourth. It runs a whole city block, did you know that?).

I miss you all terribly. And I'd be over the moon if you'd write back.

Yours,
Daisy

P.S. Please tell Amelia she was right about me eating ketchup on toast. It seems it's just as tacky as she said it was. You know better than anyone that of all my sisters, she likes saying "I told you so" the most, so please let her know I've said it to myself on her behalf.

CHAPTER XX

"Is this necessary?" I asked.

"Yes," Gatsby said. "You're attending a debutante ball. That means full evening dress. And they're going to need time to fit it to you. This is just to get an idea of how close we are."

"But a tuxedo?" I asked. "Really?"

"That *is* full evening dress," he said. "I've clearly been slacking on tutoring you."

At least the waistcoat was shorter than what I'd seen in pictures. And at least I was trying all this on in Gatsby's closet instead of a busy shop.

Full outfit on, I presented myself. "Go ahead and laugh."

Gatsby's eyes fixed on me. "Why would I laugh?" He blinked, as though coming back from somewhere. "I think we're close. Do you mind if I grab at you a bit?"

I cleared my throat. "Mind if you what?"

"No pins, I promise," he said.

"Oh," I said. He was talking about checking the fit. "Sure. Go ahead."

I kept my body still, holding off any reaction to his hands brushing my shoulders, my waist, checking the jacket, the extra fabric at the pant hem. His fingers skimmed along the loose bow tie hanging around my neck. I hadn't known where to start with tying it.

He was close enough that I could smell his cologne, something green growing under rain, like wild clary. Alongside the dark wood shelves of his bedroom, I felt the dividing pull of something between lovesickness and homesickness. The green of that cologne and the deep wood called up Wisconsin trees.

I shut my eyes for just a second. I didn't want him to see me doing it. I didn't want him worrying over that one kiss, or thinking I was in love with him.

He took hold of the lapels, shifting the seams on my shoulders. "You look marvelous."

I would have sworn to a priest that Gatsby's smile pulled light in through the windows.

———— • • • ————

The moment I unlocked the cottage door, the sight of Dechert pinned me at the threshold.

I had caught him in the act of opening a drawer.

A bowl of fruit had been knocked to the floor. A vase had spilled water and flowers onto a rug. Books I hadn't brought but that I'd leafed through splayed across the floor and sofas. Things that belonged not to me but to the owners—stationery and pens, little decorative figures—seemed to have flown around the room.

"Hey!" I yelled.

I expected him to run, and my body geared up to chase after him.

But he didn't run. He regarded me in the doorway, as though he might continue his search with me standing there.

"Get out of here!" I yelled.

What else could I yell? *I'll call the police*? I had a better chance of building Jules Verne's cannon to the moon than having the police take my side against Dechert's. *I'll report you to your boss*? I didn't know who his boss was, and even if I had, it was unlikely he'd mind an investigator tossing the place where someone like me was staying.

I nearly shouted, *You can't just do this*, except that he could.

Nothing stopped him.

He shut the drawer with a courteous air, like he was being polite. With a slow, deliberate shove of his hand, he threw one of my math textbooks to the floor. The pages landed in disarray, creasing them at odd angles. It struck me worse than Tom's elbow in my face.

"Evening," Dechert said, and took the sea-facing doors out.

My body still wanted to chase him, but I stopped it. Even if I overpowered him, the whole thing was far more likely to end badly for me than him.

He'd left the kitchen in even worse disarray. Jars of flour and sugar pushed over. The icebox left open. I'd heard anecdotes about jewelry being hidden in containers of cereal grain. But did he really think I'd just toss all those pearls in with the oats?

"Nick!" Gatsby was running across the grass.

"What are you doing here?" I asked.

"You left these." He held up a folder of papers, numbers I meant to recheck before tomorrow. "They looked like work, so I thought you might need them. Then I heard the yelling and saw a car drive off." He paused in horror at the state of the cottage. "What happened?"

I wanted to tell him everything so that he'd know how badly I needed to get my cousin away from Tom Buchanan. But I had more reasons not to tell him. First was that I didn't trust him with it. If he heard any of my speculation that Tom might have harmed Daisy, or at least used her without caring whether she got hurt, Gatsby might go right over to East Egg and start throwing his fists at Tom. However badly a fight between Dechert and me might end, that one would end worse.

Second was how little I could do. Dechert had been in here and hadn't made any try at concealing who he was. He didn't have to. I was a brown boy in a borrowed cottage, flanked by millionaires. Dechert had nothing to fear from any complaint I could make.

"It was just kids," I said, as though I wasn't, by the definition of most adults, a kid myself.

"I'll check around." Gatsby made a circuit of the cottage. The reassuring rhythm of his footsteps slowed my heartbeat.

"It looks like they didn't get to your bedroom," he said when he came back.

It was as tactful a way to put it as anyone could have; I knew what he meant. *They didn't get far enough into your things to see your side lacers, or anything else that might tell them what kind of self-made boy you are.*

"I don't think I should leave you alone tonight," Gatsby said. "Do you want to stay with me?"

"No," I said. "I'm fine."

"Then I'll stay here with you," he said.

I wanted to say yes to having another heartbeat in the cottage with me, and to that heartbeat being his. And in a locked cabinet deeper within me, I might have imagined the warmth of his body next to me, kissing him in the dark.

"No," I said. "I don't need that."

"Then at least let me help you clean up," he said.

"I've got it," I said. "Really."

His nod was hesitant, and a little sad. It seemed to hold no pity, but what else could it be? Why else would someone like Gatsby want to stay here, with me, except that he was worried? And why else would he be worried for me except that I was Daisy's friend?

"Listen," Gatsby said. "About your birthday."

"We don't have to talk about it," I said.

Gatsby blinked at me.

"It seems better if we don't," I said. "Doesn't it?"

"Sure," he said. "It's just that if I upset you at all . . ."

"You didn't," I said. "We were caught up in the moment. Nobody meant anything by it. All in good fun, right?"

I hoped he felt relief at that. I wanted him to know I didn't expect anything. I didn't want him to worry that I had attached any romantic hope to that kiss.

Gatsby loved Daisy. I was Nick. I wasn't the distant allure of a green light. I was close. I existed in the play script of Gatsby's life for no reason except to facilitate his reunion with the girl he loved.

"Good night, Nick," he said.

Within a few steps, he was a silhouette against the moonlit trees.

"Jay," I said.

He looked back, the silvered lilacs framing him.

"Thank you," I said. "For today. For my birthday. For everything."

He waved and then vanished.

CHAPTER XXI

"Wisconsin, if I were you, I'd get yourself to Hexton's office as fast as your plow can carry you," Princeton said. "He's incandescent."

"Carraway!" Hexton bellowed from his office.

"Do you need a Bromo-Seltzer?" Princeton asked. "You look like you're about to be sick."

But then Hexton followed up with "Are you riding your family's ox here? Hurry it up!"

The moment I obeyed, he shoved a sheet of paper in my face. "Remember this? Your big idea?"

I examined the numbers enough to recognize them. "Yes."

He grabbed the paper out of my hand and threw it to the floor. "Well, it was genius! Up with the wheat, just like you said! We could paper my office in money off this one!"

I stood silent, confused by the way his compliment sounded as angry as everything else.

"Rises and falls with wheat!" Hexton shoved past me and

out the door. "Benson! Go back to that hick town! I want a dozen more like this one!"

Princeton leaned against a support post, grinning. "Diamond work, Wisconsin. You just might last around here after all."

* * *

"Take those to the clubhouse, will you?" A man in knickerbockers slung a set of golf clubs into my arms. He walked off before I could object.

I looked at Jordan. "Should I even be here?"

Jordan sighed. "Every man in plus fours thinks he's Prince Edward, doesn't he?"

I noted my mistake. Plus fours were longer than knickerbockers, I remembered, and more current. Gatsby had told me that, but I didn't know how he kept it all straight.

"And you're my guest, remember?" Jordan said. "I say you should be here and therefore you should."

"I think the only reason they let me in is because they think I'm your caddy," I said.

"If they don't like you being here, they can go pickle themselves," she said. "You're the honored guest of golf prodigy Jordan Baker."

"Then what do I do with these?" I asked.

She shrugged, and the sleeve of her blouse fluttered. "Well, he didn't tip you, so in my book that must mean they're a gift. Keep them."

The golfers held their fingers to the wind, checking the direction and speed, and that wind blew the disconcerting lime of Daisy's Le Jade toward Gatsby. The two of them stood close under a spectators' tent.

Each day, Daisy had drifted across the sound from East Egg to West Egg on the breeze of a different perfume, and she and Gatsby set to work planning the debut of the season.

On the day they discussed the orchestra, she had spritzed on the orange flower, iris, and amber of Narcisse Blanc. As Gatsby's gardeners spoke like poets of their vision for the grounds, each delighted nod of Daisy's head emitted the soap-clean citrus, lavender, and rosemary of 4711. As they tasted cakes and custards for the dessert, laughing as they dotted each other's noses with frosting and chasing me with handfuls of buttercream like snowballs, Daisy's shoulder wafted the vanilla and vetiver of Shalimar. When Gatsby had his favorite florist bring a dozen towering arrangements for her to choose from, Daisy smelled of Narcisse Noir, the daffodil and lemon as fresh as nighttime after rain. Each perfume lingered in Gatsby's gardens and rooms, a dozen fragrant ghosts.

"You're staring at them again," Jordan said.

"Sorry," I said.

"What are you apologizing for?" she asked. "It's nothing to me. I just thought you should know it."

Today my cousin was wearing, of all things, a pink

gingham dress and pink stockings along with it, the stockings embroidered with floral vines so dainty they were liable to run if you looked at them wrong. Pink gingham and pink tights. My cousin might as well have been going to a costume party dressed as a white girl. But she carried it off so well, a dozen socialites would be wearing the same at the next tournament. It was Gatsby I was worried about, the pale blush of his clean-lined suit. The men around here were in those voluminous plus fours, or in chalk stripe or seersucker.

"They all make fun of him, Jordan," I said.

She started on her arm stretches. "What do you mean?"

"They come to his parties and drink his liquor and then they make fun of his wallpaper," I said.

"Never mind them." Jordan held an aluminum putter behind her, gripping it by both hands. "They all try so hard to look like they're not trying so hard. See that one showing off his spectators? Or that one over there, so subtly taking his pocket watch out of his vest so everyone can see how expensive it is? And don't get me started on the girls here. Did you know they buy dresses from Paris and leave them in their closets untouched for a year?"

"Why would they do that?" I asked.

"They call it curing," Jordan said. "So nothing appears too new, too eager. It's a hilarious amount of effort not to seem eager, if you ask me. Give me a new frock, I'm wearing it to my next party." She twisted her body, still holding the club.

"And as to the wallpaper, let them talk. They're all proud of those fortunes hoarded in their accounts. They'd buy diamonds heavy as wrecking balls but won't replace their own peeling wallpaper. Old Mayflower values. They think it's such an accomplishment to be old money. And that's how they say it too. Not that they *have* old money, but that they *are* old money. What does that tell you?"

A white woman in a sky-blue dress waved a gloved hand to Jordan, and Jordan waved back. I hoisted the golf bag onto my shoulder, hoping Jordan wouldn't notice me hauling it toward the clubhouse.

On the way past the spectators' tent, I snuck a glance at Gatsby and Daisy. The sun threw shards of light through the cut crystal of her glass, and he was looking at her like she was condensing all the stars into a cluster of ice cubes. To Gatsby, the fine dust of Daisy's powder compact suggested a world that could be softened at the edges. Her voice dripped of money she didn't have. The lightness with which she carried herself promised a lifetime of roses on the breakfast table.

When Tom joined her at the tent, Daisy peered out from under her hat, the brim the color of the sky.

"Is that your car out there, Gatsby?" he asked. "Interesting color. I prefer myself a blue coupe and leave the pretty shades to the girls, right, Daisy?"

"Afternoon, Tom," Gatsby said.

Tom pointed at Gatsby. "You'd better be careful with the sun—you're almost as brown as Nick."

Tension came into Gatsby's fist, the one alongside his trouser leg. If I hadn't been carrying a set of clubs, I would have told him not to bother. Tom had worn me out at the beginning of the summer. When I could help it, I didn't listen to half of what he had to say.

"A pink suit," Tom said, eyeing Gatsby up and down. "That's something, isn't it? Have you got a wristwatch to go with it?"

By the time I got back from the clubhouse, Daisy had left Tom's side. She and Jordan were off in a pool of dappled shade. They were holding hands, and even though I couldn't hear her from this distance, I knew from Daisy's smile that she was talking in that soft, reassuring way of hers. Jordan was nodding, breathing deeply enough that I could see it.

I may not have known much of how friendships between girls worked, but the scene was calm and sweet in a way I couldn't miss—Daisy was helping Jordan settle her nerves. She was both talking her up to the task in front of her and making her laugh so that she'd have a moment of forgetting it. It had the even quality of a routine, something they might have done before many past tournaments.

Daisy squeezed Jordan's hands and then let them go. With one last nod, Jordan took on her socialite's posture and walked out toward a crescent moon of waiting reporters.

"Jordan Baker, what cold cream do you use?"

"Over here, Jordan, is that a new rouge, what's the color?"

"Jordan, is it true you wear orange toenail polish for good luck?"

I knew Jordan set fashion as much as any debutante. But I couldn't imagine Walter Hagen getting so many questions about his hair tonic or whether his lucky socks were plaid or diamond-checkered.

"Ms. Baker," I called, loud enough that she looked past the reporters.

"I see we have a fan with a question of his own," Jordan said. "Young man, what would you like to know?"

"Is it true you played your first majors from the men's tees?" I asked.

"Of course not," Jordan said. "That's an outrageous lie, and I won't have you spreading it."

The crowd gasped.

Jordan's face beamed the light of a chandelier. "I drove from seven yards behind the men's tee," she said, and the crowd bore her up on their thrilled laughter.

Between holes, Tom greeted Yale friends and business associates. Daisy and Gatsby gathered up those stray moments like sunlight in their hands. They pinched away blades of grass and threw them at each other, green catching on Daisy's hat. They tried sips of each other's drinks.

When Daisy saw Tom had his back turned, she pressed her thumb to her rouged lips and patted the blush of color onto the apples of Gatsby's cheeks. "There, now you look sun-flushed."

That was enough for Jordan, who found me between the twelfth and thirteenth holes.

"Do something about your boy, Nick," she whispered, a putting cleek clutched in her hand. "He's being reckless. Look at the two of them."

"I know," I said.

"Then stop him," she said. "I can't concentrate worrying about him like this. Tom's right there. And his friends aren't all as stupid as they look."

"What do you want me to do?" I asked.

"I don't care if you borrow two sets of clubs so you can both go practice your drives," Jordan said. "Don't make me bite my nails over what a fool he's being. I have a new manicure."

The next time Tom excused himself to greet an acquaintance, I blurted out, "You know, I had a teacher who taught me all about the physics of golf." Nerves nearly made my voice crack. "It's very interesting."

Tom laughed. "You really are just a head and nothing else, aren't you, Nick? Well, I suppose we need a few like you watching the markets."

But it worked. I involved Tom, Daisy, and Gatsby in an intermittent conversation about the arc of the swing and the angle of the shot, cementing myself as an absolute bore. Tom stayed, his presence dulling the shine of the afternoon, so much so that Daisy and Gatsby stood an arm's length apart.

"We had to wait out your adoring public," Daisy told Jordan after the gloved clapping ended.

"Jordan Baker the Tournament Taker," Tom said.

"Oh, as though you were watching," Jordan said. "You treat every country club as an office."

Daisy looped her arm through Jordan's. "I know you're the best at it," she said. "But really, how do you stand this game? It's punctuated walking."

"Only to those who don't understand the art form," Jordan said. "Come on, I need to change. I'm just soaked from being out in the sun."

"No false modesty," Gatsby said. "You're fresh as a lemon blossom, and you know it."

"Stop trying to get me to marry you, Jay Gatsby." Jordan grinned over her shoulder. "I'm never going to fall in love with you."

"You can't blame a man for trying, can you?" Gatsby asked.

Jordan leaned into Daisy. "I have my blue Lanvin, the one with the peach flowers. I've been too many hours in sensible linen. Let's sparkle a little."

"I brought my gold rayon floss," Daisy said. "The Madeleine Vionnet. It's rose and copper all at once. It's glorious. What do you think of all the going back and forth between rich colors and the pastels? Do you think it'll keep?"

"Oh, I think it's seasonal," Jordan said. "Is that a new handbag?"

"I needed something big enough to hold that cute little pistol Tom gave me," Daisy said. "All the purses I had were barely big enough for a compact and a lipstick."

"You're carrying it around with you?" Jordan asked.

"Of course," Daisy said.

"Not loaded, I hope," Jordan said.

"Yes, loaded," Daisy said.

"Whatever for?" Jordan asked.

"In case Tom wants to go to the range at a moment's notice. He thinks I don't like a present unless I fasten it to my person at all times." Daisy gave Tom a playful look back. "Remember that pair of yellow shoes he bought me? The ones with the double straps? He was awfully offended when I didn't wear them days in a row."

"Well, didn't you explain it to him?" Jordan asked. "Cora practically writes love letters to those green d'orsay heels and even she knows you can only wear a bright shoe like that a few times a season."

They went on murmuring about hats and the smallest bags a woman could carry, gloves and summer-weight jewelry, curved heels, dropped waists. I knew skirts and shoes from my mother and cousins, but this was a language as unknown to me as shorthand directions around the city.

"What are they talking about?" I meant to ask Gatsby but accidentally aimed the question at Tom.

"Who knows?" Tom said. "They change clothes a thousand times a day. It seems you need a different dress to write a letter than to go for a stroll than to take a telephone call. Don't try to understand women, Nick. You never will. I gave up years ago."

"I don't think they're so hard to understand," Gatsby said.

"You hear that, Nick?" Tom asked. "Mr. Pink Suit's here to give you the finer points of ladies' day dress. Ruffles, collars, bows, embroidery, all of it."

A laughing song rose from the space between Jordan and Daisy.

"Nicky." Daisy rushed over to me. "Jordan and I just remembered the most amusing thing and now I have to know." She circled around the back of me so she could put her hands on my upper arms. "Have you ever been inside a revolving door?"

"There's one in the building where I work," I said.

"But have you gone in it?" she asked.

"There are perfectly good ordinary doors on either side of it," I said.

"So that's a no?" she asked.

"That's a no."

Daisy got that look that always told me to brace for what was coming next.

CHAPTER XXII

"I'm not going in that thing," I said.

"Don't you want to write your mother back home and tell her that you spun in the revolving door of the Plaza itself?" Daisy asked.

"Was this really worth going out of our way?" Tom asked.

"Hush, Tom," Daisy said, and then returned to me. "Nick, you're a man of science, so you should appreciate that revolving doors have a scientific purpose. I thought you of all people would want to engage close up."

"I know the purpose," I said.

I'd read a paper about revolving doors. They had them in Chicago too. The way they spun pockets of air helped relieve the stack effect inside a building, the pressure that grew more intense the taller a structure got. That didn't mean I wanted to get inside a moving door that could knock you down as easily as it could take you anywhere.

"I'm not going in on principle," I said. "It seems like you might never come out."

"But you do, and I'll prove it." Daisy shoved the first panel of brass-framed glass. She picked up speed, singing a song that bounced off the interior doors too much to be understood.

Daisy's charm flew out those revolving doors. Hotel guests looked on, amused by this diaphanous girl.

Daisy slowed to a stop. "See, Nick? Now come on in with me."

"No, thank you," I said.

She gave an actress's sigh with her whole body. "Fine. Then who's coming in? Tom?"

"I'm not participating in this," Tom said. "This whole affair, it's just silly. Nick didn't even want to come."

"Fine," Daisy said. "Jordan?"

"And risk tearing the Lanvin?" Jordan ran her fingers over the organdy of her skirt. "Not even for you."

Daisy tossed a glance toward Gatsby. "Jay? Care to help show our Wisconsin boy that there's nothing to be afraid of?"

Gatsby hesitated.

"If one of you doesn't come in here with me right now I'm making a terrible scene," Daisy said. But it was Gatsby's arm she reached for, and she pulled him in.

As they spun, they threw their heads back. Her honeyed hair and her rose skirt floated behind her. His enchanted laugh sounded distant filtered through the glass. Every few seconds they spun near enough to leave nothing between them and us, and his laugh was clear and close. Then they kept spinning, and he went away again, and his laugh sounded as far as another planet. That laugh was a lighthouse beam, illuminating me and then leaving me unseen in alternating seconds.

I was a moon for him to throw sunlight on. In the glow of Gatsby's gaze or laugh, I was luminous. When he directed the ray of his attention on my cousin—my beautiful, white-passing cousin—I was a cold and forbidding landscape.

The pursing of the lower half of Tom's mouth stood in perfect opposition to the widening of his eyes. He wore such a scandalized look you might have thought Daisy had removed her dress and danced through the lobby in her slip.

Daisy and Gatsby had done something that not even Tom could miss.

In this moment, Tom Buchanan, this man I loathed, was my awful, unlikely companion. We had each noticed something truly inconvenient.

Tom had just realized that Daisy was in love with Jay Gatsby.

I had just realized that so was I.

• ◦ •

Daisy and Gatsby tumbled out of the revolving doors breathless, Daisy's sterling-silver laugh tinseling the lobby.

The revolving doors kept turning, holding the last of their momentum. As they slowed, my thoughts still spun.

Was a boy like me even allowed to love another boy? What did that make me? I had parents who'd respected me telling them that I was a boy, and who'd helped me live as the boy I was. Shouldn't that have been enough? Shouldn't I like girls as more than friends by now?

I should have wanted Jordan. Jordan was stunning and wry, with a shell of sarcasm around her open heart. She was neither as cynical as I knew myself to be nor as recklessly romantic as Gatsby. I should have been taken with her. But I adored her like a cosmopolitan older sister. I admired her without envy, indifferent to who she laughed with or smiled at. I had grown attached to Jordan without feeling any trace of desire.

Even if los santos descended from heaven and blessed me loving another boy, that boy could not be Gatsby.

That boy was in love with my cousin, who had decided not to be my cousin.

I wanted Daisy away from Tom. And Daisy had fallen back in love, or more deeply in love than ever, with Gatsby. This had been the best outcome all along, hadn't it?

"Tell you what," Tom said. "Why don't you two girls go for some shopping? Try on hats. And, Nick, I'm sure you have some numbers to go over at the office, don't you? Endear yourself to your boss come Monday morning. You'll thank me. I promise."

My relief at not being folded into the category of "girls" lasted only until he added, "That should give Mr. Pink Suit here and me a chance to get better acquainted. What do you say, Gatsby? Should we turn one of the rooms here into a smoking parlor? Have you ever had a Cohiba?" Tom clapped Gatsby on the back hard enough that Gatsby had to brace the heel of his shoe into the floor. "A Romeo y Julieta?"

I cringed. Usually I didn't pay much mind when someone pronounced Spanish wrong. But there was a certain blunt sound to when someone wasn't even trying. I could hear Tom crushing the words in his mouth.

Through glances, Jordan and I had a silent conversation.

If we leave them alone together . . . , Jordan's worried face said.

I know, my eyes said back.

All it took was my nod, and Jordan burst into sparkling life. "You two think you can have a party without us?" She wedged herself between the two men. She threw one arm around Tom's shoulder, the other around Gatsby's. "On the day of my victory? And you call yourself gentlemen!"

"She's right," Daisy added. "There's no party at all without me. Why, Nicky, tell them what they've done in my hometown since I left."

"They do nothing but pine for her," I said. "They sigh in droves in front of the greengrocer's. They weep that she's not there to dance with them."

"I knew it!" Daisy said. "And to think anyone imagines

they can have a gay afternoon without me!" She offered a hand to Jordan, and when Jordan took it, Daisy twirled Jordan into her. They laughed with the abandon of young girls and the reckless grace of rich young women.

"That settles it," Daisy said. "Tom, be a dear and get us a room. One big enough for the five of us."

The flush of Tom's annoyance climbed up his neck. It rose higher as Daisy twirled Jordan again.

"Really, Tom." Daisy caught Jordan, wrapping an arm around the waist of her dress. "It was so dreadfully rude of you, and Jordan's feelings are so very hurt." Daisy looked at Jordan, who answered the cue with a crestfallen expression that the back row of a theater couldn't have missed. "See what you've done? Now book us a parlor suite. It's the least you can do."

For the first few minutes in the brocade-papered suite, Daisy and Jordan twirled around the room. Gatsby and I sat on opposite sides of a sofa a few shades deeper than his suit.

Daisy and Jordan fell laughing, dizzy, into the space between us.

"I'm just the worst ballerina in the whole world," Daisy breathed.

"You're the belle of every ball, and you know it," Jordan said.

They both draped themselves on chaises upholstered in matching periwinkle satin.

"Tom, what a dreadful idea you had." Daisy leaned back her head. "It's hotter up here than on the sidewalk."

From his place in an armchair, Tom gave his best imitation of a smile. The glass in his hand sweated whiskey. He had one leg propped up on the opposite knee and seemed to be trying to scuff the sole of his shoe against the pale pink of Gatsby's pant leg. But Gatsby wasn't quite in range, no matter how Tom leaned.

From floors below, the cheer of a wedding rose to the open windows. The perfume of the bride's bouquet trimmed the air in petaled lace.

"Should we try to spot the bride?" Jordan drifted over to a window. "For good luck?"

"Too hot," Daisy crooned.

"Oh, she looks very pretty," Jordan said. "I do love a Juliet-cap veil. It is long though, I hope she doesn't trip."

"You sound like you're calling a race at the downs," Tom said.

Jordan ignored him. "Long-sleeve lace dress. They're everywhere this season, aren't they? Daisy, when do you think the brides are going to start going sleeveless?"

"My mother would faint," Daisy said.

"Yes, so would mine," Jordan said.

"My mother thinks we should have the wedding here," Tom told Jordan.

"Your mother thinks you should have a wedding here but to another woman," Daisy said, closing her eyes.

Tom added a few more ice cubes to his glass. "Maybe if you'd lift a finger over the plans, she'd warm to you."

"Why would I do that when you haven't even asked me?" Daisy said, sounding more bored than annoyed.

"I've just got to work it all out with my family, you know that," he said. "And besides, a few months ago I couldn't shut you up about dresses and azaleas."

"Gardenias," Daisy and Gatsby said at the same time.

An ice cube I'd swallowed a few minutes earlier roiled in my stomach.

"Oh, there's ages to plan the wedding," Daisy said. "First, an engagement, n'est-ce pas? And before that, my debut."

Jordan stared out a window. "Which do you think is going to win?"

Gatsby took a sip from his glass of seltzer.

"Which of who?" Tom asked.

"All those buildings out there," Jordan said. "They're all racing to get to the sky. Which do you think's going to win?"

"I'll bet they'll have revolving doors," Daisy said.

Jordan pulled the rose from the drinks tray and threw it at Daisy.

Daisy caught it and got up from her chaise. "Oh, let's don't go wasting blooms." She lifted a pearl-headed pin from the hat she'd worn this afternoon. Gatsby watched, enraptured, as she pinned the yellow rose to his vest, a boutonnière.

The disdain on Tom's face thickened the heat in the air.

"How do you even get alcohol in a hotel?" I asked, my voice pinched with how badly I wanted to change the subject. "The man brought it up on a tray and everything, and I thought that was against the law. Aren't they worried about getting caught?"

Jordan looked at me with a mix of fondness and pity. "Oh, Daisy, how do you stand it?"

"Stand what, dear?" Daisy asked.

"How sweet our Nick is," Jordan said. "He's like a baby chick. Or a little lamb."

"He's no little anything, Daisy," Tom said. "I'd say he's the only one of the four of you not making a fool of himself. In fact"—now he stood—"I think it's time we moved the party home."

"Oh, Tom, no," Daisy said. "We're having a good time."

"I think you've had a bit too much of a good time." Tom brushed bits of mint off his slacks. "I can hear the ice rattling in your head."

"Don't be sore on account of the heat," Daisy said. "We could hire four more rooms and get ice baths."

"We can do that at home," Tom said. "Plenty of bathtubs there. Even a blue one, if you can believe it. The silly things my mother wanted put in. And the liquor's cheaper. Come on, Nick, you're riding with me."

The heat stuck my shirt to my back. A sheen of worry crossed Gatsby's forehead.

"Why don't I go with you both?" Gatsby said. "Then the girls can drive back together."

I shook my head mildly enough that perhaps Gatsby would notice and not Tom, a forewarning for what I'd say next.

"I think you're the most fit to drive of the three of you," I told Gatsby. Daisy and Jordan were whirling back into their shoes and hats.

Gatsby and I had been the only ones drinking seltzer. Even if Tom wouldn't let me at the wheel, at least there'd be someone sober in each car. So we left in the city twilight, Tom and me in one car, Jordan and Daisy and Gatsby in the other, the smell of hotel starch clinging to our bodies.

We weren't even out of the city before Tom started in.

"I asked around about your neighbor Gatsby, and do you know what I heard? He's in with a ring of drugstores and coffee joints that sell grain alcohol right over the counter. I bet he doesn't put that on his business cards."

For miles more, Tom worked himself up.

"I know that kind of man. He has no respect for propriety at all. Those parties of his, they just breed intermarriage between the races. All that mixing together."

I watched the Ash Heaps come into view in the distance. Those gray peaks dyed the blue of the sky, deepening it into night as we moved through the valley.

"Now don't go looking at me like that," Tom said. "I told you, you're one of the good ones. I don't think you're as bad as the rest."

"The rest of who?" I asked.

He didn't hear me over the roar of the engine and his own voice. He kept up his steam through the Ash Heaps, past the mountains of gray and the specter of Myrtle Wilson at the gas station window, all the way to the wide, curving drive of the Buchanans' East Egg estate.

"And him throwing this ridiculous debut," Tom said as he jerked the car to a stop. "As though he's some old-money prince. It's all just laughable. You're too trusting, Nick. I'm telling you that right now. He'll pull you into all that nasty business. Where does he even come from? Who is his family? Nowhere and no one." Tom got out, slamming the door behind him. "He was an enlisted man in the war. No rank at all."

Maybe it was the heat, or the smell of ash mixing with hotel mint, or the relieved rush of getting out of that car. But I said, "And what rank was your great-grandfather?"

Tom paused while trying to work his lighter. "What was that?"

"Your great-grandfather," I said. "Wasn't he the one who paid someone to fight in his place in—what was it, the Civil War?—so he could stay home? Profit off all that lucrative bloodshed? What rank was he?"

Tom shoved me against the polished door of his car. "Just who do you think you are?"

My instinct to smooth over, to apologize, uncoiled. But that instinct had grown slower and weaker with every word out of Tom's mouth. It wasn't active or quick enough to pull me back anymore.

"You drive through that valley and you think nothing of it," I said. "Sure, sometimes you think of Myrtle, maybe. Sometimes. But the land, all that ash, you don't even realize what it is."

"It's an ash dump from all the coal furnaces," Tom said. "How simple do you think I am?"

"It's what's left of all the work and the lives and the wreckage that keep your precious city and your precious estate running," I said, striking each word harder than the one before. "You amuse yourself with a woman who thinks you care about her. You leave mountains of ash behind you, and you can't even look at them. The very people you despise make your life possible."

"If people like me disgust you so much, why come to New York?" Tom asked.

"If Gatsby disgusts all of you so much, why do you come to his parties and drink his liquor?" I asked.

Tom's sneer showed more in the pinch around his nose than in his lips. "I'm disappointed, Nick. I really thought you were different."

"Than who?" I asked.

"The rest of you," Tom said.

"Nick," Gatsby called out.

I hadn't heard the second car arrive.

Gatsby ran ahead of Daisy and Jordan, who were a night

breeze of chiffon and organdy. The garden lamps blew through their skirts, turning the hems translucent in the dark.

Tom glanced their way. "Tell you what," he said quietly enough that only I heard him. "You're clearly not yourself at the moment, so I'm willing to forgive this little outburst. For Daisy's sake."

"For Daisy's sake," I said. "And you holding on to her without actually proposing, is that for her sake too?"

"I'm warning you," Tom said.

"Or you living in the city and leaving her here?" I asked. "I'm sure that's a great sacrifice for you."

"One more word," he said. "And I'll have you out of that little house before daylight."

"Go ahead," I told him. "I don't want anything from you."

Gatsby, Jordan, and Daisy reached us.

"I think we're all a little overheated," Gatsby said. The casual tenor of his voice was a mismatch to the heaving of his breath under his shirt. "Nine at night and it still feels hot as noon, doesn't it?"

"Your friend's right." Tom took hold of the collar of my shirt, as though to make a friendly gesture of smoothing it. But in a small, efficient motion, he crushed it in his hands, wrinkling it past the point the collar stays could keep it taut.

The flare had been lit in me. It was a dock light bursting, spilling its filaments everywhere. My cousin and Gatsby were holding the shimmer of their former lives between them, their dance-hall laughs caught in each other's hair and within the glass of revolving doors. But Daisy still wore Tom's emerald on her finger, even as Gatsby planned the grand affair that would crown her as a top society girl.

And I was sick to death of it all.

Daisy could deny me, but she couldn't deny what was happening with Gatsby. It was one farce too many. She couldn't keep pretending that Tom Buchanan was the beau she'd once dreamed of while staring out the window of the room she shared with her sisters. This couldn't be the man she imagined as she picked the brightest winter stars from the Wisconsin night like they were diamonds.

"Daisy," I said once she floated close enough to hear me. "Tell him. Tell Tom."

CHAPTER XXIII

"Tell him what?" Daisy asked.

"Tell him why you've stopped asking about the engagement," I said. "Tell him the truth."

Tell him that a man who hates anyone brown or Black is no man you want for a husband.

Tell him that a man who keeps an apartment for a woman you don't know isn't worth a diamond-adorned veil.

Tell him that a man whose love requires you not to be my cousin isn't a man whose love you want.

"You know I've been crazed with planning my debut," she said. "Why, I've been working poor Jay into exhaustion." She gave Gatsby a sweet, apologetic smile. "There's just been no time for the wedding. But there will be after. I'll have acres of time for it. I'll plan a wedding like New York has never seen. After my debut."

"Your debut," I said. "And whose arm do you want to be on for that? Is this"—I threw my chin toward Tom—"who you want leading you out into the world?"

In time with Daisy's pained expression, Tom chuckled. "Who else? You have some little friend at work who's dumber and better-looking than I am? You think I'm too ugly for the society pages?" Tom's expression was good-natured enough. It was the languorous self-deprecation of a man who'd never been too ugly, too short, too poor, for anything.

Jordan's uncomfortable glance drifted toward Gatsby.

Tom followed it, quick as swinging a polo mallet.

"What kind of joke are you all making?" Tom asked. "You all thought for a second she'd come out on the arm of Mr. Pink Suit? No offense meant." He said these last words to Gatsby with the perfect calibration between politeness and sarcasm. "Daisy's very grateful for the little get-together you're planning for her; you know that, of course."

I stared at Daisy, silently pleading with her.

Do it. Now. Tell him you want to come out on Gatsby's arm. Tell him you want to come out on mine for all I care. Just tell Tom you don't want to parade down a staircase with him. Once and for all, renounce this man who hates everything I am and who would hate everything you are if only he knew you.

Beneath my wordless pleading I hid a deeper, more desperate hope. It had nothing to do with Jay Gatsby and everything to do with Daisy and me and the grain of Wisconsin earth under our feet.

Remember how I helped you hide from your older sisters after you borrowed their lipstick?

Remember flinging ourselves into the pond together?

Remember how I stayed under so long everyone else gasped, but you threw your wet hair back and laughed, knowing I'd always come up again?

Remember how you were the first cousin I told I was a boy?

Please, claim me. Claim the brown of my skin and the black of my hair and my eyes that are a darker version of yours.

Daisy Fabrega-Caraveo, admit that I'm yours.

But Daisy Fay kept her demure silence.

I nodded at Gatsby and Jordan. "Let's get out of here."

"Now why would you do that?" Tom asked. "We're all having fun here, aren't we? There's plenty to drink inside."

I met Gatsby's eyes, but the stoic set to his face told me nothing.

"We've cleared things up, haven't we?" Tom asked. "Mr. Pink Suit over here and I are just getting to know each other."

For a moment Gatsby was still, save for the hitch in his throat as he swallowed.

"Of course," he said.

I took off down the drive and toward the road, no word over my shoulder until I heard the clicking of heels. It wasn't the tapping of my cousin's trotting steps but the certain, light striking of shoes on brick paving.

"Why do you let him rile you like that?" Jordan asked.

I paused at the last hedgerow before the gate. "Why do *you* put up with them?" I asked. "You're better than all of them."

As I said it, I realized how much I meant it. Jordan had neither Tom's cruelty, nor Daisy's apathy, nor Gatsby's senseless optimism. She was the only one who knew anything.

"Why bother with them?" I asked.

She looked at me strangely and asked, "You know it's not your job to look out for Jay's heart, don't you?"

"But it was my job to make sure he wasn't reckless with Daisy?" I asked.

"When it interferes with my golf game, I should say so."

For just that moment, the laugh we shared brightened the garden lamps.

When it fizzled, I said, "I don't care about his heart."

"Of course," Jordan said. She kicked at a round stone. It went skittering into the grass. "The thing is, there's more to your cousin than you know."

I was about to take off on telling her that I knew plenty about Daisy.

Then I realized what Jordan had just said.

"Wait," I said. "You know she's my cousin?"

"Of course I know," she said.

"But how?" I asked.

"Girls tell each other things they won't tell their beaus." Jordan smoothed the pin-tucked film of her skirt.

"And you still want to be her friend," I said, "knowing she's like me?" Disdain tinted every word as lightly but clearly as the dye on Daisy's dress.

Jordan picked a leaf out of my hair. "What do you mean?"

I looked back up the drive. As much as I despised my cousin at this moment, I didn't want to announce to Tom the blood and color she shared with me. But they were distant enough not to hear us. Tom and Daisy and Gatsby were talking as though they were the best of friends. Tom gestured up at the architecture.

"You've heard Tom plenty," I said. "His speeches about the mixing of races. How everyone might intermarry. Well, what do you think Daisy and I are? We exist because our colonizers screwed our ancestors in more ways than one. We're mixed." I spread my arms, presenting my body, my skin, as evidence. "We're the awful harbingers of everyone intermarrying, Jordan, haven't you heard?"

"Yes," Jordan said in a dry voice. "And wouldn't that be terrible?"

My arms fell to my sides.

"You're a dense little thing, aren't you?" Jordan asked.

"What do you mean?" I asked.

"Mírame," Jordan said.

I went still, beginning with the blood at the center of my

heart, then out to my fingertips. In that second of hearing Jordan's Spanish, the sound flawless and familiar, I was so still that the gust off the ocean couldn't move the strands of my hair.

"Look at me, Nick," Jordan said. "Really look at me. Not like Tom and all those other men look at me. You. Really look at me."

So I did. I looked at the cool tones of her skin, the peach varnish on her nails, the hair she'd smoothed into a neat bun the same way Daisy did. And I saw her.

Jordan Baker, the woman who was just as much a harbinger of Tom Buchanan's nightmares as I was. Jordan Baker, the woman passing as white just as successfully and probably with just as much effort as Daisy.

"Oh, Jordan," I breathed out.

"Oh, stop," she said. "I don't want your pity. Would you want mine?"

"It's not pity," I said.

"Well, I don't want your admiration either," she said. "Do you think I enjoy teeing up in front of a world that thinks I'm marvelous but wouldn't let my own father attend my tournaments?"

Maybe there was something foolish in thinking I should have known. My own cousin was proof that it was foolish to think you could know just by looking at someone. But Jordan had told me without telling me, when she'd told me about her family, only I hadn't caught on quickly enough to realize. Her brother. The 65th Infantry Regiment. The number had called up something in my mind that I couldn't place, but now I could. It was the unit I heard about in news of older cousins and of neighbors' sons. In the ice-cube turn of my stomach, I imagined her brother coming home to a country that would never thank him for defending it and that loved his sister without ever knowing her. I imagined her father's pained pride as she told him about the tournaments he never got to see.

Still, the questions reverberated in me. *How did I not know? How did I not know you?*

But when I opened my mouth, the first I spoke was another question entirely, the one I'd wanted to ask Daisy since she'd met me at the train.

"Why?"

"Why do you think?" Jordan asked. "I wanted better for my family. I was good at something that could help me get it for them. And I wasn't just good at it, I loved it. I still do. Daisy will complain until the moon goes to bed about how boring it is, but I love it. The precision of it. How quiet you've got to be in order to be good at it. But if I wanted to do it, if I wanted what I wanted for my family, I had to let everyone make me into what they wanted."

Jordan studied her nails, the shine of the lacquer. "So as you might imagine, I would be the last to judge what your cousin's doing," she said. "The problem is that she hasn't truly reckoned with it, what it means to live as she's living.

She talks to her family, your family, as though nothing has happened, as though life is just as it was. I couldn't do that. I had the conversations. Hard as they were, I had them. We had them. But she hasn't done that with her family. I doubt she's truly even done it with you."

In trying to make my face show nothing, I suspected I was accomplishing the opposite.

"And she thinks she's sparing you and them something by pretending there's nothing to talk about," Jordan said. "But that pretending . . . that's what's going to break their hearts. Because they're supposed to be the ones she doesn't need to pretend with. *You're* supposed to be someone she doesn't pretend with."

Jordan turned, and it seemed less as though she was turning away from me and more like she was looking for something, like in what direction the moon might be.

Both rumor and newspaper print debated where Jordan was from, without clear consensus. She was a Chicago debutante. She was a small-town beauty from the Hudson Valley. She was raised in Boston, where Massachusetts cold dissuaded her neither from the golf course nor from going out dancing. So I didn't know where Jordan was from. And I wouldn't ask. She would tell me if she wanted to. The thing was that she knew. She hadn't forgotten and wouldn't forget. But I wondered now if, one day, Daisy might. She might stay away so long that the name Fleurs-des-Bois would elude her memory, the town she grew up in as vague and distant as the name of an old friend she hadn't seen in years.

Gatsby might have glanced my way, trying to hide it. But from this distance, and by the intermittent light of the garden lamps, I couldn't tell.

"What are you getting out of all this?" I asked Jordan.

"I don't follow," she said.

"Not the golf," I said. "I know what you get out of that. I mean putting up with people like Tom. What is it you want?"

"You came here, didn't you?" Jordan kicked another stone, turning her back to me. "So don't you know?" When she turned back, a pair of tears, tasteful as twin pearls, glinted at the inner corners of her eyes. "Don't you already know all the things we want and can't have?"

———— ✷ ✷ ✷ ————

Querida Amelia,

Mamá says you're going to have another baby, which is just the most marvelous news. Less marvelous is hearing you've been sick with this little one just like the last. Mamá said that you're up with the sun cooking and cleaning and seeing Rodolfo off to work, but that you're sick in bed by sundown. (Why do they call it morning sickness anyway? It's not as though it observes the clock.)

I thought you could use a little entertainment while stuck in bed, so here I write some of the ridiculous things I've witnessed at parties lately.

Some producer told us he lived so close to the Hollywood-land sign that the bulbs were too bright to let him sleep. He thought the complaining would make his bragging subtler.

And you should see all the girls trying to get in front of the cameras! They stroll past the photographers as though they don't care a thing about being named in the society pages. They're all elbowing one another out of the way to be in the frame, but when the bulb pops, they give the camera a wide-eyed "Oh, I didn't know you were there, how you've surprised me!" expression. They're all trying to be famous by chance. Your eyes would roll right back in your head, and mine right after.

Don't get me started on the endless critique of debuts. Who can keep up with half of it? It seems that maidenhair ferns, roses, and carnations were the style of the moment yesterday, but woe to any girl who adorns her hair and banquet hall with them tonight. Pink and white roses with gold ribbon is some sort of mark of a country girl, but I think that sounds lovely, don't you?

A couple of awful little socialites were making fun of a third for having her party at a restaurant. And it was Delmonico's, for goodness' sake! How much more elegant could it be? They all consider judgment some competitive sport. As though the world waits in breathless anticipation for them to decide whether sapphire pins worn in the hair is chic or a sign of the nouveau riche.

I think it's just wonderful that the new times are bringing so many new kinds of debuts. It's no longer just les bals blancs. There's the bal rose, with married women. Women who drove ambulances for the war in their teenage years are having theirs now. Last month there was even a stylish old woman—all her hair was silver!—who decided she was going to have a debut for her sixtieth birthday. She wore long white gloves, carried a fan, and wore a dress with enough seed pearls that she must have strong bones. She even topped her silver hair with the loveliest tiara! And she's a grandmother! Can't you picture that's something Abuela might have done if she'd had the chance?

It's all such a refreshing change from the only debutantes being girls who sit prettily in their window seats embroidering from breakfast until dinner.

If you'll let me, I'll send you the most beautiful dress—I think you'd look divine in a Hilda Steward—and you can wear it and pretend you're in New York with me. It won't matter how pregnant you are, Rodolfo won't be able to stop staring.

I hate to ask for anything when you're in your condition, but would you ask Mamá and Papá if they're getting my letters?

Yours,
Daisy

P.S. I've sent you all perfume again, but so the smell won't bother you, Mamá's holding yours until you're feeling better.

CHAPTER XXIV

"I'd offer to take you home, but Daisy's my way there," Jordan said. "I'm sure she'd drive you too."

I didn't want to get into Daisy's car. And I didn't want to ride home with Gatsby either. He would always choose watching my cousin across the sound over anyone close enough for him to touch.

"It's okay," I said. "I'm walking."

"Nick," Jordan said. "It's miles."

"Have you ever been to Wisconsin?" I asked.

Jordan puffed a low, crisp laugh into the night air. "Do I seem like I've ever been to Wisconsin?"

I smiled. "No. You really don't."

Knowing Jordan better, and knowing what she had in common with Daisy, hadn't made her glamour any more approachable to me. She still seemed polished with money in a way that made me feel rough as sackcloth. The black of her hair and the near-black of her eyes held all the elegance of a satin dress.

"Where I'm from, it's not Milwaukee or Madison," I said. "It's hours away from anything you'd call a city. If you need to get anywhere without a car, you're walking a ways. I'm used to it."

"Are you sure?" Jordan asked.

I turned back to see Jordan lifting her chin toward the pearl-gray clouds. "It looks like rain."

With hands in my pockets, I gave her a shrug. "I'm not water-soluble."

About half a mile out, the rain had soaked me, the wind blowing sheets of it across the road. I tried to think of it as something cleansing, a washing away of any instinct to help Gatsby or Daisy. But the more I walked, the more my clothes dragged, heavy on my back and shoulders. The weight of my pant hems pulled at my hips.

A car slowed. On instinct, I moved off toward the trees.

"Is this what all the young men do these days?" Martha Wolf called from the driver's seat. "Go on long, brooding walks in a downpour?"

I came back toward the shoulder.

"May I offer you a drier form of transportation?" Martha asked. "I think I'm going your way."

I squinted through the rain. "He's not at home."

"You think your boy's the only one I ever come to see around here?" Martha asked. "I know everyone in both Eggs. I know every egg in the carton. Now get in."

"I'll soak your car," I said.

"It's seen worse." Martha threw the passenger's side door wide. "Now hurry up or it'll really get soaked in here."

So I did.

"I can taste certain things about rain, did you know that?" she asked. "Like I can taste that this is going to last through the morning and then clear right up."

"You're putting me on," I said.

"Maybe," Martha said. "Maybe not. We'll find out in the morning, won't we?"

"So it is true?" I asked. "What Gatsby said about your palate?"

"Everything around here gets at least a little exaggerated, but yes," she said. "I can tell what kind of flowers bees made honey out of. Hand me a glass of wine, I'll tell you the vineyard's life story. Everyone needs a spectacular talent. That's mine."

"Have you always been that way?" I asked.

"Yes and no," Martha said. "Some people talk like I was just born with it, but here's what they don't think about sometimes. Talent takes practice. You can be born with perfect pitch, but that doesn't mean you're born knowing how to play an instrument."

"So how did you learn?" I asked.

"My grandmother taught me," Martha said. "My mother is an excellent cook, and don't you ever tell her I said anything else, but it was my bubbe who taught me to truly taste things. To go slowly enough to find the layers. I'm better with drinks than I am with food, but my grandmother, she could take a bite of something and know everything that was in it."

This enraptured expression was something I'd never before seen on Martha. She had such a cosmopolitan air, as though nothing in the city or the sky could surprise her, and I liked knowing that what sparked her wonder was her own abuela.

Another half a mile down the road, Martha looked over. "Now's your chance. Go ahead and ask."

"All right," I said. "Does your mother know you're a lesbian?"

She let out a surprised laugh. "That's not at all what I thought you wanted to ask me."

"Oh," I said. "I'm sorry."

"Don't be," she said. "I like when people surprise me sometimes. And yes, my mother does know. I won't say she's had an easy time with it. She certainly wishes I were still observant. But she loves me. And we both know that if I want to keep coming home, which I do, then who and how I love is something we can't exactly talk about with our friends and neighbors and even some of our family."

I thought of the relatives I hadn't seen since I started living as the boy I was. That I'd told my parents and they'd taken it as well as they had, and that Daisy's parents and sisters had taken it as well as they had, that was already more miracles than I thought I'd ever get.

Martha adjusted her grip on the wheel, a pair of driving gloves helping her palms slide. The cuff of her sleeve slipped back, revealing a thread that looked white and then blue when the rain-silvered light hit it. That was the place she had touched so delicately the first day I met her.

"It's from my grandfather's tallis," she said. She still had her eyes on the road, and when she smiled, it seemed as much to herself as to me. "Most people don't notice. But I was almost certain you had."

"So is that what you thought I was going to ask?" I said.

"No," she said. "I thought you were going to ask exactly what kind of work Jay and I do together."

"Oh," I said. "Well, if you're offering."

As Martha spoke, the reflected light off the road glossed her lipstick. "When I met Jay, he didn't have much. It was something, but nothing near what he'd need to buy that house or throw those parties or any of that. But he had just gotten a little bit of money from the officer."

"What officer?" I asked.

"He didn't tell you?" Martha asked. "Of course he didn't. Jay doesn't tell much of the good things about himself. Speaking of which, I think you should know that the people who work for him, he pays them for the whole week but only calls them in on the weekends for those parties."

"What does that have to do with anything?" I asked.

"It doesn't," Martha said. "But he'll never tell you that,

so I'm telling you. He's a decent man. Don't let the Tom Buchanans of the world tell you what to think."

"I never do," I said.

She turned down another road. "Anyway, there was a man in the war, an officer, and Jay saved his life in the trenches. And when that man died, he left him something. By then Jay was already in New York. Meanwhile, I was making my living by teaching men like Tom Buchanan and his friends and their girlfriends how to sound smart when they talked about wine. And Jay thought that if we put our heads together, we could get somewhere."

"So you already knew each other?" I asked.

"Oh, not at all." Martha looked over. "We hadn't even met at that point. Before then he'd been working as a breaker boy in the Ash Heaps. Do you know what a breaker boy is? Do they have those in Wisconsin?"

"I know what they are," I said. I wished I didn't. In years that harvests were so bad my abuelos couldn't get work, they'd been breaker boys themselves. Hours of separating coal from slate and sulfur, from ash and clay, had ruined their hands and lungs. My mother blamed the industry for how I never got to meet her father. "They're still using breaker boys here?"

"Not so much anymore, thank goodness," Martha said. "But there were a few still when Jay was doing it. That's why he doesn't have any fingerprints. They made the boys work without gloves so they could handle the slicker pieces better. And when the coal was washed, it made sulfuric acid. Burned their prints off. When you do work like that, you don't even get to keep the ridges in your skin that tell who you are."

Martha's words threw light on that shame I saw in Gatsby sometimes. It wasn't just from growing up poor in North Dakota; it came from the coal dust he'd forever feel under his fingernails. His guests could speculate all they wanted that he'd gotten his fortune from Nevada silver or Montana copper. Gatsby knew that silver and copper and coal were things that got their shine from being slicked with blood.

"Then how did you meet?" I asked.

"He was eating a lot of his meals at the speakeasies," Martha said.

"How could he afford that?" I asked.

"You can eat well in those places for below cost, because the real money's in the liquor," Martha said. "But if you're going to eat that way, you have to do it fast before they realize you're not drinking. He rotated where he went, which was smart of him, because a boy with soot stains on his clothes tended to be remembered. It turns out he wasn't just doing that to get away with not buying drinks. He was looking for me. Apparently my reputation preceded me, or the reputation of my palate anyway. And he knew that what I'd been doing meant I already knew something about the polo pony set. Even though I'll never be like them. Or love like them."

I tried not to look over at her suit, the skirt with the menswear jacket she'd had altered. I'd seen the way girls looked at her—with thrilled interest, like they hadn't known until that moment that anyone like Martha was possible.

"And no one ever makes you feel like you need to apologize for that?" I asked.

"Oh, they do," Martha said. "Of course they do. There'll always be someone trying to make you apologize for something about who you are. But you learn not to feel it quite as much. It helps to choose my own company whenever I can. People who don't want those kinds of apologies. That's something I liked about Jay right away. He doesn't think anyone owes him an explanation."

As the headlights turned the rain to a million sewing needles, Martha told me about Gatsby's idea, how it put together her talent and the money the officer had just left him. She told me about the art of importing champagne and limoncello. The liqueurs made with violets and roses, with elderflowers and lavender. Martha could tell even from the scent whether a bottle had been faked, sure as a museum curator could tell a forged painting.

They had competition, of course. There was already a brisk business in Cognac, which grew more and more popular. People were catching on to the fact that it was nearly impossible to fake, and so less likely to be contaminated with the poison of denatured alcohol. A similar principle apparently held with champagne and wood alcohol. But Martha's reputation meant that she and Gatsby could import anything and know upon arrival whether it was counterfeit, and as word spread of how nothing false got past Martha Wolf, few even tried it. If rich New Yorkers wanted an illegal bottle of Aperol or Sauternes, and to know it was genuine, they knew who to get it from.

"We're selling the stuff the rich people will pay anything for," Martha said. "The bottles they want to show off to their friends. If Jay hadn't found me and talked me into this, I might still be tutoring at eating clubs."

The rain came down harder, then softer, and Martha took inventory of my face.

"You like him," she said.

"Sure," I said.

"I didn't mean you think he's a fine citizen," Martha said. "I mean you're in love with him."

I shifted to look at Martha. The bounce of the headlights off the wet road showed me her face.

"You think I'm gay?" I asked.

"Aren't we all?" Martha gave me a smiling glance. "Young and gay and radiant, and ready for all sorts of gay exciting things?"

I tapped the window as though starting a toast. "Gay and radiant, all of us."

Gay was far from the only word I ever heard for boys who loved other boys, but it was the nicest one I knew. It was the only one I had ever been able to live with considering.

"I don't know if I'm gay," I said.

How could I have asked my parents to do everything they'd done for me so I could live as a boy, as a young man, if I was just going to go love another boy, another man? Most of the men like me I'd read about, the ones who had lovers at all, had lovers who were women. Some even had wives.

Were there any who loved other men?

Did those kinds of self-made boys exist?

If I loved another boy, did that make me less of one?

"Maybe the word doesn't matter so much," Martha said. "Maybe the person does. The person you are. The person you love."

"I don't love him," I said.

"All right," she said.

"It wouldn't matter if I did," I said. "It'll always be her."

"That's all a mess, isn't it?" Martha asked. "Boys get funny about girls like that. They think a woman like that proves something about what kind of men they are. It's the other side of the coin from the Tom Buchanans of the world. The Toms want the Daisies the same way they want an expensive watch."

"You're honestly comparing Tom and Gatsby?" I asked.

"I'm not comparing anybody," Martha said. "I'm telling you everyone in this picture has their problems. The Toms want to slip the Daisies onto velvet alongside their cuff links. The Jays want the Daisies to prove something to them about themselves. If you really want to know what I'm telling you, I'm telling you that if I were Daisy, I'd leave them both alone."

I shifted on the seat. "Are you going to tell people?"

"Tell them what?" Martha asked.

The smoke-tinged thought of a single word drifted toward Manhattan. If it landed there, I'd be out of a job before I could neaten the papers on my desk. Martha may have had the power and glamour to survive rumors, but I didn't.

"That you think I'm gay?" I asked.

"Are you kidding?" she said. "First, it's none of my business deciding what you are. Second, every word they call people like us is an insult. That really tells you something. Even *gay*, they say it as an insult. Even *lesbian*. But I don't much care how they use it. It's our word." She shifted her path to avoid a car drifting over the center.

I tried to acquaint myself with the idea that an insult could be reclaimed into something softer, something fit for the space inside a heart or between sheets.

"Of course, I've also been told I'm dreadfully boring," she said. "I have to fall at least a little in love with a girl before I can let her smudge my lipstick."

"Why would that make you boring?" I asked.

"People always find something wrong with how much or how little women are doing," Martha said. "We don't do as much as they think we should, we're boring or frigid. If we do more than they think we should, we're easy or fast. There's no winning. So I kiss exactly as many or as few girls as I want."

"No lavender marriage for you?" I asked.

"Those sorts of things are best done in twos if you can manage it," she said. "A sort of lifelong double date if it works out."

I remembered the couples at the bar, wives staring into each other's eyes as husbands did the same a table over.

"But that would require me to act enough like a proper wife to play my role in the whole dramatis personae," she said. "People are very threatened by women who do well for themselves, especially women like me."

I wanted to ask her more questions. How old she was when she knew. How much of her family knew; if she even knew for sure how much of her family knew, or had guessed. If they saw her as fashionable in her tailored jackets, her lipsticks brighter than the deep Bordeaux of the typical shade, and thought she was some incorrigible daughter, just a different variety than the ones in beaded dresses and pink side lacers.

But then we were on the tree-crowded lane just before the cottage.

"I'd take you closer," Martha said, "but I don't care to lose an axle in the mud."

"This is fine." I reached to open the door. "Are you sure you don't want to come in?"

"I thought I made it quite clear that I don't like boys," she said.

"I didn't mean it that way," I said.

"I know." She flashed me an older sister's smile. "I have somewhere to be."

Just before I opened the door, I said, "I hope you find her."

"Who?" Martha asked.

"A girl you want to smudge your lipstick."

<hr />

I started packing. I wasn't waiting for Tom to send someone over who'd throw my suitcases into the sound and trample the pastel heads of the tulips Gatsby had planted.

Whatever the Tom Buchanans of the world let you have, they could take away with little more effort than dialing their desk phones.

I threw in everything without making sense of it. Suspenders and side lacers. Shirts and books.

It didn't matter if I made my way as a quantitative analyst. It wouldn't matter if I made a hundred thousand dollars. I would still be a brown boy from a family of betabeleros. I had come into the world smelling of red beets and damp earth. I would forever vanish into the shadows of men like Tom Buchanan and his family's aged money.

"Nick!" Gatsby's voice parted the rain.

I took it as fact that I was imagining that voice. Gatsby

wouldn't be calling my name. Faithful suitor of Daisy's as he was, he must have been watching for her at the edge of the sound. Or still in East Egg, under the one stretch of shore-line where the moon came through the clouds, turning his pink suit to rose quartz.

"Nick!" His voice cut through the rain again.

A car door slammed, the headlights left on.

Gatsby came running toward me. "I've been driving the roads looking for you. Jordan said you took off on foot."

"Martha brought me home. I"—I cleared the knot from my voice and knocked my heel against a suitcase—"I think I'd better head out."

"What?" he asked. "No."

He came closer, and behind him the beams illuminated the silver confetti of the rain.

"Stay," Gatsby said. "Please."

The rain soaked the pink cloth of his jacket.

"Your suit," I said.

"I don't give a wheel spoke about my suit." He stripped off the jacket and threw it aside, leaving a pale shirt over the pink trousers. "Don't leave."

"Why are you here?" I asked.

He brushed past my question. "You don't have to decide anything right now. Just stay the night." He blinked through the rain. "I think I might have the room."

He wanted me to laugh, and I wanted to laugh. But neither my face nor my throat managed it.

"Come here, will you?" He drew me in slowly enough that I could have pulled back easily. I didn't, even as my heart rivaled the sound and force of the rain on the flagstones.

The downpour soaked our shirts and lacers so they felt filmy as water. They were nothing but veils of ocean between his skin and mine.

But I knew what this was. His firm grip on me, the curt way he'd patted his hand twice against my back, the hold that was more strong than intimate. This was the embrace of friends, nothing more.

The only Caraveo who would ever have Jay Gatsby's heart had already broken it.

"Please," he said. "I don't know what I'd do without you here."

His hand was still on my back, and trails of rain crossed between our bodies.

One night. I would sort out the rest in the morning.

———— • • • ————

Querido Nicolás,

I'm absolutely furious at Tom and his little fit of pique. I'm just fuming.

I've vowed not to speak to him from now until the night

*of my debut. If I need communicate with him at all, I'll post
a note on one of my letterpress cards.*

*I know he regrets speaking to you that way, and I know
he didn't mean to threaten you, not really, but his pride
won't let him do a thing about it. He stands outside my bedroom door with his exhortations. "Oh, come on, Daisy."
Or "Nick's all right, you know that." Or "I just get carried
away sometimes." Or, most nauseating of all, "I'm better
with you, Daisy. You make me better." Why must it be up to
me to make a man better?*

*He keeps sending me little gifts. A set of periwinkle lace
gloves. A seed pearl necklace that wraps around three times,
as though he means to tell me I can now be trusted with
pearls and not to fall off a boat with them. Some perfume in
an angular bottle that smells pink with flowers, and another
in black glass that smells of peaches and geranium (I made
a note of the name. I'll have to get a bottle for Mamá and
your mother).*

*But I refuse to be placated about how he's treated you. You
might be amused to see it, me turning away his offerings like
a soignée house cat unsatisfied with a dish of food. (Today
brought a rare orchid. I don't even like orchids, doesn't he
know? They're so temperamental. I'm just sick to death at
the thought of destroying anything so beautiful on account
of my carelessness.)*

To happier subjects, Jay says you're staying with him now, and I'm just over the moon about it. You two are such a pair, and I think you should get to know each other better. You're so terribly serious and practical about everything. Perhaps he might help you have a little fun?

It will be such work teaching Tom not to be so spiteful. But I'm glad his deplorable behavior at least had the welcome benefit of throwing you and Jay together. So really it all worked out, didn't it?

Yours in eternal devotion,

Daisy

CHAPTER XXV

"You're really still going to do this?" I asked.

"I still want her to have the option of something other than a life with Tom," Gatsby said. "Even if it's not a life with me."

Gardeners carried in wooden crates filled with dark earth and topped with bulb flowers. By afternoon's end, a river of grape hyacinth deeper than the blue of the bay ran through the grounds. The indigo flowers clustered so closely and densely, the ocean breeze rippling the stalks, that a few drinks might have made them seem like real water. Banks of daffodils shouldered either side. Islands of coral tulips and fields of hyacinths in every shade of pink broke up the expanses of grass.

"And what do you think of how it's coming along?" the lead gardener asked.

"Absolutely splendid," Gatsby said. "I wish you could landscape my dreams themselves."

The man pulled off his gloves, letting his hat brim shade his proud smile. "We'll get to shaping the cypress trees tomorrow."

"Oh, I think they're fine," Gatsby said.

"Do you trust me or not?" the man asked on his way out.

Once we were alone, I asked, "And you're sure about this? You're publicly admitting defeat. You know Tom can't wait to flaunt his victory in your own home."

"This isn't my home," Gatsby said. "Not really."

"What do you mean?" I asked.

He surveyed the mansion. "I can't hold on to this place. The upkeep alone would ruin me."

I looked at him. "What?"

"With what I'll have left after this and the parties," he said. "It'll be enough for a good life, but not a life like this."

"Then why did you buy it?" I asked.

"I suppose I had something to prove," he said. "It all sounds a bit silly now, doesn't it?"

"No, it doesn't," I said. "But I don't understand. It seems like things are going well for you and Martha, aren't they?"

"Oh, yes," he said. "But the money's not infinite. It's real, and it's written down, and it has limits."

The way he said it was so plain and full of sense that I felt instantly foolish. I had always thought the wealth of places like East Egg and West Egg was endless, that if you were rich, you were rich in some infinite way. But now I realized that was as misguided as assuming that the price of wheat or gold would never fall.

"This is my fault," I said.

Concern struck Gatsby's face. "What do you mean?"

"I talked you into giving Daisy a debut," I said. "And from the looks of what you're doing, it might bankrupt you."

"It might mean I have to leave this place," he said. "But so what? I will have done all I can do. She'll be a debutante with enough standing to know she has choices other than Tom. If that choice isn't me, then I'll still know I've done my best. She deserves that."

"Then what?" I asked. "You'll leave West Egg?"

"Maybe," he said. "Or New York altogether."

"You just talked me into staying but you're thinking of leaving?" I asked.

"As long as you're here, it's bearable." He looked almost sad as he said it.

I wished he wouldn't say things like that. To him, I was a good friend. But my heart now followed his the way his followed Daisy's. She was the sun around which his being orbited, and I was his moon, shadowed and undetected.

A green-coated stretch of floral wire had been dropped or forgotten alongside the brick path, and I had an idea of how to brighten the mood.

"Could you get some dish soap and water?" I asked.

He went inside, and I loved him a little more for not asking why.

By the time he came back, I'd twisted the wire into a honeycomb frame.

"I'm intrigued." Gatsby set the bowl on an umbrella-shaded table.

"Have you heard of minimal surfaces?" I asked.

"No," Gatsby said. "What are they?"

I dipped the wire frame into soapy water. "It's the smallest possible surface within a bounded area." I held the bubble-filled honeycomb to the light. "It minimizes the area within a prescribed shape."

Gatsby stood alongside me, both of us studying the colors that swam over the iridescence.

"Is there some great lesson I'm failing to grasp?" he said.

"Does everything have to have some sort of significance?" I asked. "I just wanted to do this." I blew through the honeycomb, and bubbles flew at him.

He laughed, lifting his hands toward the bubbles as though offering butterflies places to land. For the thousandth time since meeting Gatsby, I marveled at how a boy could have such a beaten-up heart and still have his wonder so untarnished.

I dipped the wire back into the dish. "Think of if the surface of the pool could stretch as tight within its shape as you can imagine."

Gatsby blew through the soaped honeycomb, and bubbles floated toward the pool. On the floor of it was a spiral of iridescent white against the deep blue. Looking at it now with math in mind, I understood the shape in a way I hadn't during the noise of the parties.

I lowered the wire frame. "It's a spiral shell," I said. "Like a sea snail."

"Good eye," Gatsby said. "No one notices. They just notice the bits of light it throws off when everyone's splashing around in it fully clothed."

I'd seen it. Guests put on bathing costumes for the beach, but the pool always seemed to be a more impulsive decision. They jumped in wearing gowns and fine suits.

"The man who built it had that pattern set down with little bits of opal. Can you believe that?" Gatsby seemed to be looking for something under the water. "You know, I haven't used it all summer."

"Why not?" I asked.

"Do you really think I'm going to during a party?" he asked. "I have yet to find a side lacer I can hide under a bathing costume."

"If your guests go in with their clothes, why can't you?" I asked.

"I don't like to encourage that," he said. "Especially among the intoxicated."

"So go in now," I said. "It's just us here. Why not?"

He considered the pool, the same blue I imagined the Mediterranean might be.

"Will you come in with me?" he asked.

"Now?" I asked.

"I have an extra costume."

I hesitated.

"Do you not swim?" he asked.

"Oh, I swim," I said. "I'm an excellent swimmer."

Gatsby gave me a challenge of a smile. "Show me."

I stayed down at the bottom, the blue so deep I could imagine myself on the floor of an ocean. Or, if I trailed that spiral of opal, inside a shell.

As I surfaced, the blue brightened, the sun pleating into layers as delicate as tulle.

I splashed through it and shook water from my eyes.

"How do you do that?" Gatsby treaded water near me. "You were under for a hundred years."

"I had a lot of practice in the pond back home," I said. "I can show you how."

"No, thank you," Gatsby said. "I prefer staying where I can breathe."

"Come on," I said. "You got me in here."

Gatsby's hands slid through the blue, as though fidgeting with the water itself. "Fine."

He came close enough to let me tell how the salt changed his scent. It sharpened it, like he was coming to life in water.

"Are you ready?" I asked.

At his nod, we went under.

We regarded the blurred versions of each other. Identical black bathing costumes covered us from our shoulders to the middle of our thighs.

He looked toward the surface, like he might be considering kicking up toward it.

I took his hands, calming him into being still. I'd learned from older boys that I could hold my breath longer than I thought I could. If I could keep Gatsby down a few seconds more than he thought his lungs could manage, he'd know the rush of doing a small thing you once thought impossible.

Strands of light adorned our bodies and the bottom of the pool, like the bowing strings of chandelier crystals.

Gatsby drifted toward me. He shut his eyes, and in my watery vision he looked as though he might kiss me.

I had kept him underwater too long, and now he must have been light-headed. I wrapped an arm around his waist and pulled him to the surface.

"Sorry," I said. "Did I keep you too long?"

"No," he said, breathing hard enough that I knew he was lying. "Not at all."

<hr />

Querida Mamá,

I was thrilled to get your letter, though I will admit, I wish it was about more than to ask whether I'd cut my hair. I haven't. I know it's too curly and full for a French bob. But there are such neat little tricks. If I put my hair in a chignon, I can style the pieces in the front to give that same sort of look.

And no, I'm not plucking my eyebrows too much. Not too much eyeshadow or mascara either. I'm keeping it all on the rouge and lipstick.

Mamá, Amelia told me the most awful thing. She told me you think I'm ashamed of you all, and that's why I haven't brought you all to New York or brought Tom to meet you. Of course I'm not ashamed of you. I'm heartbroken you could even think so. I'm not ashamed of Nick either. Would I have convinced Tío and Tía to let him come here if I was ashamed of him? Everyone here knows him as one of my oldest and dearest friends.

Yours,
Daisy

CHAPTER XXVI

By day I worked in the city, making sense of a universe of numbers as men lobbed trading instructions and college footballs over my head. I practiced the words Gatsby taught me (*jam* not *preserves*, *writing paper* not *notepaper*, *wireless* not *radio*). And Gatsby attended to business with Martha and to adorning the grounds.

We spent our nights in salt water. The moon turned the wet sand to silver, and we lay on it, looking up. The edge of the tide inched closer to our bare feet, the biggest waves lapping at our heels.

"Will you tell me about where you're from?" he asked.

I laughed. "Where I'm from, we tell directions by barns."

"You mean, 'take the road after the third silo,' 'turn after two red barns and a green one,' that kind of thing?" Gatsby asked.

"Exactly," I said.

"We do that where I'm from too," he said.

The angle was wrong to see the green light across the bay. Instead, our view was the moon and its cape of stars.

"What about your family?" he asked. "What are they like?"

After I'd introduced myself as a son of the Beet Patch Caraveos, there was no reason not to tell him. "A long time ago, before we came to Wisconsin, we were where Texas is now," I said. "Then it became part of this country. My family lost what little land they had left. Then it wasn't long before they started north, looking for work as jornaleros, betabeleros. The Midwesterner growers, they were recruiting workers from Texas to harvest beets."

I kept expecting Gatsby to sit up, to make sure the green light was still there.

"Do you miss them?" he said.

"The beets?" I asked. "Not a bit."

He reached across the sand and lightly shoved my arm. "Your family."

"Sometimes," I said. "I miss playing chess with my father, and losing every time. I miss how my mother can hear when a fox is getting near the chicken coop."

"She can?" Gatsby asked.

"Oh, yes," I said. "It's just a sense she has. She'll scream without warning and run outside. She'll even wake up from full sleep like that and go right out the door."

Gatsby laughed. "Really?"

"It still startles my father, even after all this time," I said.

In the dark, Gatsby talked of growing up poor in North Dakota, raised by his aunt and the woman his aunt called her roommate. He hadn't seen them in years, and since they had no telephone, they corresponded only in letters and the money he sent them monthly.

"They gave me my uncle's name," he said. "When I told them I was a boy."

He talked of enlisting, and this time he told me how old he was. Fourteen, same as I'd guessed.

"And before I knew it, I was with the Sixteenth Infantry," he said.

"Didn't they know you were too young?" I asked.

"I think they probably did," Gatsby said. "But when I said I didn't have my birth certificate, they didn't think anything of it. A lot of us didn't have them. And they wanted anyone they could use. They just checked that I met the minimum measurements."

"Minimum measurements?" I asked.

"Five-foot-three for height," he said. "Thirty-four inches for chest." With a hand to his chin, he gave a self-effacing laugh. "You'll appreciate this. Have you noticed how few beards you've seen?"

He was right. The most I saw on any man younger than Mr. Benson was a pencil mustache. But this had been one of a hundred details about Manhattan men and their heads. The smell of wax, hair shined straight back, the sheen of sharp parts. How they had specific dates on which they switched from summer hats to winter (felt hat day) and back again (straw hat day), and stuck to them even if the autumn chill or spring thaw was late coming.

"Yes," I said. "Why is that?"

"Gillette razors were standard issue during the war," Gatsby said. "Since they encouraged shaving, my lack of any significant facial hair simply made me look well-groomed. So after the war, the clean-shaven look became something of the fashion. Same with the close-shaved sideburns."

"They cared how neat you looked when you were fighting?" I asked.

"It wasn't so much that," he said. "Shaving made it easier to seal our gas masks."

"Oh," I said. "Of course." How had I asked something so obvious? How many men in my county had come home with lungs singed from phosgene, or not come home at all?

Gatsby spoke of the Argonne Forest with its hemlock and pine, the relentless rhythm of the trenches—six days in, then rest if they were lucky. He didn't mention the cold and the mud, the weight of wet clothes, the rats and the smell of death, the influenza that ripped through camps in the last seasons of the war, taking soldiers even faster than it had taken my grandmother. But he didn't have to.

While Daisy and I had been children, Gatsby had been a child acting as an adult. Daisy and I had mourned cousins and uncles and neighbors, but we had been spared the bitter gallantries of what Gatsby had witnessed. He had lived in that poison and mud.

"You think I do all this for her," Gatsby said. "This house. The parties."

"Don't you?" I asked.

"I'm more selfish than that," he said.

"How?"

"Because this is how I forget," he said. "This is how a lot of us forget."

Like the iterations of a fractal, I understood how Gatsby could wear such a haunted expression at his parties and still want to have them. The glitter of paillettes, the floating sparkle of dresses, the trombones and clarinets, the whispering of beads—it all pushed back the thick gray of the Argonne Forest.

"But doesn't it scare you?" I asked. "All the noise, the bright lights? Doesn't it just remind you?"

"Yes," he said. "But that's some of the point. I'm hoping that if I get used to noise like this, and bright flashes at a party, then something being loud or bright won't be as frightening. I'll remember all this noise and forget the noise I want to forget."

I knew he was giving me something he would never give Daisy. This was a raw, rough corner he hadn't polished to enough of a shine to present to her. And this made me want to hold it carefully, gently, all the more.

"They don't much like talking about it, and who could blame them," Gatsby said. "But at every party here there's a lot of us. We came home to a world we didn't know anymore and a country that didn't know what to do with us and didn't much care to. Boys like you and me knew we'd have to work harder to be considered men, and we'd still have to no matter what we'd done in the war. Black soldiers came back to a country that didn't value their lives any more than the day they'd left, even though they'd just risked them for it. The government still hasn't given Bhagat Singh Thind and Marcelino Serna citizenship."

For a moment I saw a thread of light in him, a crack in all that romantic hope. It left me feeling, in equal measures, sad and safe. Sad because I didn't want to see that hope for how fragile it might truly be. Safe because of how much this boy saw outside of himself.

Tom could go on making jokes about how tan Gatsby was getting this summer. It didn't matter. Gatsby would always be white, and I would always be brown, and that left a distance between us that could never quite be closed, like the inevitable space between atoms. But Gatsby noticed the things that were wrong in the world alongside the things that were beautiful. Perhaps there was no white boy in New York who might understand someone like me, a family like mine, better than Jay Gatsby.

"None of us has the same story," Gatsby said, "but a lot of us are after the same thing. We're looking for ways to make a bright light or a loud sound be just a bright light or a loud sound, and not a hundred things we don't want to remember."

Gatsby was a self-made boy, in so many ways. He had sandpapered down his accent and taught himself to say *sofa* instead of *couch*, to toast *good health* instead of *cheers*. But Gatsby's life, the dazzling parties and pressed shirts, were as much a reaction against what he'd lived as it was a display for Daisy or anyone else. He was now a version of himself so utterly incompatible with North Dakota dust and blood-tainted mud that he might think of these things as belonging to someone else. He had carried the shame of it and then beat it back into the past with the light of a hundred chandeliers.

Gatsby blinked into the night sky. "Do you know that we'll send rockets to the moon? It sounds like Jules Verne, but it's really going to happen."

He'd already turned the compass of his heart. All it took was the moon beholding itself in the mirror of the sound to give him back his dreams. And how could I blame him? If I'd seen what he'd seen, known what he'd known, I'd grasp at whatever beauty I still found in the world.

I wanted this boy to have what he wanted, even if what he wanted was a chance at my cousin's heart. I had offered my help making her a debutante whose very name carried the scent of a cascading bouquet. I had helped clear the way for them to fall into each other's arms. Daisy might have been hesitating now, but she might still choose him. What kind of man could I call myself if I interfered with their happiness?

When we went into the night tide, I kept my distance. Under the dark water, we couldn't tell how far apart we were, so Gatsby's hands brushed my arms. His ankle grazed my shin. I could have floated closer, pretending our nearness was the fault of the current. But this was as close as we could ever be, sharing this piece of the ocean.

Gatsby and I may have been nothing to men like Tom Buchanan, but men like that did not know we were as divine as the heavens. We were boys who had created ourselves. We had formed our own bodies, our own lives, from the ribs of the girls we were once assumed to be.

CHAPTER XXVII

"You're still here," Princeton said on his way out.

"You sound surprised," I said.

He leaned against one of the file cabinets. Everything from his hair to his tie pin gleamed of money. "If you start staying late, you're going to make the rest of us look bad. It's no way to make friends."

"I'm not trying to make anyone look bad." I turned through a few pages. "I'm trying to find a way to look at this that makes it look better."

"I imagine I'll regret asking," Princeton said. "But hell, why not? I'm asking."

I rested my elbows on the desk. "Have you ever heard of Mandelbrot?"

The man lifted an eyebrow.

"Fractal geometry," I said.

He lifted the other eyebrow.

"Think of shorelines." "The irregularities found in

nature. The market is a little like that, at least as far as I can tell."

"A market like a shoreline," the man said. "That's a nice picture. Tell Benson that. He'll like that." He stretched a conquering hand out toward an imagined horizon. "It sounds like all our ships are coming in."

"It's not good," I said. "Fractal markets have more unpredictable events than anyone ever accounts for."

"And?" the man asked.

"And that means the stock prices everyone's so optimistic about won't hold," I said. "It means this spectacular rise will, in all likelihood, end with a catastrophic fall. But no one's hedging for that. Everyone's making decisions like it's all going to rise forever."

The man looked behind him, as though checking for eavesdroppers.

"Listen." He was whispering now. "I know you're new around here, so I'll tell you this in case no one else has." He leaned close enough for me to smell both his lunch and his eau de toilette. "There's no room for that kind of gloom around here. Benson and Hexton may be as different as wheat and steel, but they want go-getters. Idea men. The way you're talking, you'll never last."

He left quickly, as if the coal dust of my skepticism might end up on his suit.

The whole train home, I thought of these men's reckless

optimism, and I seethed against it. But as the Ash Heaps gave way to trees, a sickening feeling rose in me. How could I condemn the idealism of men on Wall Street and yet think so highly of Gatsby's infinite romantic faith?

Everyone is partial to their own reasons for despising other people. Mine was the unchecked optimism in the young men around me, watching the numbers like Jules Verne's cannon. But there was no judging their dauntless cheer without judging Gatsby's.

Gatsby was foolish enough to believe that earning the heart of a particular woman would grant him a life as gilded as Daisy's hair. He didn't recognize that both kinds of gold were fake.

But Gatsby wanted Daisy. How I felt for him, he didn't feel for anyone except her. And if he felt any shadow of that longing for me, it was only because I was some convenient substitute for Daisy. I was desirable for no reason except that I was on his side of the bay. I was more reachable than the ribbon of green light cast on the water.

There were just some charmed, beautiful people in the world, and they were always destined for each other. Gatsby and Daisy. Jordan and whichever man one day captured her attention. The couples in the club behind the florist.

I wasn't one of them. And it had nothing to do with the brown of my skin or being the kind of boy I was. It had to do with the splinter of cynicism I carried in my heart. Some people wore their broken hearts with careful grace. I didn't. The pieces of mine scraped against everything, and everyone could hear the grinding noise, even if they didn't know what it was.

"It's still warm out," Gatsby said later that evening. "Do you feel like a swim?"

"No," I said. "Not tonight."

＊＊＊

Querido Papá, querida Mamá,

You really don't have to keep sending letters just to thank me for money. I've told you it's not necessary. I'm your daughter. I want to do it.

I'd really rather you not mention it at all, but if you must, why not save it for when you write me with all the news of home? I miss every one of you (yes, even Gloria; please tell her that I am, in fact, watching my figure).

Yours,
Daisy

CHAPTER XXVIII

I wasn't much of a fighter. But when you were a bookish child in Wisconsin who understood mathematics better than you understood the girl you were expected to be, you had to either run or fight, and I was never very fast.

This came back to me as I noticed the shadow of a man moving across the grass, coming nearer to me.

It wasn't Gatsby. I knew his shape and the sense of him, how the air shifted bluer and greener when he was close. And it wasn't anyone who came in on the weekends. I had picked up from things Martha said that almost all of them were like her or like Gatsby and me or like someone who'd been there at my birthday. We all didn't belong in some way, and we were forever announcing ourselves or clearing our throats when we entered rooms so we wouldn't startle each other. We all had reasons to startle easily.

I kept my path in the shadow of the cypress trees. I pretended I didn't notice the man. I'd never won any fight without surprising my opponent.

When he was close enough, I whirled around. I grabbed his arm to try to flip him in the fulcrum way my father taught me (he got furthest by interesting me in the physics).

The man threw his other arm at me. I grabbed hold of it and used it to lever him toward a retaining wall. I let him go just in time for his momentum to tumble him over.

As he fell, I gauged my options. Gatsby was out. No one else was here. I didn't like my chances reaching the nearest neighbors, let alone getting them to care.

I settled on running for the shore, hoping any bathers might scare him off. And in case I did have to fight, I grabbed two crystal glasses from a wooden crate. The faceted pieces were for my cousin's debutante ball, and I smashed the top of the flutes on a stone statue. Bits of crystal flew everywhere, carrying the pink and blue of the evening with them. I held out the crystal stems, a jagged sepal topping each one.

Dechert rose from behind the retaining wall. "Easy." He shied away from the broken crystal, and fell backward again. "Where'd you learn to fight like that?" He sounded more impressed than bothered.

"Try being the math teacher's pet in farm country," I said. "I took class with kids five and seven years older than I was."

"If you ever need a job"—he got to his feet—"you're hired." He surveyed the grass stains on his suit.

"You here to search my suitcases this time?" I asked.

"Listen," he said. "I didn't want to have to do that. But you weren't giving me anything."

"Because I don't know anything," I said.

"I'm on your side here," Dechert said.

"Then why were you sneaking up on me?" I asked.

"I did nothing of the sort. I said your name three times."

"What?" I asked. "No, you didn't."

"Yes, I did," he said. "I swear on my mother's cooking. You were somewhere out in the cosmos. I'm starting to worry about you."

The role of concerned older brother. I wondered what number technique that was in the Port Roosevelt Limited Investigator's Handbook.

"If I were you, I'd rethink the company you keep," he said. "It makes you look guiltier."

Guiltier instead of *guilty*. But at the moment, my defensiveness was more for the *company*.

I set down the glass stems. "What's your trouble with Gatsby?"

"Gatsby?" Dechert looked around the gardens and the pool like they amused him. "I don't care anything about this circus here. He can import vineyards whole cloth from France if he wants. It's none of my business. I meant Miss Fay. But no matter what it is she's gotten you into, we can figure everything out if you just tell the truth."

"You think I stole it?" I asked. "Is that why you were

going through the cottage? You thought I had it and just threw it somewhere?"

"Not in one piece, no," he said. "I don't think you're that stupid."

"What do you mean not in one piece?" I asked.

But the question answered itself.

"You think I'm a fence," I said, and the words had little air in them.

That's what he'd been looking for in the cottage. Not money. Not a whole necklace. Pieces of it. Bags of loose pearls, or smaller strands, broken up enough to sell without attracting too much attention.

"Try to see it from my perspective," he said. "You show up out of nowhere. You have this unusual kind of relationship with Miss Fay. She trusts you. Clearly. She visits you, unchaperoned, without her boyfriend. And you just happened to come to New York at just this time?"

"Even if you thought I'd do something like that," I said, "why would you think Daisy would?"

"That's where it gets really interesting," Dechert said. "Because I can't find out anything about Miss Fay before a couple of years ago. It's like she came out of nowhere, too. At least you can tell me where you're from. Any answer she gives, I try to run down, and no one's heard of her. You can see how that wouldn't look good. You can see how she might look like some sort of confidence woman."

"And what about Tom?" I asked. "You said he had debts he doesn't want to tell his family about."

"He does," Dechert said.

"Well?" I asked.

Dechert laughed as though grasping a joke. "You're not trying to tell me Tom Buchanan stole the necklace he bought?"

"Why wouldn't he?" I asked. "He could get away with it, couldn't he?"

"It doesn't make you look innocent to accuse an upstanding man," he said. "It makes you look worse."

"Then why did you bring up his debts?" I asked. "What did you want me to think?"

"That your friend Daisy doesn't know her own beau," Dechert said. "He has enough that he doesn't want his family to know about. How do you think he feels about this mess? She doesn't know what he might do when he finds out what she's done."

"You don't know that she's done anything," I said.

"You know how this works," Dechert said. "If you start talking, this goes easier. If she does, it gets a lot worse for you." He walked off. "You have my card if you find yourself feeling chatty."

The collapse was coming on fast, the deflation after a fight. Before it hit, I gathered up all the crystal I could find in the grass. The deepening light turned them to rubies and sapphires.

By the time I'd gotten all the pieces I could find, the garden lights were coming on. I sat on the edge of a fountain and shut my eyes.

The gravity of existing this close to Gatsby was tearing my being to pieces. And his love for my cousin was as glittering as all those crystal glasses.

I'd come to New York for the possibility of a future but had only gotten drawn into Daisy and Gatsby's past.

"Nick?" Gatsby's voice pulled me back. He stood near the fountain, framed by green and garden lights. "Are you all right?" He sat next to me, putting a hand on my back. "You're shaking."

I jumped to standing. If he kept touching me, I'd kiss him again, and this time there'd be no confetti, so he'd know it was serious.

"Please," I said. "Just stop. Whatever you're doing, whatever we're doing, just stop."

"I don't understand," he said.

"This is a transaction," I said. "You're helping me. I'm helping you. We're here for what we can do for each other, aren't we? Can't we stop pretending it's anything more than that?"

He looked so pained I nearly took it back. But I'd meant it. So I let it stand.

"All right," he said. "I'm sorry."

I stayed still. That was all I knew how to do when he got close to me now. I didn't say anything about how he looked in evening attire, hair slicked back out of his face, the light catching the stripe of satin down the side of his dress pants.

I held my body tense as he adjusted my jacket on my shoulders. I didn't breathe when he took hold of my bow tie hanging slack on my neck. He tied it with a few flicks of his wrist, with the same graceful efficiency of juicing a grapefruit.

It was the night of Daisy's debut, and thousands of candles bounced their glow between crystal goblets and chandeliers. Each glass held the blush of a Lady Rose, or the citrus and lavender of a secret garden. Olives from Italy and Spain filled the gilt-edged dishes, and guests raved that the oysters tasted like eating the sea.

"Oh, Jay." Daisy floated through the gardens between Gatsby and me. The twinkle of the fairy lights—pink and lilac and mint green tonight—cast their color on her dress. "It's a dream. A perfect dream."

"I'm glad you like it," he said.

I looked for some longing in him, but he seemed pleased at her delight.

From gardens to ballroom, Gatsby's mansion had become an enchanted world. Outside, the stars looked like diamond-headed pins, and inside, tapestries of blue velvet dotted with tiny crystals gave the sense of the night sky rushing inside.

Daisy's dress was oddly simple, pale blue satin that fell to her white shoes.

"You're surprised at my restraint, aren't you?" She spun in a circle, and the short, fluttering sleeves belled out. "I wanted to greet my guests in a simple spring silk, but don't you worry. I don't plan to disappoint. I'll change just before my entrance."

Except for her letter, I'd heard nothing from her since the day of Jordan's tournament, and it took all my gentlemanly efforts to smile for her now.

As Daisy drifted from the rivers of tulips and irises and into the house, the smell of roses and jasmine went with her. She drew a pause of admiration from every guest. The chairman of a cable corporation. Men in top hats and bowlers who thought any land ribboned with silver ore belonged to them. Women in emerald green and ermine.

Between the swell of the orchestra and the hum of the lights, blond hair shined against silver satin. Ruffles bristled against bows and embroidery. And the word *club* peppered all conversation. Yacht clubs, hunt clubs, country clubs—the mentions were as thick in the air as the ruddy smoke of cigars and cigarettes.

Daisy took me by the shoulders and turned me so that a strawberry blonde was in my line of sight.

"There's Virginia Muldoon," Daisy said. "Her debut will be in November."

"Won't it be cold?" I asked.

"No, it'll be festive," she said. "And it's a sign of how pretty she is and how rich her father is. No girl pencils in her ball that late in the season unless she's confident everyone will come. Ellen Hornbeam's father just bought a building the length of a block for four million dollars. Her debut's on December twenty-third. She knows she can get away with it too. Only the girls at the very top can have Christmastime balls."

Daisy peered over platinum and graying heads. "Now where's Tom?"

"Complaining about what he called the 'girly liquor,' last I heard." Jordan now stood next to me. She held a drink that matched the violet of her dress, a gown with the same plain elegance as Daisy's. "It didn't stop him from having a few."

"Well, help me look for him, will you?" Daisy asked. "We've got to get the boutonnière on him before my entrance."

We scattered to the halls, searching parlors and corners. My steps felt unsteady, dress socks slipping inside my polished oxfords. They were thin and sheer as ladies' hose, and I didn't know how all these men looked so sure of themselves in socks that felt like you'd forgotten to wear socks altogether.

Each time I opened a door, I felt relieved to find only drunken conversation. Gatsby's parties usually carried the risk of interrupting some passionate embrace.

At the next doorknob, the sound of two voices, intimate and thrilled, stopped me. I recognized Tom's, the same tone in which he talked to Myrtle. But the second voice wasn't Myrtle's.

"Who are you eavesdropping on?" Daisy's whisper startled me.

"No one," I said.

I couldn't let her see this, no more than I could have told her about Myrtle. Even when I despised Daisy, I couldn't break her heart or watch her break her own.

She reached for the knob. "You're being so strange tonight."

"Daisy, no—" I said.

She threw the door open.

Tom and the woman were tangled up on a dark velvet couch. Sofa.

"Daisy." Tom scrambled to his feet. "This isn't anything."

The woman's hair was as dark as Daisy's would have been without peroxide, and her dress was as pale as her complexion. It seemed a rude gesture to wear white to a debutante ball, and the woman lifted her chin at Daisy.

But Daisy laughed. A gloved hand flew to her mouth as though she'd giggled in church.

"Daisy." Tom pulled on his tailcoat. "Why don't we talk?"

She turned from the room.

"Daisy!" Tom yelled after her. "Daisy, stop! I've got to show you something."

At that, she did stop. "Another birthday pistol? Because I'd welcome one of those about now."

"I had plans for tonight." He adjusted his silk scarf, and his cuff links flashed his initials. "I was going to ask you. Truly."

"Oh, were you?" Daisy looked past him. "Was she helping you rehearse?"

"I mean it." He fumbled a small box out of his pocket, dyed leather patterned with gold leaf. "I know I can get a little confused sometimes." He opened the box, and the diamond within threw off needles of white light. "But I love you. You know I love you."

Daisy blinked into that sparkle, and I held the word *no* in my throat so I wouldn't shout it. The dazzle of that jewel and all it promised might blur away what Tom had done right in front of her.

Daisy laughed, loud and silvery as the tinkling of the celesta in an orchestra. She laughed louder and louder, and Tom and the woman on the velvet couch looked increasingly concerned.

When Daisy's laughter calmed enough to let her speak, she looked right at Tom. "You're no good to me."

But I could see, by the trembling in her chin, that all this bravery was a gloss, thrown over so she could put on a good show.

With small, hurrying steps, she rushed away.

"Daisy," I said as she passed me. "Daisy, wait—"

"Oh, look at your worried face," she said. "Did you really think I didn't know?"

Her smile was fond and pitying, and I despised myself for being both cynical and naïve.

Daisy kept going.

"Wait," I said again.

She turned back. "You're a dear for worrying, but I'm just fine." She smoothed her skirt. "I don't need him anymore."

"Then why do you need any of this?" I asked. "You don't have to do this."

"Don't be silly," she said. "I've dreamed of this. And look at the trouble Jay's gone to. Do you really think I'd let Tom ruin it?"

I stood with the haunting emptiness of getting exactly what I'd wanted and finding it hollow. Finally, she was casting Tom aside. But she still wanted all of this. It wouldn't end with Tom. She'd be the prize of the next man who'd have her. She'd keep making herself into a smaller, paler version of herself. She'd keep shoving Daisy Fabrega-Caraveo into the shape of Daisy Fay.

The only man I knew who wouldn't do that to her was the man I, selfishly and shamefully, wanted for myself.

He loved her. He would be good to her. He would let her be Daisy Fabrega-Caraveo. It was his arm she belonged on tonight. But I didn't know if she was thinking clearly enough to know it.

I followed after her. "Daisy."

She only stopped when she found Jordan.

"I'm going to go dress," she said, and flitted off.

"Daisy, listen to me," I said. "Please."

"Nick," Jordan said. "Stop." It was as much reassurance as command.

Daisy squeezed my hand. "I know what I want." Her laugh was an echo of that laugh in the hall, and she said with delighted surprise, "I truly know what I want."

"I'll take care of her," Jordan told me. "We're very good with each other. She takes care of me every time I panic before a tournament. I took care of her before that ridiculous party with the Buchanans. We've done this a hundred times."

CHAPTER XXIX

"Gatsby?" I had looked for him, and now I had called his name a dozen times. But his name was on so many lips that my voice vanished into the chorus.

"Jay?" I tried instead.

The guests were so drunk on champagne and beauty that there was no use asking anyone.

Then all conversation condensed into a single shared gasp.

Daisy stood at the top of the curved staircase, radiant as a fairy queen. Her skirt was a cloud of tulle, and each step revealed another layer in a slightly different shade of pastel pink or blue.

Tiny roses—were they real, or well-made fabric flowers?—trimmed the neckline of her gown. Garlands trailed each seam of her skirt like seaweed. The cape flowing from her shoulders gave the effect of enormous wings that flashed between powder blue and green. Pink and white peonies and what I thought were water lilies crowned her hair. She even carried a scepter of a wand topped with a gold-edged bloom. In her other hand, she held a bouquet so enormous she had to brace it against her waist. It was a globe of the same peonies and water lilies, with a train of blue ribbons that each ended in a rose or a bow or a cluster of orange blossoms.

She made a perfect, demure bow. Her skirt billowed as she lowered herself, and then she rose.

She looked like she was floating. She looked like a water lily who'd taken the form of a girl. I couldn't have been the only one thinking it. She seemed to be the living equivalent of Monet's paintings. *Nymphéas, Reflection of a Weeping Willow.*

The mischief in her smile told me everything. By looking like a flower grown from water, Daisy was reminding everyone that she had braved the sea. Her dress harkened to the image everyone had of her underwater. By morning, every paper would sing not only of her beauty but her dauntlessness. She would be the debutante who laughed in the face of her own mortality. And really, what did anyone here want to be except young and lovely and fearless?

Every camera rushed to capture her. And any camera that didn't flashed in the moment after, when Jordan Baker appeared next to Daisy Fay.

Daisy shifted to one side to make room for both their skirts. Jordan had changed from her simple dress to a gown as spectacular as Daisy's. It was the blue of a gas flame, and even with the weight of the lavender beading, the skirt moved and floated. It turned to deep purples and greens toward the hem, the colors of a peacock wandering a garden by moonlight.

Magnesium cubes popped in every direction. The sharp smell filled the air alongside delighted gasps and thrilled murmuring.

"Is that . . ."

"Who is that?"

"It's Jordan Baker."

Before the end of the night, they would call it the fashion statement of the season. An upstart socialite had burst onto the social scene with a golfer whose style matched her skill. The Muldoons and Hornbeams would express their pity for any other girl debuting this summer.

Within days, newspaper columns would herald Jordan and Daisy as an illustration of the new age, one in which girls and women forged their own paths across ballrooms and into the world.

——— ❋❋❋ ———

"Nick." Tom shoved his way through the crowd. "What's going on here?"

In that same moment I spotted Gatsby. He stood near the base of the stairs, watching Jordan and Daisy descend.

I expected him crestfallen, wondering why, if Daisy wasn't alongside Tom, she couldn't be alongside him.

But Gatsby looked contented, filled with new and endless pride.

On her way by, Daisy clasped his hand and squeezed it, and then she and Jordan progressed toward the gardens.

"Good for her." Gatsby said it so wistfully I thought he might have been talking to himself. But he turned to me and said again, "Good for her."

Adoring guests gathered close to Daisy and Jordan, giving them only enough room to sweep out into the flower-scented night.

When Tom couldn't get to them, he settled for me. "What's the meaning of all this?" he asked.

Gatsby's smile was catching. I was smiling with him now, both of us watching Daisy and Jordan.

"I don't know," I said. "I really don't know."

"You think this is funny?" Tom asked. "If Daisy had had a debut at my family's country club, you and half these people wouldn't be allowed in unless you were serving the drinks."

Gatsby snapped away from his tranquil state. "Get out of my house," he said.

"Excuse me?" Tom asked. "Everything's gone to hell since the two of you came into her life, and you want me out of your house? And you." He looked to me now. The louder he spoke, the more his voice blurred, showing just how drunk he was.

This was what I thought of as he threw a slur at me. He'd probably been holding it back since the night I first came to

East Egg. I thought of how drunk Tom sounded so that the full weight of the word wouldn't strike me.

Pulling back from the moment slowed it down. But then it sped forward, and I saw Gatsby grabbing Tom and shoving him toward the door.

Tom threw a punch, but in his stupor he'd lost his polo player's aim. His fist hit the banister, and he howled at the impact.

"Do you need help finding the way out?" Gatsby gripped Tom's jacket and turned him. "I'm happy to oblige."

Tom elbowed Gatsby in the stomach.

The crowd was pulling back from the fight, leaving room, and I rushed forward.

Gatsby grunted with the impact. But he straightened up in a way that revealed a soldier's bearing and readiness. It was in such contradiction with his typical leisurely stance, as though the specter of fourteen-year-old Gatsby had come to see Daisy's debut.

Martha took Tom Buchanan by the tie of his tuxedo. She stood two stairs up. The gentle slope of her skirt looked like a dark sea she was rising from. The scalloped hem moved like the edges of waves.

The world slowed again, and the only thing I saw clearly was the intricate embroidery on Martha's dress. It encircled her sleeves and swept along the skirt, and I thought I remembered her telling me that it was patterned after the embroidery on a family challah cover. I remembered her telling me about how she slipped pieces of her life with her family into her clothes. A pocket square matched to a headscarf of her grandmother's. Lace chosen because it was nearly identical to the veil her mother had worn to light Shabbat candles. And always, the thread from her grandfather's tallis on her wrist.

Martha carried her family with her. She wore their history on her body.

How could I face my own family now, when I had heard Tom say that word, and I couldn't even move my own body from where I stood?

The world only sped up when I heard Martha's voice.

"You touch him again," she said, "you touch anyone here again, my heel's going up your ass. And I'm quite fond of them. They're new. Don't make me waste a Louie heel and an almond toe on someone like you."

• • •

Tom didn't leave the house so much as stumble out of it. He shoved away each partygoer who tried to sway him from his car. *A little too much embalming fluid? Maybe we should call you a cab.* He flicked his hands at the women as though shooing away moths. He pushed the men aside, slurring about Yale and the fine whiteness of the Buchanan line.

"Jay." Daisy flitted up to Gatsby, her gown a cloud around her. "We can't let him go like that. He's practically liquid. Could I borrow your car?"

"I'll go with you," Gatsby said.

My anger felt woven into my shirt fabric. At nothing more than my cousin's request, Gatsby was again mired in the mess that was Daisy and Tom.

Within seconds of ignition, Tom ran the blue coupe into a stone retaining wall. When he backed away from it, it looked like a wheel had fallen off, but still, he drove it. The blue coupe listed on one side, the scrape of metal growing louder as he sped off.

"Come on." Jordan pulled me outside.

"What are you doing?" I asked.

She led me toward the cream finish and chrome of her car. "They're going after a Buchanan on wheels." Graceful as Daisy's bow, she opened the driver's side door and slipped into the green interior. "Do you really think they're not going to need our help?"

We were too far behind to see the blue of Tom's car. But sometimes we caught glimpses of Gatsby's, a distant point of lavender. We raced past West Egg village and toward the Ash Heaps.

Jordan watched the road with such focus it cinched her eyebrows, but she spared a moment to scrutinize my face.

"What are you sulking about now?"

"He's still following her," I said. "He'll always be following her. No matter what she does."

Jordan readjusted her grip on the wheel, as though steeling

her patience. "Who did Jay get into a fight over tonight? Daisy? No. You."

"Because Tom was ruining Daisy's party," I said.

"Wrong," Jordan said. "It's you, Nick. Which you'd already know if you'd stopped to think about it." She looked over again. "You're safe with him. And I don't say that about people easily."

The landscape around us grew gray. Hills of ash rose from the ground. The windows of houses and a café punctuated the dark. So did the lights of the service station where a lavender car sat parked. Tom's blue coupe was nowhere in sight.

Jordan pulled to a stop.

A group of young men, all red- and blond-haired, were cornering Gatsby. Two women stood by, a golden blonde I soon recognized as my cousin—more by her dress than her features—and a red-haired woman I placed as Myrtle Wilson.

Myrtle noticed us before Daisy or Gatsby did, and she ran toward us.

"What happened?" I asked.

Myrtle flapped her hands. "They've got it all wrong, you've got to do something!"

"What happened?" Jordan asked.

"I don't know what to do." Myrtle fiddled with the bracelets on her wrists. "I saw Tom's car, so I ran out to try to catch him, but he just kept going. He didn't even stop. And then that purple car came out of nowhere right behind him, and the woman, she braked so hard, she stopped so fast so she wouldn't hit me. But I was already running out of the way. I really thought she was going to hit me."

I thought she might snap the bracelets off her wrists. "I was trying to run out of the way," she said, "and I fell, and that boy"—Myrtle pointed a varnished nail in the direction of Gatsby—"he got out of the car to help me up and make sure I wasn't hurt, and my brothers saw it, and now they think there's something between us. Oh"—she bent her knees and then straightened up again—"they know something. They know I've been going out. They just don't know the right thing."

Myrtle's brothers were talking at Gatsby, the flood lamps showing the motion of their mouths.

One of them shoved Gatsby's shoulder.

I ran toward them. "Lay off."

Jordan followed, her polished shoes kicking up ash. "What seems to be the trouble here, gentlemen?"

"This character's been ruining our sister," one of them said.

"And what would make you think a thing like that?" Jordan asked.

"She's been sneaking off at all hours of the day," another said. "Are we supposed to think it's some kind of coincidence that she runs right out and this guy is holding her hands like he's about to recite Shakespeare?"

I looked at Gatsby, begging him with my stare. *Tell them it was Tom. Just tell them.*

"He thinks he can just come in here with his fancy car and disrespect our sister," another said. "Not so long as she's got us." He shoved Gatsby's other shoulder.

I lurched forward.

Jordan caught my elbow so hard it was almost a slap. "Yes, why don't you turn this into a brawl?" she whispered at me, and then returned to her usual voice. "Boys, I think we've got a whole misunderstanding here. Don't we, Daisy?"

She looked at my cousin, who was frozen in all ways except how the ash-filled air stirred her hair and gown.

Jordan gave a nod, encouraging and prodding.

Daisy's stricken expression warmed.

"I'm so very embarrassed," she said.

Every one of the Wilson brothers found the source of that lovely voice and the girl who went with it.

"It's me, not him." Daisy tilted her chin with great apology. "I've just been taking your sister into the city to have a little fun. We've struck up a bit of a friendship, that's all. I didn't mean any harm. I thought we'd see the park, and I wanted to buy her this lipstick at B. Altman. Oh, she reminds me so much of my sisters back home, and I miss them so very much."

Myrtle's brothers looked almost sedated by Daisy. She would be the ethereal dream that floated across their closed eyelids tonight.

Daisy didn't so much cast spells as she was them, and the enchantment of her had saved us. But I despised it. There was something monstrous about the way my cousin breezed through the world. Maybe she didn't care about what burned up behind her. More likely, she didn't know. She never looked back to check.

CHAPTER XXX

When Daisy left the ring of light around the service garage, I followed her.

"You let him do this," I said.

Daisy turned around. "Excuse me?"

I caught up with her. "You followed Tom, and then you let Jay take the blame for all this."

"First, I didn't follow Tom for Tom's sake," Daisy said. "He was under the table. I followed him for everyone else on the road. Second, I didn't let Jay take the blame. I just told them I'm Myrtle's friend, didn't I?"

"As though you'd be friends with anyone who's not in the society pages." I watched the night air fill the petals of her skirt. "Are you still going to marry him?"

Her laugh was in tune with the stirring of clouds above us. "I doubt it. Goodbye to all that if this is how he behaves."

I nodded.

"Oh, you can jump up and down if you want," Daisy said. "Don't pretend you're not overjoyed."

But I wanted more than for Daisy to shove Tom aside.

I wanted Daisy to either love Gatsby or let him go.

And maybe that was why I said, "He did this all for you. Do you know that?"

"What are you talking about?" Daisy asked.

"The debut," I said. "All of it. It was for you. To make you the debutante of the season."

"Oh, is that what it was for?" Her laugh was a cutting chirp. "Good of you to tell me. I'd be so lost without young men like you standing by to tell me things."

"What does that mean?" I asked.

"It means I'm not your little soap bubble," she said.

"Whose?" I asked.

"Yours," she said. "Jay's. Everyone's."

"You came here to become exactly what you are," I said. "You wanted this. You wanted to be the beautiful girl everyone's talking about."

"So what?" she asked. "Am I not allowed to want that?"

"Of course you are," I said. "And we were trying to get you that. We were getting you everything you wanted."

"I don't care if you were getting me the blessing of the archangel Gabriel himself," she said. "You should have told me what you were doing. I'm not about to be the center of any of your little machinations without my knowledge."

"Oh?" I came closer, the ash-bitter night between us. "Is that why you didn't bother telling me you'd disowned me before I even got to New York?"

"I didn't disown you," she said.

"To everyone here you did," I said. "I wasn't good enough for you."

"Yes, you were." Her voice softened into pleading. "I brought you here. I convinced your parents. Don't tell me you weren't good enough."

"Fine." My voice grew a hard shell. "Then too brown."

"Don't you dare," she said.

"You told Tom that I was your housekeeper's son," I said. "You could not have made it clearer that I didn't belong to you, that I wasn't part of your family."

Daisy's brown irises shivered in their fields of white.

Daisy Fay had distanced herself from my brown skin and black hair. She had denounced me like a false religion.

"You used me to make yourself look like some rich family's daughter," I said. "And then you broke Jay's heart."

Now her laugh was unguarded and piercing. "I'm sorry. *I* broke his heart?"

"Didn't you?" I asked.

"You need to talk to Jay." She glanced past me. "He needs to tell you the truth, and you need to hear it."

"Are you angry at him?" I asked.

"I'm not angry at him at all," she said. "I'm angry at you. I care deeply for Jay, don't you ever forget that. I love him. But not that way. And he doesn't love me that way either. I know that."

"Then you don't know anything," I said.

"Of course not," she said. "Why would I? I'm not supposed to know a thing for myself." She leaned forward, her skirt lapping at the night. "Men love beautiful, useless, expensive things. So I'm meant to be one. I'm not supposed to be anything but a beautiful little fool."

"Nick," Gatsby called from the light of the service garage. "Let's go home."

"Daisy'll go with me," Jordan said. "I think we could all use some sleep."

Daisy's eyes stayed on me. "Talk to him."

For once, her posture didn't speak of pale blue cosmetic tins printed with pink flowers. It didn't speak of her imitating advertisements of virginal blondes on tree swings.

This was the Daisy I knew, the one who jumped from the highest trees into the pond when everyone else was still gauging the distance.

"Please," she said. "Just talk to him."

⁂

Gatsby drove us out of the Ash Heaps and toward the lush green of West Egg.

"Have you ever heard of la luz mala?" I asked.

"I don't think so," he said. "What is it?"

"It's light that looks beautiful," I said. "Enchanted even. But it's around something decaying. It's light that results from something decomposing on the ground just underneath it. It comes from the vapor off that decay."

A ribbon of ash twirled through the air.

"So you get these beautiful wisps of green light, but then they lead you into a marsh that might drown you, or a meadow full of snakes, or a forest you might never find your way out of."

"Have you ever seen one?" Gatsby asked.

"No," I said.

"Then how do you know?" he asked.

I could taste my own smile, bitter as gin. "Daisy's mother warned me about them." The irony of it, how Daisy's mother had been so diligent in cautioning her children and nieces and nephews. *Escucha, beware something bright like that, just out of nowhere.* Daisy, her own daughter, had bleached herself so pale that all that was left of her was a green glow.

"From far away, it looks like something you want," I said. "But if you get too close, it's poison."

⸺ ● ● ● ⸺

To my truest heart in the world,

I can't believe what we've done. I can't believe we came out together that way. None of those men who'd been bragging about their millions could lift their jaws from the floor.

Everyone has such ridiculous questions, like if it was Brussels lace on your dress, or if it's true that I wore gold garters with diamonds (where do they get these ideas?).

I won't tell a soul that the only thing on my garters was the orange blossoms you pinned there. I won't tell how those petals crushed their scent to my thighs as I greeted every fawning guest.

With every picture I see of us, I'm delirious with happiness. There's no one else on earth I would have wanted to come out with. You are every dazzling thing in the world. Do you know that?

Yours, entirely enamored,

Daisy Fabrega-Caraveo

CHAPTER XXXI

"Gentlemen." Another of the Ivy League men who said what college he'd gone to more than his name—I thought this one might be Harvard?—poured a 4:00 P.M. champagne toast. "It's all up from here."

Everyone raised a glass in a murmuring agreement except me.

The Princeton man noted my empty hand. "Nobody got you a drink? Strange, since you always look like you need one."

"I don't drink," I said.

"You one of the Mormons?" He swallowed half his glass. "I didn't know they had Mormons in South America."

I ignored the array of incorrect facts. "I tried it as soon as I got off the train in New York," I said. "It turns out I don't hold my liquor very well."

"Know thyself." The Princeton man raised his glass. "I respect that."

The Harvard man went on. "If you think we've summited

the highest peak, get ready to go to the stars. And after the stars, the moon!"

Everyone burst into applause.

They were careless with facts about me, and the moon, and they were careless with other people's money.

Before I could think better of it, I said, "The moon is closer than the stars."

Scattered laughter replaced the dying applause.

"Something you want to say, Carraway?" the Harvard man asked. "Care to give a lecture on geometry?"

"I was just thinking about your toast," I said. "And I guess we're not going to talk about the potatoes."

A few of the younger men, ones who were shrinking freshmen at Yale and Cornell when men like Tom Buchanan were seniors, did laugh. But the rest of them looked at me with curdled expressions.

"The overbuying of potatoes last week because no one double-checks their paperwork?" I asked. "How much money did that lose?"

"Everyone makes mistakes, Carraway," the man said. "Even you, I'm sure. You'll never get anywhere if you're afraid of them. Besides, you're from Idaho, aren't you? Shouldn't you have warned us about the potatoes?"

"And the Canadian dollar futures?" I asked. "How about those? The men you bought them from weren't even Canadian. They didn't know what they were talking about."

"How were we supposed to know they were crooks?" another man asked.

"They bought the futures right before they convinced you to buy them, and when you bought them the price went up and they sold them." I spoke to the questioning man now. "And you would have known what they were running if you'd asked around about them."

The traders averted their gaze, as though talk of logic or linear algebra might stain their silk ties.

I could learn the right words and the right colors for shirts. But this was where I stopped. The next step was one my body resisted.

"The market won't hold forever," I said. "That's how markets work. And if you keep assuming it will, a lot more people than you are going to lose a lot."

"We're going to be captains of the universe, my friend," he said. "And you're going to be back in Minnesota."

"You're going to be broke, or you're going to be rich off other people's backs," I said.

"Carraway!"

I turned around to the sound of Benson's voice.

"My office," he said.

I followed.

"Looks like Benson's finally about to clean house," someone said, but I didn't look to see who.

Benson shut his office door. "What in the hell do you think you're doing?"

"You're the one who hired me to look at numbers," I said. "Wheat prices predicting silver prices. How much gold investors buy when they're worried about inflation. Trend lines. Models. Why did you ask me to play this game of dots and boxes if you didn't want to hear what I saw?"

"Because nobody wants to hear it," he said. "That kind of talk can take down a whole place, Carraway."

"That's not my name," I said. "It's never been my name."

"It doesn't matter." He got out his checkbook. "I won't remember it anyway."

He scrawled out the sum of my last pay.

"You know I'm right," I said. "There are things you can do now so that when the downturn comes, it won't ruin everyone."

Benson ripped the check off, blew on the ink, and handed it to me. "I wish you the best of luck."

———— ▪▪▪ ————

Mr. Jay Gatsby
West Egg, New York

Dear Jay,

I know I've probably disappointed you to no end, and I think it's time I give you a clear answer. I should have weeks ago.

I can't do what you're asking of me. You see, my heart goes where Jordan goes, and the rest of me follows. I think you know that by now.

It occurred to me that I never told you how I fell in love with Jordan, and since you're a fellow romantic, I thought you might want to know.

Did you know that Mrs. Buchanan's private bathing room has a glass bathtub? Can you believe it? I swear that woman would put in a crystal floor with a fishpond underneath just so she could say she had one. Anyway, the first time Tom left me alone there, I showed it to Jordan, and I told her we should go in. I undressed right down to my camisole and knickers, lavender bubbles and all. Jordan stayed fully dressed, so I thought that meant she wasn't coming in. But then she did, still wearing her ice-green charmeuse. She looked like a siren among sea foam, and I realized I'd been in love with her for a long time and hadn't known it, and that she'd been in love with me for a long time and had known it.

Maybe sometimes I'd known a little, when I saw the bloom of her lipstick on a champagne glass, or when she told me that bridal bouquets were getting so enormous I'd have to take a course of serious exercise in preparation to carry one. But I hadn't truly known before Mrs. Buchanan's glass bathtub.

And that was that. We threw bubbles at each other like snow, and there was no getting my heart back. You know just what that's like, don't you?

Yours, still,
Daisy

CHAPTER XXXII

With that pale leaf in my pocket, I left the building. I stepped out onto the pavement in time to hear the far-off whistle of the National Biscuit Company. The paper grew heavy in my pocket from the damp air and the knowledge that I had failed at being a grateful son, a man who took care of his family.

I walked, and the bells of St. George's Church sounded. I passed through the shadow of the Flatiron Building, where men gathered at Fifth and Twenty-Third, waiting for currents of air off passing traffic to ruffle skirts. I continued north toward the park, where the glass gleam of the Plaza's revolving door stopped me.

There's a moment before jumping into water where you don't have enough of a chance to hesitate. If you go past that moment, you might not jump at all. It was in this spirit that I held my breath and shoved myself into the revolving door.

I spun around once, and kept going, through the lobby and then out again. Marble-cooled air and then hot evening and back.

"Sir?" a voice said.

I spun, my world nothing but metal and glass.

"Sir?" the voice said again.

I kept spinning, trying to throw myself into orbit.

"Sir." The voice came resolute and loud.

I slowed, falling to earth.

A pane of glass stood between me and the worried face of a concierge.

"Sir, you can't do that here."

"No se preocupe." I caught my breath. "I'm leaving." I spun the half turn toward the street. "There's something I have to do, anyway."

• • •

Mr. Nicolás Caraveo
West Egg, New York

Dearest Nick,

By now you must be awfully confused. I suppose I'm a bit confused myself.

But here's the best I know how to explain: I think some- times you do the same thing so many times, you get tired of it. Maybe not if it's the right thing. If you do the right thing over and over, I imagine it becomes part of you, like your own breath. But when it's the wrong thing, there comes a point where you try it on for a thousandth time and realize how ill it's been fitting all the while.

You see, I spent half my life trying to get everyone to

like me, trying to be what it was everyone would like. But do you know what I found out? If you turn yourself into someone everyone can like, you'll probably end up not liking yourself much. If everyone in the world loves you, then really nobody does.

That's why you go after it, Nick, the star that helps you find your way. Everyone needs something that's worth risking everything for. Even if the world doesn't think that's the right thing, even if the world thinks you should be going after something else, you have to *know*.

I hope you and Jay have had it out by now. Why, that sounds ominous, doesn't it? I didn't mean it that way. I mean I hope you've discussed things.

Do you know what I said to him last week? I told him, "You know that one day I'll be old, don't you? I won't be as lovely as I am right now, at least not to the world. The world might think I'm harmless and sweet and a pretty sort of old lady, but it won't be so impressed that I'm on your arm. Will I still be beautiful to you then?"

And do you know what he told me? He said, "Yes, of course. No matter your age, you'll still be a dream to me."

I think he meant this to be sweet, but all I could think was, my goodness, I'd still be a dream at that point? I wouldn't be a fulfillment yet? That sounds exhausting. Does he have any idea how tiring it is to be someone else's dream?

He's been trying so hard to convince me what delirious fun a life with him would be, and I'm sure it would be.

But I worry about him. I worry that chasing after me or some other girl like me is something he's done for so long he doesn't know how to do anything else.

So be sure that you know, Nick. Know the light you're following.

Yours,

Daisy

CHAPTER XXXIII

I found Gatsby in the library, cutting the pages of a book with a letter knife.

"Do you still love her?" I asked.

He looked up. "What?"

I wished he hadn't worn the shirt he had on. As I'd been borrowing his clothes, he'd thrown different ones at me to try. That one, wine red, hadn't fit me right. But now I thought of it being against my back and then against his.

"She let you take the fall for Tom," I said.

"I wanted to," Gatsby said. "I didn't want her humiliated by everyone knowing he was stepping out on her."

"And you still love her," I said. "Even after that?"

"Yes." Gatsby's fingers traced a set of uncut pages. "Of course. Why would I want to spend my life with her if I didn't love her?"

Daisy's green lamp was a luz mala, a luring light that would pull Gatsby out into the bay.

"What is it about her?" I asked. "What keeps you so in love with her no matter what she does?"

Gatsby fumbled the book. "In love with her?" He recovered his grip. "Nick. I've only ever fallen in love with one person."

"Yes, I know," I said. "We all know."

"I really don't think you do." He set both the book and scrolled letter opener down. "Nick."

The light of a nearby lamp threw amber onto one side of his face.

"Do you not know I'm gay?"

The green of his eyes turned to twin luces malas, a bright lantern glow across a pond. Everything about Jay Gatsby pulled me into a marsh, a meadow, an ocean, and I was lost there.

His time as an underage soldier in the war.

His history as a breaker boy.

How he'd come to say the words *I'm gay* with so little hesitation.

How had he managed it? I hadn't even known for sure that boys like me—like us—were allowed to claim the word *gay*.

There was so much under the surface of this boy. He seemed to hold everything out in front of you so you could see it all, but he was simply giving you a mirrored surface. Like the smooth glass of the sea, the reflection concealed everything underneath.

"If you're gay," I said, "then why were you chasing Daisy?"

He slipped the partly cut book onto the shelf. "Do I really have to draw you the whole picture?"

"Yes," I said. "You do. You've been pining for her for

years. You bought this house. You had these parties. To win her heart."

"No," Gatsby said. "Not to win her heart. So she'd accept my proposal."

"Why did you care so much if she accepted your proposal?" I asked. "If you don't love her, why?"

"Because I'm gay and—" He hesitated, stopped cold in the middle of the sentence.

I breathed the rest of it, the truth, before I even understood it.

"Daisy likes girls," I said.

Gatsby would never have said it out loud. He would never tell that about someone else. But he didn't have to tell me. The kinship I'd always felt with my cousin flew into pin-sharp focus.

"Daisy's been trying to tell me she likes girls," I said. "And I haven't listened at all."

You see, Nicky, boys are always falling in love with me, but I don't much fall in love with them.

Of course Daisy wouldn't fall in love with Gatsby. He was a boy.

"So what was the proposal for?" I asked. "If you're not in love with her and she's not in love with you, then why?"

"Because that's what you do if you can," he said. "Someone like me marries someone like her. I didn't want her that way. I wanted the life we could have together."

It had been dawning on me slowly, but then it broke.

"A lavender marriage," I said.

"Yes," Gatsby said. "We could make a way for ourselves in the world, and she could be with whoever she wanted, and I wouldn't mind because I'd be with whoever I wanted. And then I fell in love with you, and she was in love with Jordan."

"Daisy's in love with Jordan," I said, as though my mind needed a repetition to absorb the fact.

"You really haven't noticed?" he asked. "Did you think them strutting out together like that was just a performance? That's the way Daisy always wanted it. That was her wildest debutante dream. She wanted Jordan on her arm and she wanted to be on Jordan's arm. And they did a fine job of making it look like a show, but they love each other."

Daisy holding Jordan's hands. The two of them twirling in their organza skirts until they were dizzy. The artful way they found excuses to touch each other.

It had all been right there. Without knowing it, I had been a spectator to their romance this whole time.

Gatsby traced the scrolled brass on the lamp. I hadn't noticed until now that the letter opener nearly matched it.

"And when you and Jordan struck up your friendship," he said, "it seemed like a kind of fate."

The lamp shifted the green of his eyes to the same bronze as the letter opener.

"I could marry her and if you and Jordan liked each other as much as you seemed to, you might be able to do the same thing for each other one day," he said. "We could all offer one another the protection the world will never offer us.

That's why I went along with your idea about Daisy's debut. Because you were right. It would give her a kind of power women like her don't usually have."

"You all wanted me to marry Jordan?" I asked. "When did you all decide this?"

"Nobody decided anything," he said. "I wanted to marry Daisy so she and I could both be happy. You and Jordan, that was up to the two of you. I only started thinking of it when you took to her so much and when I fell in love with you."

I reached out to the wall to ballast myself. "When you what?"

Mr. and Mrs. Darío Fabrega-Caraveo
Fleurs-des-Bois, Wisconsin

Dearest Mamá y Papá,

If you believe the papers around here, I am the most famous—and yes, perhaps a little infamous—debutante in all of New York. A man wants to write a movie scenario of my life. The chatter around New York is that because of me, every debutante will be wearing peonies in her hair. Mamá, I can't wait to show you the pictures.

I'm happy. I'm almost sure of it.

But I'm afraid that since I've come to New York, I've gotten a little out of practice telling the truth. I tell the pretty parts and try to forget the rest. You taught me to do that, so that no matter what I would notice the things that are good. But I fear I've taken it and turned it ugly.

I did something terrible to Nick. You knew I had done it. And I knew I had done it. But what's even worse is that I couldn't see what was so wrong with it. I couldn't imagine why it was so awful you wouldn't want to talk to me.

Papá, do you remember the day you caught me telling the girls from school that we had royal blood, that we were descended from Moctezuma himself?

You told me that deception is an untamed thing. You think you have it, that you can hold it, like a lit match or a wild horse. But then the horse runs away with you. The match flame catches into a wildfire. It takes you with it, and suddenly, you're not leading it anymore. It decides where you go.

First, you start lying.

Then, you become a liar.

Then, you become a lie.

But here, I'm going to tell the truth, because I can't bear becoming a lie to you.

I'm sorry I never told you I have a heart for other women. I wasn't sure myself until lately. But now the word "lesbian" feels like a beautiful song on my tongue and I just want to sing it at all hours.

I thought maybe I could love a man if he was sweet and sensitive enough. But I've met the sweetest, most wonderful man, and I can't even manage to fall in love with him. It's the queerest thing. He's everything I ever would have said I wanted, anything any girl would want. If a fairy godmother had asked me to make a list of all I'd like in a young man, he's what she'd cook up. But I love him only as a friend, or as a sister loves a brother. It's as though I had all the ingredients set out to make Eton mess, or Mrs. Sanderson's tomato soup cake, but I couldn't follow the recipe. The ingredients wouldn't come together.

When I realized I loved my friend Jordan, it was as though that kitchen, where before I couldn't make a cake or a pavlova, turned into a land of sweets. The air burst into powdered sugar and fairy floss. All of a sudden the world was tres leches cake, sugar plums, and the gingerbread puerquitos we all make at Nochebuena.

I sound lovesick and ridiculous, don't I? But I love her, and if watching you both taught me anything, it's that loving someone is worth making a ridiculous spectacle of your own heart.

I may seem a fool sometimes, but I'm no fool. I know that if we make a life together, we'll have to do it with the most artful discretion on earth. But people do it, don't they? We could. Couldn't we?

Yours,
Daisy

CHAPTER XXXIV

"Nick."

The way Gatsby said my name made me hold on to a bookshelf to stay upright.

"I don't care if you don't love me back," he said. "I want you to be happy. I want Daisy and Jordan to be happy. All of us, we have to find ways to live. So yes, Daisy was my dream, because my dream was for us to get to love who we love without having to answer to spouses we're keeping secrets from or the whole world when it's none of the world's business."

He leaned down, and his hair went into his eyes. "We find the ways we can to make ourselves. Ways to be ourselves. You know that. But Daisy doesn't want that. And I need to respect what she wants. I held on to that dream for so long. But it's not mine to decide."

I stood in wonder at how this boy lived in both dreams and details. Jay Gatsby's romantic heart was far more practical than I'd realized.

He threw elaborate parties hoping Daisy would stroll in, wonder-struck, but those same parties fueled his work with Martha.

A life with Daisy was his version of an American boy's dream. He couldn't marry another man, no more than she could marry another woman. But he could marry her, and they could switch beds after turning off the light.

He could be a successful man with a beautiful woman on his arm, and their hearts could be a little less afraid than if they shared a mailbox with anyone else.

His dream was to let her be herself, and to be himself.

"You're in love with me?" I asked.

Gatsby smiled. "Good," he said. "That was the second time I'd said it. I was beginning to think you were ignoring me."

"You're in love with me?" I asked again.

"Since we met on that dock," he said.

"Why didn't you tell me?" I asked.

"I thought there might have been something between us, but I haven't had the nerve to ask you. And then you kissed me on your birthday, but after it seemed like maybe you wished you hadn't. I didn't want to push it. I didn't want you doing anything you didn't want or weren't ready for. Especially since you started staying here. The last thing I wanted was for you to think you owed me anything."

"You've wanted to kiss me again?" I asked.

His smile held that infinite hope I'd never seen in anyone else. "Couldn't you tell?"

A handful of green lights in me broke loose. I grabbed Jay Gatsby by his suspenders, and I kissed him with the reckless enchantment of following a thousand luces malas. He kissed me back like I was the light of every bulb and chandelier in his gardens.

I held my hand against the nape of his neck, and his skin smelled like the mint and moss of his aftershave. He spread his palms over my back, and mine slid over the red cloth of his shirt. His fingers found the hollow under my shoulder blade, the exact point he'd touched the day we stood outside the cottage. The desire I'd stored up in my brittle heart flew out, loud as those summer evening parties.

I was a boy kissing a boy. Our fingers slipped into the starched belt loops of each other's trousers. Our thumbs glided over the close-cut hair on the back of each other's heads. We grabbed suspenders and shirt collars and the buttons on undershirts like the only way to hold each other together was to tear each other to pieces.

We kissed between rivers of blue hyacinths and gold daffodils.

We kissed in the tide of the sound, still in our clothes, and the ocean dusted its reflected stars onto our skin.

We carried salt and the moon on our bodies, sprinkling light and sea onto Gatsby's sheets.

———— ❖ ————

"Fairy," Jay said.

"What?" I asked. We were lying in the dark, but I still shifted to face him.

"Fairy," he said. "It's a word I forgot to tell you about. It's a word they use for boys like us. They mean it to be an insult, but I take it to mean there's something magic about us and they know it."

He kissed me, and I felt the contours of that reclaimed word in my own mouth. He kissed me, and I saw the tinsel flashing in his hair at that first party. He kissed me, and those silver threads bloomed into heat and fire.

I came to New York as a handful of Wisconsin earth, but it was that precise earth, this precise body and heart, that Jay Gatsby wanted. Falling stars may have been spectacularly misnamed, but in this moment, I understood the impulse. The earth I was made of blazed like cosmic dust, lighting up brighter the faster I fell.

Yes, there was inevitable space between all atoms. When my palm lay flush against his, when his lips pressed the perfect imprint of his mouth against my jawline, I knew there was still invisible distance between the charged particles of his body and mine. But I couldn't feel that distance. We were electrons flying across each other's orbits, throwing off quanta of light and energy.

Learning this boy, touching him—it was as fractal as measuring a coastline. Within every corner and curve, there were countless more. Every feature of him I learned, I wanted to learn in greater depth and detail, every bay and channel and shoal.

I could never learn all of him. It was as impossible as finding the true length of the shore along the sound. But I wanted to get as close as I could.

CHAPTER XXXV

When Jordan saw me, her expression was both knowing and relieved, and I knew she knew.

"Did he have to tell you or did you figure it out?" she asked as we sat down at one of the coffee shop tables.

"He had to tell me," I said.

"And us?" she asked a few moments later. She stirred a spoon through her cup, the metal sound dainty against the porcelain. "Did he have to tell you about Daisy and me, or did you figure that much out?"

"He had to tell me," I said again.

A couple waved to Jordan on their way out, and Jordan waved back until they were gone.

"So now you know everything." Jordan crossed her ankles, and her knees moved the pleats of her damask dress.

"And you know that Daisy's chosen you, don't you?" I said.

"What gives you that idea?" Jordan asked.

"Her debut," I said.

Jordan shook her head, lifting the spoon from the cup. "Everything you saw, sure, it was a lot of fun, but it was a spectacle. An act. On both our parts. I don't take it seriously because neither of us meant it that way."

"I think she meant something by it," I said.

"Half of Daisy Fay is performance," Jordan said. "You can't take seriously what she does in front of an audience. You must know that by now."

I'd learned to tune out the shrill call of Jay's telephone. Between the lead-up to Daisy's ball and Jay's work, it was always ringing.

"It's for you," Jay told me, his voice soft as the morning. I knew from that voice, and the slight smile he gave me as he pushed his hair out of his face, that yes, it had really happened. The night before last, it had happened. Jay Gatsby had told me he loved me.

"Who knows I'm here?" I asked.

He smiled. "Your mother."

"What?" When I picked up the phone, I nearly dropped the handset. "Mamá? Where are you calling from?"

She told me about the telephone just installed in their hallway. The house and the equipment paid off. Daisy had wiped out the debts of my family, her family, and several other branches. My mother sounded uncomfortably grateful, as though our priest had honored us with a personal visit but she'd been in her dressing gown when he'd arrived.

My stomach curdled. I had only my last paycheck to send to my parents, and this eased the weight of me losing my job. But was this Daisy's way of making herself feel less guilty for distancing herself from us?

"How was the wedding?" Mamá asked. I could hear her making an effort to be cheerful.

"What wedding?" I asked.

"Your tía said this was some kind of wedding present from Tom," Mamá said. "Was it?"

A wedding present. What a magnificent lie. Or were they mixing up the wedding and the debutante ball?

My silence went on long enough to make my mother laugh.

"Or doesn't she tell you anything anymore?" she asked.

"Not so much," I said.

"Qué lástima," my mother said. "You two were always so close. She's the only one who could keep up with you. And your only true rival at the pond."

In an instant, I was in sunlit water with Daisy, sinking down toward the dark. She was the only one who could go half as deep as I could. I heard her laughing through the water, and in that laugh, her bathing costume became a filmy dress. Her hair turned pale. She transformed from a girl in a Wisconsin pond to a socialite who knew she could swim to shore.

The debutante mermaid of East Egg.

As soon as I'd hung up with my mother, I called the Buchanan estate. I could see it across the water, the manor looming over the shore as though it might ford the distance between the Eggs.

"Is Miss Fay there?" I asked.

"She's gone out," the woman on the Buchanans' phone said.

"No, I've missed her?" I exaggerated my own distress.

"She's on her way to the train," the woman said with sympathetic regret.

"Well, thank you," I said. "No message."

"What's going on?" Jay asked once the call was over.

"I need a favor, but you can't ask me why," I said.

"All right," he said.

I thought of the timetables in my head. "How fast can you get me to the train station?"

I'd always known there were disadvantages to being as beautiful as my cousin was. And I'd always known the first, probably the biggest, was unwanted attention from men.

But another—I was just now noticing—was how easy she was to spot on a train platform. The layers of her dress, each a different shade of rose, fluttered as the train came in.

On board, I didn't approach her. I knew better than to be

a brown boy in a shirt, suspenders, and trousers (in the heat, I hadn't even grabbed a jacket) approaching a rich-looking white girl.

But I followed her on, and I followed her off. The same sidewalk crowds that made it difficult to keep track of her made it impossible for her to know I was trailing her. Under shop window displays, the smell of cedar blew into the streets, their basements filled with barrels and boxes of liquor.

It got a little more difficult to follow Daisy when she turned onto a side street. Tony apartment buildings beamed their pristine faces. Immaculate brownstone alternated with whitewashed buildings, and the plant-lined balconies of penthouses looked out over the street.

Daisy's skirt, fluffed by her steps, settled as she looked over her shoulder. "You've always been the loudest walker on earth, did you know that?"

CHAPTER XXXVI

"This is the one for your mother." An elderly woman I'd just learned was called Ruth set a necklace on a low wooden table. The long strand alternated peach, pink, and gold pearls.

The necklace looked at home against the apartment's rich palette, black and silver accenting the yellow, green, and deep mauve. Round mirrors on opposite walls threw back endless copies of Ruth, Isabella—the old woman Ruth called her *dear friend and roommate*—Daisy, and me.

"And these are for your sisters, your cousins, your aunts," Isabella said. "You decide which. You know them better than we do." The strands mixed almond and rose pearls, wine and light blue, deep brown and powder green, berry pink and champagne, olive and apricot, more colors of pearls than I knew existed.

With each strand, my throat tightened, like the weight of them was building at my neck.

"Daisy," I said, with barely enough breath for her name. "What have you done?"

"Would you like to try some orange-blossom honey?" Isabella pushed back the lid of a rolltop desk and took out a glass pot. "It goes wonderfully with that kind of tea."

"Isabella," Daisy said in a forbidding voice. "Please don't poison him. He's my cousin."

The women crooned in identical fond sighs. "How lovely."

"I can see it," Ruth said. "Now that you've said it, I can see it, especially around the eyes."

Isabella put the pot back in the desk and closed the top.

I leaned back against the sofa, dizzied.

Daisy had taken the necklace and had it broken into pieces. She'd admitted I was her cousin. And she'd admitted it so these brooch-wearing little old ladies wouldn't do me in.

"And this one's for that favorite aunt of yours." Isabella arranged a shorter strand of stone blue, celery, copper.

"You think she'll like it, don't you?" Daisy asked me.

"I don't care." I went to the open window, hoping the breeze would clear my head.

"And this one." Ruth lovingly presented a length of pearls in lavender and eggplant-purple, deep blue and silver-blue. "You know who this one's for."

I set my hands against the windowsill. "Why did you do it?"

Ruth gave Isabella a look. "Could you help me with that contraption in the kitchen? It's a devil of a thing."

"And how!" Isabella said. "Always sticks."

The two women gave us their parlor.

"It's all a bit of a story, Nicky," Daisy said.

"Not this." I shrugged away the sight of the pearls. "My parents' house. Why did you do that?"

"Aren't you happy?" she asked.

"No," I said. "I'm not. No one asked you to do that."

"But isn't that what you came to New York for?" she asked. "So things would be better for them?"

"I came to New York so *I* could make things better for them," I said. "*I* wanted to do it. *I* wanted to give them that. *I* wanted to pay them back for . . ." The words caught in my throat.

"For what?" Daisy asked.

"I owe them everything," I said. "Just like I owe you everything. I told you who I was before I told anyone else, and you accepted what I told you. You accepted me as a boy. And then you told me to tell them even though I swore you were wrong, but you were right. I told them and they accepted me and they made me"—I gestured ineffectually at my own body, my men's clothes—"this. I couldn't make myself because I needed you and them to make me, so I wanted to make something for them. For you."

Ruth and Isabella stood in the kitchen doorway, chiffon shoulder to chiffon shoulder. "Is everything all right in here?"

"I think my cousin might need some air," Daisy said. "Mind if we come back in a few minutes?"

If Daisy noticed the looks we were getting as we walked

along the park, she didn't let on. But a young woman as well-dressed and seemingly white as Daisy, alongside someone like me, drew anything from curiosity to scorn.

"I'm sorry," she said. "I didn't know how much it meant to you. I should have."

I couldn't remember if I'd ever heard her say the words *I'm sorry* for anything more substantial than stepping on someone's foot or knocking over a sugar bowl.

"So did you figure it out?" Daisy asked. "Or is this all a big shock to you?"

"Just today," I said. "How did you do this?"

"Two little old ladies out for a nighttime row on the bay," she said. "All I had to do was find their boat, leave it with them, and then swim for the beach. It was a heavy thing, that part was true. It would have drowned me if I'd tried to get to shore with it."

"But why?" I asked. "You're not a thief. Your sisters' accusations about their combs and lipstick notwithstanding."

"I always returned them promptly!"

"Daisy," I said.

Her sigh was light as the breeze. "If I wasn't going to be Mrs. Buchanan, I needed something to walk away with."

"You're the one who's been putting off the engagement," I said.

"Yes," she said. "Because I found out about Myrtle. I realized what I should have realized months earlier: That he might never ask me to marry him. He could promise me a diamond and a dozen yards of alençon lace, but if his family didn't come around, he'd never propose, and if he did, he'd never make it to the altar."

"Dechert thinks we engineered the whole thing," I whispered.

"But you were in Wisconsin," she said.

"It doesn't matter," I said.

"It does," she said. "He can't prove anything."

"He doesn't have to," I said.

Daisy grabbed my hand. "I'm not going to let that happen."

"How can you be sure?" I asked.

"Because you don't know the rest of the plan," she said. "I do."

"Oh?" I asked. "What's the rest of it? Earrings? Bracelets?"

Two pictures came to me at once. First, the last necklace the old women had set out.

Second, Jordan alongside my cousin at the top of Gatsby's staircase.

The necklace perfectly matched Jordan's magnificent dress.

"The purple-and-blue one," I said. "That's for Jordan, isn't it?"

Daisy lowered her head, her hat shading her face. "Violet is her favorite color."

"So this is what you did with it?" I asked. "You had it made into jewelry for everyone else? Can they even wear them anywhere?"

Daisy laughed and leaned into me. "That's a fraction of what was in the necklace," she whispered. "The rest was broken up and sold. What do you think Ruth and Isabella do? They make and sell pieces."

I kept us walking. "Daisy, they're going to follow the money."

"No," Daisy said. "They won't. Because you see, when you like meeting people like I do, you make friends, and some of those friends are the most creative accountants in New York."

"And why would you trust them?" I asked.

"Because some of them are like us," she said.

Only Daisy would find such a tactful way to put that.

"And they're good," she said. "If they want to hide something, it vanishes. Our family's debts look like they were paid off by generous local benefactors who, incidentally, each made large philanthropic donations to churches and shelters and charitable organizations in the area at the same time. It's all very meticulous and it's all about numbers. You'd like it."

Daisy had given this the same careful attention she'd given her transformation from Daisy Fabrega-Caraveo to Daisy Fay.

She kept a gloved hand on my arm, glaring at anyone who stared. "So all that with my debut?" she asked. "You thought you needed to pay me back?"

"How else was I going to do it?" I asked. "How else could I ever repay you? How else could I ever repay my family?"

"Why are you trying to pay anyone back for something we always meant as a gift?" she asked.

I flinched under the question.

"And as for the other thing," she said. "We're all going to get out of this."

"How?" I asked.

"Because you're going to do a math problem for me," she said. "You'll like it. It's even more involved and boring than the ones you're probably doing at that job of yours."

I hadn't told her I'd lost it.

"But if you want to get the math problem, you've got to help me with something else," Daisy said. "Do you promise?"

"Let me be sure I understand," I said. "You want me to do some mathematical calculation for you, and in payment for the privilege of doing so, I get to do something else for you?"

"Yes, that's exactly right," she said. "Because you're curious enough now that you want to know what the math problem is. I know you. You won't be able to stand it if you don't know."

I sighed. "Fine. I'll help you with something else. What kind of math is it?"

She smiled. "Modeling currents and debris distribution within a tidal estuary."

I stared at her. "What?"

CHAPTER XXXVII

The something else, it turned out, involved Daisy borrowing the key to the empty cottage and the two of us filling it with the perfume of flowers and sugar. But this time, instead of the peonies and lilacs Gatsby had brought for Daisy, we set up vases of purple sea holly, drifts of blue hydrangea, lavender roses edged in pink, the blue clouds of love-in-a-mist. The macarons and cakes matched so precisely that I wondered if Daisy had brought blooms to the pastry chefs so they could dye the batter and icing.

"Oh, don't go, please," Daisy said when we'd finished. "Wait until she gets here?"

"You're going to be fine," I said.

"Please?" she said. "She knows something's going on. I know it. I didn't sound natural when I asked her here."

"No, you didn't," Jordan said.

We both looked to find her standing in the doorway.

Daisy jumped up from the sofa, the cape of her dress fluttering around her.

"It wasn't just an act," Daisy said.

Jordan looked a little startled, and Daisy took her hands like she had before the tournament.

"Coming out with you," Daisy told Jordan. "I meant it."

I backed toward the other door, close enough that Daisy would know I hadn't left her but far enough to give the two of them the room and its thousand flowers.

"I choose us," Daisy said. "I choose you, if you'll have me. I want to go where you want to go. I want to go to every one of your tournaments because even though golf is the most boring thing I can think of, when you're the one doing it, suddenly it's the most interesting thing in the world. You make golf more exciting than any party. And if that doesn't tell you that I'm in love with you, then I don't know what will."

This was Daisy. No performance, no show for an audience, just her hopeful, guileless face as she waited for Jordan's answer.

"Why do you look so nervous?" Jordan asked.

Daisy pulled at the fingers of her lace gloves. "Because I am."

Was this how they'd been when they were first getting to know each other, giddy and hesitating in the space between friendship and flirting?

"Well, don't be," Jordan said. "Because I want you at every one of my tournaments even if you still can't tell the difference between a play club and a putting cleek. Because even if you don't understand golf, you understand what I need before I play or before I go out there and get a dozen questions about my favorite shoes or my nail varnish. And if you mean what you're saying, if you're truly ready, then yes, I'll have you."

"I'm ready," Daisy said. "I know I haven't been, but I am now."

Jordan kissed Daisy, and the orchid chiffon of Jordan's dress brushed against the cape sleeves of Daisy's. They leaned their foreheads against each other, eyes closed, their smiles lit with the same surprise they might have felt the first time they kissed each other. And when Daisy pulled off her gloves so she could drape the blue and violet pearls around Jordan's neck, it seemed as intimate as slipping on an engagement ring.

For Daisy, the most romantic a gesture could be was if it was in front of no one except the woman she loved. So I turned from the doorway as Daisy fastened the necklace's closure, and I left them alone in the cottage.

———— ❖❖❖ ————

That night, an olive pearl washed up on the beach, a pale point among a tangle of seaweed.

"Look." I picked it up and held it out to Jay.

"You're kidding." He smiled at it, and it winked blue-green back at him.

The next day, we heard about a few more found up and down the shore. Yellow and gray pearls. Pink and apricot. The surf threw one onto the sand every few miles. If you were a girl lucky enough to come across one, you counted yourself destined to be beautiful and adored.

Soon everyone wanted everyone else to think they were among these luckiest girls. Girls crowded the shores in their scarlet or yellow or blue bathing costumes. Over the next few days, Jay and I suspected that the growing numbers of stories were greatly exaggerated. Everyone wanted to have found a pearl from the necklace Daisy Fay had lost to the sound. They broke apart strands from their own jewelry boxes and cast their own pearls onto the wet sand so that they could be wondrously found. Arguments broke out over what colors had truly been on the necklace, future debutante accusing future debutante of staging her find.

In the end, the stories of found pearls would add up to far more than had ever been in the necklace. Though, of course, whenever Dechert tried to follow one down, the future debutante would say, "Who, me? I didn't find anything." No one would risk the confiscation of her treasured charm.

I suspected Daisy knew how many false finds there would be. I wondered if this had been part of her plan all along, tossing a handful into the water and waiting for the tide to bring them in, and if she had just needed me to do the math of exactly where to cast them onto the surf. A few found pearls could suggest untold numbers still lost, spinning through the dark surf like tiny planets.

Nicolás Caraveo
East Egg, New York

Dear Nick,

I doubt you'll be surprised that your mother has been talking to Daisy, and I hope you won't mind what Daisy's told her. Your cousin meddles. It's what she does.

I never told you exactly why I was so reluctant for you to take that job in New York. I didn't want you to believe that masculinity was financial. I wanted you to think of your own manhood in terms other than money. I never imagined that it was worse than this, that you thought the right to being a man was something you had to pay back with interest.

Please accept what we've given you. If you ever want us to accept anything from you, you must accept this from us. Please don't treat it as a debt you must pay off. You don't owe us anything for seeing you as you truly are.

Make your own life, Nicolás. One you're proud to tell us about.

Your Papá

CHAPTER XXXVIII

"Nick!"

I surfaced from sleep to my cousin's voice calling my name. I tried to place where I was—Wisconsin? The cottage?—and then smelled the blossom-and-grain smell of the boy lying next to me.

"Jay!" Daisy's shoes tapped across the hard flooring.

Panic tore through me.

She'd been caught. Tom, or Dechert, or someone in Tom's family, had found out what she'd done. A thousand stories of pearls washing up hadn't been enough.

Jay and I threw on our clothes and found Daisy downstairs. A beam of sun lit the mint chiffon of her skirt and showed her stricken face.

"It's everywhere," Daisy said. "The bay, the valley, the city. Everyone knows."

"Knows what?" Jay paused on the stairs, buttoning his shirt.

"They didn't believe me," Daisy said. "My lie about Myrtle and me. Everyone thinks Jay is involved with Myrtle."

The world tilted.

Not a fortune in French and Italian pearls.

The mess after Daisy's debut.

"Daisy!" Jordan's voice carried through the house. She was wearing the linen of her golf attire, and she slowed to a stop when she found us. "I came as fast as I could."

"Oh, it's awful," Daisy said. "And now Tom wants to tear down the world over this."

"Why?" Jay asked.

I sighed deeply enough that it closed my eyes. "Because *Tom* is involved with Myrtle."

"He thinks Jay ruined his almost-engagement *and* his affair," Jordan said.

"Of course he does," Jay said.

"You can't laugh this off," Jordan said. "This isn't going away. Nothing goes away when you offend a Buchanan."

"I heard he's on his way over," Daisy said. "Coming back from the city."

"How do you know?" I asked.

"I'm nicer to the Buchanans' maids than they are," she said. "Jay, you've got to leave town."

"Leave town?" Jay asked.

"I'm afraid he might kill you," Daisy said. "Tom practically has nothing to him but his polo and his pride, and as far as he thinks, you've taken the latter. He blames you for humiliating him in front of all of New York."

"You think this is going to end if Jay leaves town?" Jordan asked. "Tom's after revenge with all of us. I was your escort for your debut. Even if he's too dense to know what we are to each other, I was in the place he considered his. And he probably blames Nick for breathing the same air as him. That's about the level of logic we have to imagine with Tom. If he thinks Jay's humiliated him, he thinks that about all of us."

"So we all leave town, then," Daisy said.

"No," I said.

They all stopped talking.

"We're not running," I said. "Not from him. Not like this."

"Then what do you propose we do?" Daisy asked.

"Do you still carry around that pistol?" I asked.

"Yes," she said, wary.

"Really?" Jordan asked. "That's your plan? We're going to shoot him?"

"No," I said.

I looked at the three of them.

My cousin.

The girl she loved.

The boy I loved.

And I said, "The plan is we fight back."

———— ◆◆◆ ————

Jordan held up different bottles of grenadine. "You know this is a terrible plan, right?"

"Terrible?" Jay asked. "You really think it's all the way to terrible?"

"You know I can act this part," Daisy said. "I think months have been leading up to this performance, don't you?"

"This isn't about your acting prowess," Jordan said. "On a strategic level, this all works." She compared two bottles of currant syrup. "But on the practical details of getting none of us killed, it's awful."

Daisy's worried glance was a lighthouse beam turning from Jay to me to Jordan. "You think he might get killed?"

"We're attempting to stage a death." Jordan held a bottle of crème de cassis up to the light. "Whenever you do that, there's a chance someone might actually die. We're all relying on Daisy firing and missing while looking like she's not trying not to miss? Do you know how hard that is?"

I looked at Daisy, remembering all the times she shot close enough to those wolves to scare them away but never hit them.

"I know exactly how hard that is," I said.

———— ❊❊❊ ————

Tom came in yelling. "Gatsby!"

He shouted Jay's name from the drive and up the steps.

"Gatsby! Get out here."

He found the doors locked, so he stormed around to the back, his feet crushing bulb flowers.

The four of us stood ready as players in a stage production. Two were in position for Tom to find, the debutante and the boy in that rose-pink suit. The other two hid in the shadows, a nervous boy and a socialite whose fingers were stained with the red of liqueurs and syrups.

None of us heard everything. None of us could. So later, we put together the details of our respective scenes to understand how it had all happened.

Tom kept shouting Jay's name but now alternated with my cousin's. "Daisy! You're here, aren't you?"

The nervous boy in the shadows became an odd imitation of me. He watched the scene as though remembering it rather than living it. In that moment, he was more Nick Carraway than Nicolás Caraveo.

"Does he want to kill her too?" Nick Carraway asked. "We have to do something."

"Stop it," Jordan whispered. "And actually listen."

I waited for the next time Tom called out. Jordan was right. The way he yelled "Daisy!" was more in desperate outrage than in accusation.

"He doesn't want to kill her," Jordan said. "He wants her back."

"You're kidding."

"Everyone wants her now," Jordan said. "So of course he does. He's going to try to set it all right with her." Jordan watched out the window, open to let in the sound. "Until he sees what she's capable of."

Just in time for Tom to round the last corner of the house, Daisy was there. Daisy and the dark blue plunge of the swimming pool showed through the olive and lemon trees.

"Jay," Daisy said, with a breathless regret Mary Pickford could not have improved on. "Jay, you ruined it all!"

Keep your back to Tom, Jordan had told the boy in the pink suit. *That's the only way this works.*

So the boy in the pink suit did.

Tom saw the shell-handled Remington he had given Daisy for her birthday. It gleamed in her hand. The debutante and the boy in the pink suit couldn't see Tom's reaction, but the two of us watching from the window could.

Tom stayed back, shielded by the boughs and hedges.

"Daisy, please," Gatsby said in a low voice.

She lifted the gun. "Her?" Daisy's voice quivered, and the dark-polished wood shined. "You and Tom both loved *her* instead of *me*?"

"I didn't love her," Gatsby said. "I never loved anyone but you."

"Liar!" Daisy screamed in unison with the shot. In the moment of firing, the shell handle flashed blue.

Gatsby fell into the pool.

Turn your face away as fast as you can, Daisy had told him. So he did.

The stirring of the water turned him over so that only his hair and that pink suit showed.

Once you're in the water, keep your face down, Jordan had told him.

So he did.

Concealed within a jacket pocket, a perfume bottle waited, filled with the fake blood Jordan had made. With a quick motion hidden by the rippling water, Gatsby pulled the stopper out. Deep red rushed through the dark blue water.

Tom was still, his frightened breath troubling the hedges.

We'd hoped, in this moment, he would run. But we knew Daisy might need to scare him worse.

Daisy turned from the pool to the trees. "I know you're there." Her voice was equal parts seduction and threat, as carefully mixed as syrup and cassis.

"Come out, Tom," she said. "Or I'll shoot."

The fake blood bloomed through the water, staining Gatsby's rose-pink suit.

"Daisy, what have you done?" Tom asked.

"What's the matter?" she asked in her sweetest voice, matching the dampness of her eyes. "Didn't you come to get me back?"

Tom hesitated.

"He's supposed to run," Jordan whispered.

"I know. Why isn't he?"

"Because he thinks she might shoot if he does."

CHAPTER XXXIX

Stay under as long as you can, and then come up.

The thought became a shared breath between Jay and me. I imagined it as air moving between our lungs. I thought of holding his hands when we were underwater.

You can stay down longer than you think you can. But when you're out of air, come up.

"She's selling this a little too well," Jordan whispered.

Daisy flopped the pistol around. Tom flinched.

"Don't you love me anymore, Tom?" she asked in a voice as airy as her green chiffon.

"Now, take it easy, Daisy," Tom said.

Daisy stepped closer, trying to block the boy holding his breath. "You want me to plan a wedding? I'll plan it. We'll get the Plaza this weekend. You can make that happen, can't you, Tom? After all, you're a Buchanan, aren't you?"

"Daisy," he said in his quietest voice. "I think you're tired. You're exhausted."

"I know what you're trying to do." She pointed the pistol. "You humiliated me by carrying on with that girl, and now you think you can just end things with me?"

She advanced, her slow steps clicking on the stone deck. "Why did you push me off that yacht?"

"What?" Tom asked.

"I'm sorry," Daisy said. "Boat. Is it less garish if I call it a boat?"

"I didn't push you off," Tom said.

"Then why can't I remember anything?" Daisy lifted the gun higher.

"You were drunk." The words burst from Tom's mouth as though Daisy was scaring them out of him.

"Is that what you counted on?" Daisy asked. "So you could do away with me more easily?"

"Never," Tom said. "How could you think that?"

"You were using me!" Daisy nearly screamed. "You set it all up. Whether you meant to kill me or not, you were willing to risk it. It was just fine with you if I drowned."

"You're talking crazy," Tom said.

"I know about the insurance," she said.

"Of course there was insurance, Daisy!" Tom was yelling now. "It was $350,000. Did you think a piece like that wouldn't be insured?!"

"How convenient that I was wearing it that night," Daisy said. "That you told me to wear it."

"I wanted to show you off in it," he said.

"You wanted to show off your money more than you wanted to show me off," she said.

"Why can't it be both?" Tom asked. "A man wants to show the nice things he can put on a girl. Is that some kind of crime?"

"So what now?" Daisy tilted her head. "You got me used to those things, and now you'll forget me?"

"Never, Daisy." Tom held up his hands. "You know I'll take care of you."

As distant as their voices sounded, I could hear the opening in his words, the invitation. Daisy would take it. She'd use it to get Tom away from this house and the boy holding his breath underwater.

Before, Daisy held the power of a rich man wanting her. Now, he was suddenly afraid of her and wanted nothing more than to be free of her, and that was a greater power than him thinking her beautiful.

"How?" Daisy asked. "What will I have?"

"You'll keep the ring." The effort at persuasion strained Tom's voice. "I wouldn't ask for it back. Not after how I've behaved."

"Oh, a ring." She threw a bitter laugh at him. "What a pretty little reminder of this whole charade." She pulled it off her finger and threw it into the pool. The emerald sparkled on its way to the bottom, disturbing the water enough to hide any air bubbles coming from the boy beneath the surface.

"You can have the other one too," Tom said. "The diamond."

Daisy aimed the gun square at his chest.

"We'll get you some money," Tom grasped. "Plenty of it."

"You don't have it!" Daisy yelled.

The shock on Tom's face matched his fear.

"That's right, Tom," Daisy said. "I know about your gambling, the tabs you run up, your debts. How your family has you on a monthly allowance. Don't get me started on Myrtle's apartment and her dresses and her jewelry. You don't have the money to settle your invoice at the Biltmore, let alone anything for me."

"I'll get it," he said. "I'll talk to my parents. I'll tell them about my debts. I'll tell them everything. We'll send you on a grand tour of the continent. You won't have to face anyone here."

Daisy glanced back toward the boy in the pool.

Whispers from under the window were too faint for Tom to hear.

"I have to get him out."

"Not yet." Jordan was cool as a shined glass. "If we go in too early we'll blow all of this."

"He can't stay under that long."

"Yes, he can."

Jay Gatsby's breath was my breath. The tightening of his lungs was the tightening of mine. I needed air as badly as he did.

"You'll call the police." Daisy's lament pierced the air.

"Over him?" Tom gave a genuine laugh. "I can make this all disappear for you. My family can. My father plays tennis with the commissioner. But I doubt I'll even need to call him. Gatsby was involved with all the wrong people. It could have been any of them. Nobody would believe you did this. You could walk into the station and confess, and they'd laugh."

Tom would have wanted nothing more than for everyone to know Gatsby met his end this way. Tom's rival was dead, and Tom would have the privilege of inventing his inglorious death.

"You were right about him." Daisy cast a mournful glance at the pool. "All along."

"I know." Tom almost managed to make himself sound sorry.

"Call your bank." Daisy pointed the pistol toward the French doors, and the two of them went deep into the mansion.

For the boy holding his breath underwater, the world dimmed to darkness. The now-empty perfume bottle haloed him in fake blood. The heavy glass fell from his hand.

The last thing I saw clearly was the perfume bottle alongside Daisy's emerald ring. Through the blur of the water, it was the pink bulb of a planet next to a green star. The lines of opal inlay spinning out from the center of the pool were the spiral of a nebula.

I could hold my breath the longest, so I played the role of Jay Gatsby. But now I was running out of air, desperately holding my face down so Tom wouldn't see I was very much alive. I couldn't play Gatsby anymore. My hold on him loosened.

I wasn't even Nick Carraway, the version of me Jay had played while hiding alongside Jordan.

I was back to being Nicolás Caraveo.

I was a boy diving into a pond, staying under so long I frightened my mother and thrilled my cousin Daisy.

I was the young man hearing my father's voice on the station platform.

Recuerda esto, Nicolás: The world may look at you and see a pawn, but that just means they'll never see your move coming.

In my last moment of air, I understood.

The world expected me to move in the same direction, like a pawn. Straight all the time, forward, exactly where they wanted me to go.

So the answer was not to go straight.

It was to move like the knight I was.

When I heard the splash cut through the water, I heard it

in the distant way of dreaming. When I felt Jay's arm around me, the feeling came shrouded in haze.

He pulled me to the surface, and my lungs took over in gasping breaths.

Jay and Jordan got me out of the water. Before I could fall over, they pulled me into the cover of the hedges and trees.

"When I think they're done in there, I'm going to scream," Jordan whispered. "They'll think I found you."

Jordan pressed her back against the wall, peering into the French doors.

I lay in the grass, air clearing my head as Jay held me.

Jay touched the side of my face. "I can't believe you did that."

"Did it work?" I didn't have to try to whisper. My voice wasn't up to anything else.

"I think so." With a careful forefinger, Jay lifted a lock of hair off my forehead. It was so much paler now.

Daisy knew how to lighten dark hair, and she'd frantically grabbed bicarbonate of soda and peroxide and anything else, until she came up with something she thought would do the job fast. *Never ever do this to your hair unless it's a matter of life and death*, she'd said. She hadn't managed to lighten my hair to Gatsby's blond, but in the time it took Jordan to create that magnificent blood now staining the pink suit, Daisy had gotten it close enough to pass for Jay's.

Jay kissed my forehead. "Thank you."

"Now or never," Jordan whispered. "Brace yourselves."

She took a long breath in.

Her scream would have silenced the polite clapping of a thousand tournament spectators. It sent Tom Buchanan running out, telling Daisy to do the same. There was a faint ringing of metal—we would learn later that it was Tom throwing Daisy the cottage keys, telling her to hide out there until he sent a car for her, so they wouldn't be seen together.

Daisy made a good show of fleeing. Once Tom had sped away, she came back, running through the grass. She stopped when she saw me in Jay's arms, and Jordan standing by the pool. Relief seemed to take air out of her.

She looked down into the pool. The pink glass planet swirled with the faint shadows of fake blood. The emerald star sparkled in the opal arms of that underwater nebula.

Daisy walked down the pool steps and straight into the water. Her skirts floated up around her. She let the water lap over her head, and she was under, her hair billowing like her dress. The light went through the layers of fabric, so the water around her seemed to glow. She was again that diaphanous mermaid everyone had imagined when she'd fallen off a yacht.

She went down, and then swam back toward the stairs. Soaked in salt water, Daisy Fabrega-Caraveo held the green star, a siren coming back from the sea.

CHAPTER XL

We kept Jay away from East Egg and West Egg for a few weeks, away from anyone who might realize the great Gatsby was very much alive. Daisy and Jordan went about their socialite lives in New York. Jordan put on the air of grief for her friend. Daisy presented the callous chill of almost forgetting him, letting everyone despise or admire her for how she'd used a boy so clearly in love with her. Any remark on my absence remembered me as a waiter at the summer parties.

Jay and I had set a date for leaving but hadn't set a destination, when Martha showed me the telegram from Los Angeles.

"How did you do this?" I asked.

"If Wall Street doesn't want that fine mathematical mind," she said, "the California Institute of Technology will use it. You'll just be assisting a professor for a while. A friend of a friend. But he's going to help get you started in the program and then you'll get your degree and then you'll reinvent algebra, I imagine."

"How can I thank you for this?" I asked.

"Just mention me in all your speeches when you're a famous mathematician," she said. "Oh, and when I come visit, I demand the gayest of treatment. I don't know the clubs for us in Los Angeles. I expect you to find them."

"It's a date," Jay said.

"And you?" I asked Daisy and Jordan. "Will you visit us?"

"With you being so close to Tinseltown?" Jordan said. "You couldn't keep us away."

We'd each held the dream of this country and New York itself, even as we knew that we lived at the edges of those dreams. As long as we stayed, we were phantoms inhabiting other people's sleep.

Daisy and Jordan were off to a world beyond East and West Egg. First, so Jordan could meet Daisy's family, and then so Daisy could meet Jordan's, then off to Paris or Geneva or wherever else the world wanted two of New York's most scandalous and beautiful socialites. Ahead of them went strands of pearls in all colors, mailed off with unsigned cards.

In Italy, Daisy would let her hair grow out dark brown, trilling "When in Rome!" and Jordan would stop pulling hers back into the tight chignons of New York parties. In the South of France, they would both turn darker under the Mediterranean sun alongside so many tanning tourists. Along the Aegean Sea they would cast off their side lacers, and stop using several colors of lipstick to make their lips look thinner. With every mile they put behind them, Daisy would put less effort toward spinning herself into such pale gold. Jordan would shrug off the only Jordan Baker that

New York had let her be, now falling away like a beaded evening shawl.

With the space left by letting Daisy go, Jay marveled at the newly open landscape of his own dreams.

I would leave Wall Street, a kingdom that would inevitably fall by its own sword. I would again find the plain mathematics I held in my heart like a first love.

As Jordan, Jay, and Martha exchanged goodbyes, Daisy pulled me aside. She took a lock of my peroxide-bleached hair.

"I'm sorry I gave you such a terrible dye job," she said.

"You had a few minutes," I said. "It'll grow out before we're in California. I'll cut all the blond off."

"Good," she said. "Because you make a terrible blond. Warn your parents so they don't faint from the shock."

Daisy unwrapped what looked like a napkin from the Buchanans' estate, the cloth matched to the wallpaper. She revealed the emerald bulb of the green dock light.

"You stole it?" I asked.

"Keep it for him, will you?" She passed it to me.

I carried it away from East Egg and West Egg, as carefully as if she'd wrapped the moon in flannel.

———— •••• ————

When I first saw my father in Wisconsin, I greeted him by holding out the chess piece. I set the carved wooden knight in his hand, knowing what he wanted me to know.

In my mother's kitchen, Jay learned how the papery husks of tomatillos felt in his palms. He learned the way light fell through the hornbeam trees Daisy and I had run between on August mornings. Then, after Wisconsin, we were off to the chilled dust and wildflowered grass of North Dakota. Jay's aunt and the woman she'd loved for decades stretched out their arms and yelled, "James!" and that was how I first learned the boy's name they'd given him before he left.

Soon, we'd be on our way to California. But in the North Dakota night, we lay in a rusted boat. A reed-fringed pond reflected the moon, and swayed underneath us. My head rested against Jay's hip, and we both watched the point of green on the bank.

With the help of Jay's aunt, I'd rigged up the light to the splintered dock he'd jumped off as a child. With its leaf-bright glow, it called fireflies out from the reeds.

The constellations dipped down into the water. I thought of them in New York and California, emerging and vanishing into oceans, and here, drifting between the green light and the moon.

I thought of all those pearls floating through the sea like stars. I wondered how many new debutantes, for how many years, would hear stories about Daisy Fay and claim they'd found a pearl from her very necklace.

Within a few years, there would be rumors that Jay Gatsby never existed at all. Some would say he had been an invention of Martha Wolf. They had seen Martha closing up the mansion, readying it for sale to an unseen buyer.

Martha made Gatsby vanish, and that fueled the rumor that she had made him appear in the first place. Any question—about Gatsby, his blue gardens, his glimmering parties—she answered with a quirk of her painted lips. She was the only one left who knew for sure where we were, floating in that North Dakota night, imagining bay branches, white oleander, and orange trees.

It happened fast, Jay Gatsby becoming more legend than memory. The rich sons and daughters who drank champagne on his lawn whispered his name as though trying to grasp something, wondering if everything they remembered about the great Gatsby had been a dream.

AUTHOR'S NOTE

When I first read *The Great Gatsby* as a teen, I knew three things:

1) I was pretty sure Nick Carraway was in love with Jay Gatsby.
2) Daisy Buchanan enthralled me as much as she infuriated me.
3) I had a feeling this story wasn't done with me.

But I wouldn't find out why this story wasn't done with me until years later, when I was invited to reimagine *The Great Gatsby*. And when I was, I knew I wanted to create a *Gatsby* that included my queer, transgender, and Latine communities.

I wanted to write Jay Gatsby as a transgender young man making an increasingly infamous name for himself in 1920s New York, a boy who'd once been one of hundreds of thousands of underage soldiers who served in World War I. I wanted to write Daisy as a Latina lesbian debutante who passes as white and straight as she moves through Manhattan high society. I wanted to write Nick Carraway as a Mexican American transgender boy wanting to make a better life for himself and his family, and who falls in love with the mysterious boy next door.

I wanted to write about the American dream for what it is, a hope so many of us have but that, for so long, didn't belong to so many of us, and often still doesn't. I call this novel *Self-Made Boys* both because *The Great Gatsby* deals so much in the American dream and its myths about self-made men, and because reimagining Jay and Nick as transgender casts them as self-made boys in perhaps the most literal sense.

The phrase *self-made man* has a complicated and often problematic history that seems to date back to the first half of the nineteenth century, but the concept was later redefined by Frederick Douglass in *Self-Made Men*: "Properly speaking, there are in the world no such men as self-made men. That term implies an individual independence of the past and present which can never exist."

Nick and Jay are making themselves as boys and men, but they can't do it without each other and without their communities. As trans boys, we make ourselves, but we don't do it alone. None of us makes ourselves alone.

I started writing *Self-Made Boys* at a time when I was thinking deeply not just about my gender identity but also about my identity as a mixed-race American. I owe a great debt to another 1920s novel, Nella Larsen's *Passing*. I first read *Passing* the same year I first read *The Great Gatsby*. *Passing* was, to me, both a window book—because I will never know what it was like to be a Black woman in 1920s New York—and a mirror book—because I felt seen as a mixed-race American who sometimes passes, sometimes doesn't, and has sometimes made significant efforts to pass.

Yes, Daisy infuriated teen me. And as I reimagined her, she often still did. But she also made me face a part of myself, a part who didn't realize how much what I was doing was breaking my heart until I stopped. I had to be willing to look at the ways in which Daisy held the girl I was once, the same way I had to be willing to see how Nick held the boy I later became.

A note on identity and historical accuracy: Whenever possible, I stayed true to likely events, even when they made me cringe (like Nick's use of All Cotton Elastic; any of my fellow trans and nonbinary siblings reading this, please take Daisy's advice to Nick and don't do this). But I've also attempted to code and label race, sexual orientation, and gender identity in a way meant to fall between historical realism and contemporary consciousness. Sometimes I made decisions meant to acknowledge and question racism, queerphobia, and transphobia without putting the brutal slurs of the 1920s on the page. There are also places where I might have wanted to use contemporary wording but knew I should consider the terms used and not used in the time period (*Latino*, to give an example related to Nick's identity and my own, didn't come into common usage in the United States until later in the twentieth century).

Nick and Jay may not have had access to terms like *transgender*. Our ancestors may not have had the names for themselves and each other we have today. Regardless, we have, throughout history, found ways to know, affirm, and love one another. Without that, without the possibility of recognizing each other as we truly are, the American dream can't exist.

As you leave West Egg, I hope you leave knowing this: You are worth being seen as you truly are. You are worth imagining your life for yourself instead of how you may have been told your life must be.

You are worth your own dreams.

ACKNOWLEDGMENTS

There are many people without whom this book wouldn't exist. Here, I'll name a few:

Emily Settle, for asking me to reimagine *Gatsby* for the Remixed Classics series, and for backing all the ways I wanted to make it gay.

Jean Feiwel, for supporting making room in classic books for our communities.

Brittany Pearlman, for being as caring as she is organized and innovative.

Veronica Mang, for your thoughtful vision for this cover, Elliott Berggren, for bringing Jay and Nick to such beautiful life, and Elizabeth Clark, for the wonderful art direction at MacKids.

Everyone at Feiwel & Friends and Macmillan Children's Publishing Group: Kat Brzozowski (hi, Kat! I'm so grateful to be working with you on our next book together as I type this), Liz Szabla, Erin Siu, Teresa Ferraiolo, Kim Waymer, Ilana Worrell, Dawn Ryan, Celeste Cass, Lelia Mander,

Erica Ferguson, Jessica White, Jon Yaged, Allison Verost, Molly Ellis, Leigh Ann Higgins, Cynthia Lliguichuzhca, Allegra Green, Jo Kirby, Kathryn Little, Julia Gardiner, Lauren Scobell, Alexei Esikoff, Mariel Dawson, Alyssa Mauren, Avia Perez, Dominique Jenkins, Meg Collins, Gabriella Salpeter, Romanie Rout, Ebony Lane, Kristin Dulaney, Jordan Winch, Kaitlin Loss, Rachel Diebel, Foyinsi Adegbonmire, Katy Robitzski, Amanda Barillas, Morgan Dubin, Morgan Rath, Madison Furr, Mary Van Akin, Kelsey Marrujo, Holly West, Anna Roberto, Katie Quinn, Hana Tzou, Chantal Gersch, Katie Halata, Lucy Del Priore, Melissa Croce, Kristen Luby, Cierra Bland, and Elysse Villalobos of Macmillan Children's School & Library; and the many more who turn stories into books and help readers find them.

The fellow writers who were there during the drafting and revision process:

My fellow Remixed Classics authors. I have laughed during our chats, taken in your shared wisdom, and marveled at your stunning work. I am honored to be among you.

Nova Ren Suma, Emily X. R. Pan, Anica Mrose Rissi, Aisha Saeed, Emery Lord, Dahlia Adler, Rebecca Kim Wells, Elana K. Arnold, Lisa McMann, and Matt McMann, who shared space with me as I was writing this book while sharing about their own works in progress.

Alex Brown, for your literary brilliance, your extensive historical knowledge, and for virtually introducing me to las ratas adorables.

Aiden Thomas, for telling me how much you loved this book at the very moment I was wondering what exactly I'd done writing trans gay Gatsby.

Melissa Kravitz Hoeffner, for your help with a character who's close to my heart and with showing more of her on the page.

Lieutenant Colonel Kevin J. Stepp and Staff Sergeant Matthew Chaison, for talking me through how soldiers say who they're with, today and in the 1920s.

Taylor Martindale Kean, Stefanie Sanchez Von Borstel, the Full Circle Literary team, Taryn Fagerness, and the Taryn Fagerness Agency, for supporting how excited I was to envision my own Gatsby (and especially for Taylor's 1920s enthusiasm).

Michael Bourret, for the shared queer puns and the patience for how many questions I ask.

Readers: for spending this time in my reimagining of West Egg and East Egg. Thank you.

Thank you for reading this FEIWEL & FRIENDS book.
The friends who made
Self-Made Boys: A Great Gatsby Remix possible are:

Jean Feiwel, *Publisher*
Liz Szabla, *Associate Publisher*
Rich Deas, *Senior Creative Director*
Holly West, *Senior Editor*
Anna Roberto, *Senior Editor*
Kat Brzozowski, *Senior Editor*
Dawn Ryan, *Executive Managing Editor*
Celeste Cass, *Production Manager*
Emily Settle, *Editor*
Foyinsi Adegbonmire, *Associate Editor*
Rachel Diebel, *Associate Editor*
Veronica Mang, *Associate Designer*
Lelia Mander, *Production Editor*

Follow us on Facebook
or visit us online at mackids.com.
Our books are friends for life.